AZALEA

BRENDA HIATT

dolphin star
PRESS

Azalea
Hiatt Regency Classics #6

Copyright 1994 by Brenda Hiatt
Cover art by Fantasia Frog Designs

All rights reserved

This is a work of fiction. Though some actual historical places, persons and events are depicted in this work, the primary characters and their stories are fictional. Any resemblance between those characters and actual persons, living or dead, are purely coincidental.

This book may not be copied in whole or in part without permission of the author.

Dolphin Star Press

ISBN: 978-1-940618-66-1

Dedication

For my family—thank you for your patience!

ALSO BY BRENDA HIATT

The Hiatt Regency Classics

Gabriella

The Cygnet

Lord Dearborn's Destiny

Daring Deception

Christmas Promises (a novella)

Christmas Bride

Azalea

Americana Dreaming

Azalea

Ship of Dreams

Bridge Over Time

The Saint of Seven Dials

Scandalous Virtue

Rogue's Honor

Noble Deceptions

Innocent Passions

Saintly Sins

Gallant Scoundrel

PROLOGUE

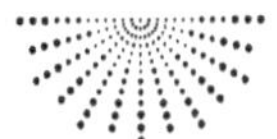

MARCH 1809

ANOTHER WAVE SWEPT ACROSS THE PITCHING DECK OF THE *Artemis,* almost wrenching Christian loose from the rail he grasped with one hand. Instead of alarm, he felt only exhilaration. For so long he had dreamed of this, his first sea voyage! The reality was even more exciting than he had imagined. Shaking the salt spray from his hair, he laughed into the screaming gale.

When his father had invited him to sail along on a business trip to America, Christian had jumped at the chance, the still-novel pleasures of London paling against the visions of adventure conjured up. What were gaming hells and cockfights, even the lights of the *demi-monde,* compared to this battle with the elements, the raw fury of wind and ocean? He had never felt more alive in all his eighteen years.

"It's gettin' mighty rough, lad. Best you go below with the other passengers." Captain Taylor, a stringy, dark-haired man with a clean-shaven, leathery face, clapped a gnarled hand on his shoulder. "I've told you what a storm at sea can do—haven't you seen enough?"

Christian breathed deeply of the fierce, fresh wind. "Not yet. It's my first storm, after all. Are we in some danger then?"

The captain shrugged. "Any storm can spell trouble this far out and I'd as lief not lose a paying guest overboard. Why, I remember a time... But there's his lordship, your father, come for you. We can talk later. I've work to do."

Captain Taylor turned to bellow orders at his crew, leaving Christian to grin after him. The captain's frequent tales of life at sea had been the best part of this voyage —up until now, anyway. Another splash of icy sea water caught Christian full in the face, making him gasp and sputter. Wiping the salt from his eyes, he saw his father beckoning him from the hatchway. With a last, reluctant look at the raging sea, he left the rail, stumbling slightly as the deck pitched beneath him.

"Here you are, Son! Let's get below, where we'll be out of the crew's way." Lord Glaedon spoke heartily, but Christian couldn't mistake the concern in his eyes. "This looks like a bad blow."

His father had spent a great deal of time at sea in his youth, Christian knew, which meant his caution, based as it was on experience, could not be ignored. Still, he couldn't suppress a cocky grin as he stepped forward.

"Sailing is every bit the adventure you promised, Father," he said exultantly. "I hate to miss any of it. If you don't mind, I'd like to stay on deck for just a bit longer. Captain Taylor doesn't seem unduly worried—"

At that moment a falling spar, torn loose from the mast

above, struck him a glancing blow on the shoulder, knocking him heavily to the deck.

For a few seconds he was dazed, not certain what had happened. Blinking as his vision cleared, he saw his father leaning over him, white-faced.

"My God, Chris, that was a close one!" He had never seen his father so shaken. "Can you stand?"

Christian nodded vigorously, though for the moment speech was beyond him. Scrambling to his feet, he followed the Earl down the ladder that led to their cabin, his enthusiasm about the storm temporarily dampened.

The next morning dawned fair; a fresh breeze filled the sails while the sun sparkled on the deceptively innocent ocean. Christian, looking out from the same rail where he'd stood the evening before, marvelled at the change. It would seem that the sea was as fickle as he'd always heard.

Perhaps with the return of fine weather, Captain Taylor would have more time to answer his myriad questions about the New World they approached. Not for the first time, he thought about what it would be like to carve out a life for himself in that untamed wilderness —a far different life than that awaiting him as second son to an earl, back in England.

"Well, my boy, we'll be in sight of land in just over a week," said his father, coming up to stand beside him at the rail. "I suppose it's high time I told you the real reason I asked you to accompany me to America."

CHAPTER ONE

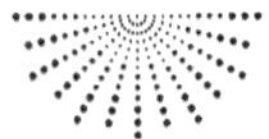

APRIL 1809

"AZALEA! ARE YOU OUT HERE?" THE HOUSEKEEPER'S VOICE floated across the paddock to the stables, where a small, trousered figure was currying a dainty, silver-grey mare with long, brisk strokes.

"In here, Swannee!" the girl answered without pausing in her work. "What is it?"

"Your grandfather wants you up to the house right away. Visitors, I believe. And just look at you!" Mrs. Swann exclaimed in dismay. Azalea emerged from the stall, grinning impishly as she ran quick fingers through her tousled red curls. Enormous, grey-green eyes of startling beauty sparkled up at the distracted housekeeper, who at this moment was more inclined to notice the smear of stable dirt across the girl's left cheek than the flawlessness of the complexion it disguised.

Mrs. Swann sighed gustily and opened her mouth in preparation for a well-rehearsed homily on her young mistress's shortcomings, but Azalea forestalled her with an affectionate hug.

"Don't fuss, Swannee! Ten to one it's just Jonathan, and he won't mind seeing me in breeches. At any rate, I can go in by the pantry door and reach my bedroom without being seen."

Mrs. Swann, plump fists on plumper hips, shook her greying blond head in resignation and gazed fondly at the glowing, untidy girl before her. For the past eight years she had been the nearest thing to a mother Azalea had known, and in truth, she couldn't have loved her more had the girl been her own daughter.

Of course, who would not love such a beautiful child, with her bright, flame-coloured curls, thick-lashed liquid eyes and sweet, winning ways? But there was also a certain wildness about her that Mrs. Swann had done her best to control over the years—a task as futile as trying to control the fresh east wind that blew in from the coast.

"All right, miss," she conceded gruffly, "but do hurry. And I don't believe it is Master Jonathan coming to call. Your grandfather has ordered supper set back an hour and an extra chicken killed. He wouldn't likely do that for one of your young friends."

"Oh, how interesting —I shall hurry!"

Azalea raced across the field at a pace that caused the long-suffering Mrs. Swann to emit another sigh and hope the girl's grandfather was well away from the back windows. At this distance, Azalea looked more like a stable-lad than a young lady of Quality.

A scant fifteen minutes later, a hastily scrubbed and gowned Azalea clattered down to the library, where her grandfather customarily received callers. She was surprised to find the old gentleman quietly reading alone.

"Oh, have they gone already?" She stopped just inside the door, disappointed. "I did hurry, Grandfather, truly I did! Swannee said our guests would be staying for supper. Were they ladies or gentlemen? Are they staying here in Williamsburg? Or was it someone I already know? Was it Jonathan, after all? Why—"

"My dear, my dear, always leaping to conclusions," Reverend Simpson said, breaking in mildly. "Taking your questions in order, they have not yet arrived, but are due within the hour. They will be staying for supper, which has been set back to eight o'clock. They are gentlemen, two in number, and are staying at Wetherburn's Tavern until rooms can be prepared for them here. You have never met them, but have often heard me refer to the elder of the two, my old friend Howard Morely, Earl of Glaedon. The other gentleman is his second son, Christian, whom I have yet to meet. Obviously not Jonathan. Did I miss anything?" The old gentleman's austere, scholarly demeanour was softened by the twinkle in his bright blue eyes.

"You know you didn't." She smiled fondly at her grandfather. "But I still want to know all about them. Why have we had no word that they were coming? How long do they stay?" Azalea fairly danced with impatience. She could not recollect when they had last had overnight visitors. And Lord Glaedon! The hero of so many of Grandfather's tales about his time in India, the one with whom he had shared such splendid adventures...!

"Very well, my dear, stop twitching," the Reverend said, relenting. "Due to a quirk of the mails, Howard's letter informing me of the date of his proposed visit arrived on the same ship that carried Christian and himself hither. They arrived in America only yesterday, and will probably stay with us but a few days, as Howard has pressing business in Richmond. However—" he interrupted himself with a brief fit of coughing "—I hope they will return for a longer visit when their affairs have been concluded."

This answer seemed clear enough, but there was something evasive in the old gentleman's manner that convinced Azalea there was more to the matter. "And?" she prompted. "What aren't you telling me, Grandfather?"

"Precocious child! Can you read my mind now?"

"If I could, I wouldn't need to ask. But I can tell when you've decided something doesn't concern me, or that I'm too young to hear all of the interesting details." Azalea almost pouted before hastily remembering that she was now too old for such behaviour.

Reverend Simpson sighed. "No, Azalea, young you may be, but this matter very definitely concerns you. Still, I would prefer to speak with Howard in person before acquainting you fully with the 'interesting details,' as you term them. I do promise to tell you all I can once I am completely in possession of the facts. Will that content you for now?"

Azalea smiled reluctantly. "I suppose it must."

"Good. Now perhaps you'd like to complete your toilette before supper —and I suggest you use a mirror this time. You missed a spot or two." He winked knowingly over his spectacles. Azalea grimaced, but hurried back upstairs to wash more thoroughly and put her hair in better order. She wanted to look her best for these distinguished visitors from England.

The warm spring afternoon was beginning to cool when Azalea returned to the library. She stopped short on the threshold, startled to find their visitors already present. Her soft surprised, "Oh!" caused all three gentlemen to turn.

"Ah, my dear, here you are," exclaimed her grandfather, coming forward. "Let me present Lord Glaedon and his son, the Honourable Christian Morely. Gentlemen, my granddaughter, Miss Azalea Clayton."

She dropped a curtsy and lowered her gaze in confusion. "I —I beg pardon for not greeting you upon your arrival! I was in the garden and thought surely I would hear the approach of your carriage—"

"No need for apologies, child," the elder of the two visitors said, interrupting her warmly. "We have scarce been here ten minutes, and you could hardly have been expected to hear our carriage, as we rode instead. And let me say that I am delighted to make your acquaintance at last, though I feel I know you well from your grandfather's letters. You are even prettier than he described you."

Azalea looked up quickly at the unlikely words to find kindly grey eyes regarding her. Timidly, she returned the Earl's smile.

Lord Glaedon was a hearty man in his late fifties, with very little grey in his thick black hair. He looked, Azalea thought, as an earl ought to: confident rather than arrogant, and dressed with a simple elegance that rendered him by far the most fashionable gentleman she'd ever seen. He was also the tallest man she could remember meeting. That is, unless she counted Judd Bellby, a local farmer's son who was certainly no gentleman.

"Thank you, my lord," answered Azalea, a heartbeat before she could be accused of staring. "Grandfather has told me much about you, also, and about the adventures you shared in India. Such wonderful stories!"

"And stories they no doubt were, for the most part," Lord Glaedon replied somewhat gruffly, glancing at the Reverend. "Gregory ever had a tendency to exaggerate. Christian, my lad," he called, turning toward the other occupant of the room, "come forward and make Miss Clayton's acquaintance."

The younger gentleman turned away from the window, where he had apparently been admiring the spectacular sunset. He advanced two or three steps towards Azalea.

Looking up—far up—as he approached, Azalea realized that Christian was at least as tall as his father, and far more handsome. In fact, to her inexperienced eyes, he was the most perfect man she'd ever seen, with thick wavy hair so dark it was almost black and penetrating blue-grey eyes.

Exciting eyes, Azalea thought irrelevantly, the colour of thunderclouds just before a storm. At first glance, at least, the Honourable Christian Morely seemed the answer to a young girl's every romantic dream.

Blinking at the direction of her thoughts, Azalea had to suppress an urge to laugh at herself. *Romantic dreams, indeed!* Between studying, riding, gardening and other pursuits, she'd never wasted time on such fantasies. In fact, she had always scorned the other girls' sighs over a handsome new student or a visiting merchant's son. But of course none of those young men had ever compared to Christian Morely.

"So this is little Miss Azalea! Not quite the child I was led to believe." His smile was condescending, Azalea thought, which immediately banished romance and put irritation in its place.

"I was thirteen in November, sir, so I am scarcely a child," she retorted, standing up a little taller. She was suddenly glad she had given up her braids two months ago.

"Isn't that what I just said? And I understand that you have had a hand in the managing of this, ah, estate for the past year, as well."

Azalea regarded the young man suspiciously. Was he teasing her? Her grandfather's house and lands, while respectable, could hardly be called an estate. However, she could detect no trace of malice in Christian's amused expression and decided that he might merely be ignorant of the extent of an American plantation.

"That is true, sir," she finally conceded. "Mrs. Swann is gradually entrusting me with the duties that belonged to my grandmother many years ago. Part of my education, Grandfather tells me." She smiled a bit wryly.

"But not your favourite part, I take it?" He smiled back, a friendly smile that allayed her suspicions and put her at ease.

"Well, it's certainly more amusing than Latin, but I find I have less and less time to spend with the horses and plants—" Azalea broke off in some confusion, not certain whether she should have revealed these pastimes, which Swannee had informed her repeatedly were less than ladylike. She glanced in her grandfather's direction, but he was deep in conversation with the Earl and appeared not to have heard.

"You like horses, then?" Christian prompted when she paused. He didn't look the least disapproving.

"Oh, yes! Above all things. Do you?" Azalea replied, caution vanishing as the conversation turned to her favourite topic. "You'll have to meet Lindy, my mare," she continued when he nodded. "She's the most beautiful thing imaginable! Perfect lines, and the smoothest trot in Virginia. Do we have time to go down to the stables before supper, Grandfather?" she asked eagerly, turning back to the older gentlemen.

"Certainly, my dear. You youngsters run along," Reverend Simpson replied with barely a glance in her direction. Azalea thought he looked grave. He obviously wanted to continue his discussion with Lord Glaedon. "Go for a ride if you wish. Supper will not be for an hour or more."

"We'll return in time," Azalea promised, then turned back to Christian with sudden diffidence. "That is, if you wish to come, sir." He didn't seem at all like a "youngster" to her.

"I'm quite counting on it," he responded with another warm smile. "And please, no more 'sirs'—it makes me feel positively ancient. Call me Chris."

Azalea agreed delightedly. "You brought a horse from the inn, you said? I can have Lindy saddled in a flash. I'll show you a bit of Williamsburg before supper."

Christian was finding young Miss Clayton unexpectedly likeable. He was not certain just what he had anticipated, but it was not this fresh, piquant woman-child.

When his father had first acquainted him with his plans, Christian had been dumbstruck and then affronted. The more the Earl told him of the girl's circumstances, however, the more curious he had become. Now, very much to his surprise, he found himself actually giving his father's outrageous suggestion serious consideration.

"Grandfather keeps some prime bloods, as well as a couple of carriage horses," Azalea told him eagerly as her mare was saddled. "Lindy, of course, is my favourite, but I will be interested to know what you think of some of the others."

Her enthusiasm made Christian smile, for horses were a passion of his, as well. It was... interesting to discover that they had that much in common, at least. "I can scarcely wait. Perhaps tomorrow I might have opportunity to try the paces of one of them. I'm certain they will cast this nag I hired from the inn quite into the shade."

A short time later, Chris accompanied Azalea down Queen Street toward the main thoroughfare of the town. He whistled tunefully as they went, to her secret delight. Whistling was something Swannee had often scolded her for doing. Still, even with his example before her she didn't quite dare to join in.

As it was late in the day, Duke of Gloucester Street was nearly deserted. "I fear Williamsburg is not the hub of activity it was before the war," she told him apologetically as they turned their horses onto the wider road. "Then, it was the capital of Virginia, and quite an important political centre for the whole country."

Chris nodded. "I read a bit of American history before leaving England. You seem quite thoroughly schooled in it, though."

Azalea could feel herself blushing. "Well, yes. I used to

badger Grandfather to let me attend classes at the college." She pointed down the street the other way, to where a fine building, designed on noble lines by Sir Christopher Wren, was still visible in the failing light. "Of course that was impossible, but he did arrange for a tutor. Dr. Jonas is so enraptured by Williamsburg's history, much of which, of course, he has lived through, that I couldn't help but get caught up in it."

"Your grandfather teaches there as well, doesn't he?"

"Yes, as mathematician and grammarian. Do you know, he actually met Patrick Henry? He was the great orator who spoke out against the Stamp Act in that very building." She pointed to the capitol building. Now, however, that once-imposing structure stood empty, and signs of neglect were beginning to be visible. The focus of Williamsburg was now at the western end of Duke of Gloucester Street, where the College of William and Mary stood.

"We British were most unreasonable, were we not?" The mildness of Chris's tone reminded Azalea abruptly that he and his countrymen doubtless viewed the outcome of the war rather differently than the Americans did. Casting about for another topic, she felt some relief when she noticed a sandy-haired youth approaching them on foot.

"Jonathan!" Azalea called, waving to the boy.

He quickened his pace. "Hullo, 'Zalea! You're out late. Who's your friend?"

She couldn't quite keep a trace of smugness from her tone as she answered. "This is Mr. Morely. He and his father, the Earl of Glaedon..." she paused to more fully enjoy Jonathan's expression of awe "... are visiting with us for a few days. Chris, this is my best friend, Jonathan Plummer."

To his credit, Jonathan recovered quickly. "Pleased to make

your acquaintance, sir," he said with a shy grin. "Does this mean our picnic is off, 'Zalea?"

"Goodness, I'd forgotten! Yes, I suppose so, Jonathan. We can do it next week just as well." She blushed again, hoping Jonathan would not mention in front of Christian that their picnic was to take place in the branches of a tree. But he merely nodded, saluted Christian and sauntered on his way.

As he retreated, Azalea couldn't help comparing her old comrade to the gentleman at her side. Jonathan's father was a wealthy planter and had been a baronet before coming to America some twenty years ago. And his mother had been daughter to an English viscount, which, she had previously thought, made Jonathan nearly nobility.

Azalea had to laugh at such a notion now. Why, next to Chris, he was a simple country boy! She did not pause to consider that Jonathan's age, a mere year greater than her own, did him no good in the comparison. "I'll show you the magazine and guardhouse," she said to Chris, turning her mare. "Then I suppose we should return for supper."

Azalea was in high spirits at breakfast the next morning. Christian and his father were due to return before dinnertime with their trunks. Rooms had been readied for them, and she and Chris were planning another, longer ride that afternoon.

She already regarded Chris as a friend. The fact that he seemed not to think of her as a mere child was a definite point in his favour. Of course, there was only a five-year difference in their ages, where Papa had been nine years older than Mama...

Abruptly, Azalea shook her head, causing the Reverend to glance up from his morning papers. What on earth was she thinking of? Determinedly, she gave her attention to the ham and eggs before her.

A few minutes later, her grandfather put his papers aside. "When you've finished, my dear, could you give me a moment of your time in the library? I'll wait for you there."

"Of course, Grandfather. I'll only be a moment."

She was not especially curious. The Reverend often requested her help in cataloguing or in reading the fine print that strained his eyes. He might even have a game of chess in mind, and Azalea had to admit she could use the practice. Quickly, she finished the last of her biscuit and milk and followed the old gentleman into the library.

"Yes, Grandfather? What is it you wish me to do?"

She breezed in, fresh as the bright spring morning in a pale green gown, her coppery curls bouncing at her shoulders. Reverend Simpson regarded her almost wistfully for a moment, then coughed and became very businesslike.

"I'd like you to take a seat and listen carefully to what I am about to tell you, with a minimum of questions, at least until I have finished."

Her curiosity now thoroughly aroused, Azalea sat in the chair he indicated and looked at him expectantly.

"After supper last night," he began, "I had a very long talk with Howard. As you know, my health is not what it once was. This infernal cough becomes worse by the month, and the doctor says that my heart is weak as well. No, no, my dear, I do not say this to alarm you," he said quickly when Azalea gasped with dismay, "but merely to help explain what I am about to suggest.

"Howard also acquainted me with some particulars regarding your English inheritance, which he looked into at my request. The means by which your uncle, Lord Kayce, gained possession of the properties is suspect, to say the least. So far, he seems unaware of your existence, but we cannot assume that he will remain so forever. Therefore, Howard and I both agree that you need stronger protection than I can provide you, especially given my present state of health. The most reasonable solution involves a marriage—"

"Marriage! Me? But I'm only thirteen! How—" Her grandfather stopped the flow of questions with an upraised hand. "Azalea, please hear me out," he said in a firmer tone than usual.

Squelching her curiosity, she nodded meekly and he continued.

"Shortly after your birth, Howard and I discussed —not very seriously at the time, I must admit —the possibility of your eventual marriage to one of his sons. He has now made you an offer of marriage on behalf of his second son, Christian."

Azalea opened her mouth, but the Reverend forestalled her with a glance.

"This would be an excellent match for both of you in worldly terms, of course," he went on, "but more importantly, it would give Howard legal authority to set about protecting your birthright. In addition, your marriage would afford you another kind of protection against your uncle, who may be less than pleased when he learns about you— which he will do, once Howard puts his plans into motion. Add to that the fact that Howard is my oldest and dearest friend—"

"You have betrothed me without my consent?" Azalea

broke in indignantly, no longer able to contain herself. "Am I to be shipped across the ocean just like that? Grandfather, how could you?" She couldn't decide whether to scream or cry.

"You have been reading novels again and neglecting your studies, I perceive," the Reverend said drily. "Nothing so melodramatic as that, I assure you. One reason I waited until this morning to broach the subject was to give you an opportunity to meet Christian and form an opinion of him before being prejudiced by the reason for his visit. It *seems* that you like him quite well. In any event, no irrevocable steps have been taken, nor will they be, without your consent."

Reverend Simpson paused for a moment and made a great business of polishing his spectacles before continuing.

"Considering your youth, the marriage would be, ah, in name only for several years. It is my hope that you would remain here for at least a portion of that time, after which you would join Christian in England. You may now ask questions," he concluded, looking up at her with a resigned expression.

With that encouragement, Azalea found herself, for the first time since she had learned to talk, devoid of questions. Her mind was a whirl. With the fear of immediate removal from the only life she had ever known allayed, she began to view the prospect of marriage as exciting, rather than frightening.

And to Chris! Surely, even if she waited years and years, and had her pick of all the men in the world, she'd never find anyone so perfect, so handsome, so...interesting! Already teetering on the edge of her first romantic infatuation, Azalea tumbled headlong at the thought.

But what had Grandfather said? That the Earl had made the offer "on Christian's behalf," whatever that meant.

"Does Christian know about this, Grandfather?" she asked, suddenly fearful of the answer.

"Why, of course. He was with us in the library after supper, if you recall. He offered no objections, if that is what worries you."

No objections. But also no assurances that she was the girl he would have chosen for a bride.

But she was being silly now. Of course Christian could not love her after only a few hours in her company. But once she was his wife, she thought blithely, she could surely win his heart. And as for herself, if she was not a little in love with him already, she knew that she soon would be.

"All right, Grandfather. I will marry him."

"Well, Son, have you decided then?" Lord Glaedon enquired as the last of their luggage was loaded onto the hired carriage. "Don't feel that you have to take this step for my sake, or even the girl's, although I admit that is more of a consideration, in my opinion."

"Yes, Father," Christian replied, "I intend to go through with it— partly for your sake, partly for hers and even partly for my own. She's a taking little thing and shows promise of growing into quite a beauty. And I'm quite certain she won't bore me!" He grinned, recalling how her outspoken enthusiasm had led her into more than one social blunder at supper last night.

"In any event, I won't precisely be giving up my freedom for four or five years yet," he continued. "And if any of the young Marriage-Mart misses become too warm, I can always frighten them off with sentimental stories of my little American wife. An enviable position all round, I think."

His father glanced at him sharply, pausing in the act of climbing into the carriage. "I hope you intend to be discreet when we return to England, Christian. I'll withdraw the proposal at once if your recklessness is likely to cause Azalea pain. Gregory is my closest friend, and I feel rather a strong responsibility for his granddaughter, under the circumstances."

"As well you might, since you dreamed up this situation," retorted Christian, his smile fading. "But your worries are groundless, Father. I would never intentionally hurt a young innocent like Azalea. Indeed, I have hopes that in a few years we may deal quite famously together. She appears to be unusually intelligent and we share several interests already."

"Both horse mad, you mean," said Lord Glaedon with a chuckle, apparently reassured. "I suppose couples have entered into the married state with less in common, and still made a pretty good go of it. Do you plan to make her an offer in form?"

Christian swung up into the coach beside his father. "Why not? I know she's very young, but she'll no doubt enjoy it. And besides, every girl should have the right to at least one proposal of marriage in her life, shouldn't she?"

Christian smiled to himself, imagining Azalea's reaction when he proposed. Really, she was a most engaging child.

"I hadn't considered it quite in that light," said the Earl, "but you are probably right."

~

Dinner was a rather uncomfortable meal for all concerned, as no opportunity had yet occurred for the Reverend and the Earl to compare notes on their private discussions with their respective charges.

Azalea kept stealing surreptitious glances at her soon-to-be betrothed, and Christian did likewise, attempting to discover from her manner whether her grandfather had mentioned anything to her.

This was going to be deuced awkward if he hadn't, Christian realized belatedly. Imagine proposing to a thirteen-year-old girl out of the blue—she would either swoon or think he had run mad. He was determined to get some indication of whether the ground had been prepared before proceeding, and began directing questioning looks, accompanied by much throat clearing, at Reverend Simpson.

Upon receiving a knowing wink and a slight nod in return, Christian was able to relax and enjoy the remainder of the meal. He realized, on reflection, that Azalea's very silence should have told him what he wished to know.

Shortly after dinner, the horses were saddled and brought round to the front of the house for the ride the young couple had agreed upon the previous evening. Azalea had changed into a charming grey riding habit that perfectly matched her silvery mare, Lindy. Chris was attired in a deeper shade of grey, his gleaming black boots mirroring the spirited stallion he was to ride.

"You so admired Spartan last night that I thought you might like to try his paces. He's the best mount in Grandfather's stables— excepting Lindy, here, of course." Azalea seemed to be recovering some of her usual animation with the arrival of the horses.

"You were very perceptive," replied Chris. "I was nearly drooling over this fellow yesterday, but didn't dare suggest you mount me on such an obviously valuable animal."

"Yes, I suppose he would bring a small fortune if he were sold, but of course we have no intention of parting with him. He was bred here, as was his dam. I daresay Grandfather's cattle would compare favourably with any stable in Virginia —and perhaps even in England."

Chris could only agree. Chatting comfortably once again, they both mounted and started down the broad gravelled drive at a brisk trot.

Azalea led Chris along one of her favourite routes, pointing out the particular beauties of the landscape. The apple and dogwood trees were in full bloom, transforming the country-side into a fairyland of white and palest pink.

Presently, they turned off into a narrow lane with a daisy-strewn field on one side and a large apple orchard on the other. The subject of horses and horsemanship had been temporarily exhausted, mainly because Azalea's thoughts were too busy for her to be her usual talkative self.

"Do you mind if I ask a rather personal question?" Christian asked after a brief pause. Azalea's heart beat faster and she shook her head, hoping that the blush she could feel rising to her cheeks wasn't noticeable. Her reins slipped slightly in her suddenly damp hands.

"Well," he continued, "it's your name. I've never heard it before and I wondered what it meant. Is it a family name or something?"

This was so completely opposite to what Azalea had expected to hear that she almost choked on a laugh.

"A family... No, not exactly. You see, my mother was very fond of the flora of the New World and experimented extensively with some of the wild species. Her favourite was the azalea, a flowering shrub. Surely you've noticed the large bushes round the house?"

"Yes, now that you mention it. The ones with the pink and purple flowers along the front, you mean?"

"Yes, those are the biggest ones. My mother planted those when she was only a year or two older than I am now. She also had some white ones brought down from the mountains by a friend of my grandfather's. I'll show them to you when we return." Next to horses, Azalea loved to discuss botany and gardening, which, perhaps in memory of her mother, she had studied in depth.

Christian nodded, but did not pursue the topic. They trotted along for several minutes, Azalea in silence and Chris whistling a stirring march. Azalea almost wished that her grandfather had never mentioned that marriage business. Then she'd be enjoying this ride as she had yesterday's, delighting in her new friend instead of worrying over how she ought to behave when—or if—he broached the subject.

"You are a very good whistler," she ventured after a moment.

Chris broke off with a laugh. "Funny you should say that. I consider it rather a guilty pleasure, since Father discourages it and Herschel, my older brother, positively loathes it, mainly because he's never learned himself. But here, why do we not take a rest for a moment?" He gestured toward a broad, mossy rock.

They both dismounted to rest on the cool surface in the shade of an unusually large and gnarled apple tree. Azalea spread her skirts about her, resisting the impulse to draw her knees up to her chin as she usually did.

Desperately, she tried to think of something else to say. The silence progressed from companionable to uncomfortable. Inspiration had yet to strike when Christian turned to her and said, "I assume, Azalea, that your grandfather has spoken to you about the possible, er, alliance between our families?"

He was watching her a bit anxiously, and that unaccountably put her more at ease. Realizing that Chris was nervous too made him less an object of awe. Her heart warmed towards him with an affection that was more sincere than the infatuation she had already admitted to herself.

She nodded silently, unable to meet his eyes. Had he changed his mind? She waited for him to continue.

"Now that we are alone, I'd... like to take this opportunity to ask you to marry me. Will you, Azalea?" he concluded in a rush.

Startled, she turned her eyes to him, unable to believe that she had understood him correctly. "You... you're actually proposing to me?" she asked incredulously, unable to hide her sudden joy. This was much more romantic than the dry agreement she had expected. Perhaps he really did care for her a little.

Christian tried not to flinch at the expression in her eyes. How could he ever live up to such expectation, such adoration? He vowed silently to do his utmost to spare her disillusionment in the years ahead.

"It's appropriate that we settle this matter between ourselves, don't you think?" he asked in as casual a voice as he could manage. "After all, we are the ones who will be sharing forty or fifty years together, not the estimable gentlemen who concocted this rather unconventional arrangement."

Taking a deep breath, he continued. "I'm by no means perfect—" he frowned, for it seemed somehow imperative that she understand this "—and cannot promise to become so, but I would never knowingly cause you pain. Consider, also, that by marrying me at so young an age you will be cheating yourself of the chance to be courted by other, possibly far more worthy, gentlemen later on."

Why should such an idea suddenly bother him?

"I want you to fully realize what you would be agreeing to," he concluded. To his surprise, he found himself holding his breath as he waited for her reply, watching her face closely to gauge her feelings.

"I realize," she said solemnly.

Christian let out his breath.

"I realized before I gave Grandfather my consent this morning, for he also wanted me to be very sure. I am. Yes, Chris, I will marry you, if you really don't mind being tied to a thirteen-year-old wife. I promise to grow up as quickly as I can!"

"Don't grow up too quickly, Azalea," said Christian quickly, surprising himself by his seriousness. "I may deprive you of other suitors, but I refuse to deprive you of your childhood. Enjoy it while you can. Promise me?"

"All— all right. I promise," Azalea answered, plainly startled by his earnestness.

"Thank you." The innocence in her wide green eyes moved him in a way he found hard to understand. "In return, I promise to make you as happy as I possibly can." He spoke it as a vow.

The wedding took place three days later at Bruton Parish Church. Due to Azalea's youth, only the rector and his wife were present in addition to the four people principally concerned.

The usual announcement had not been placed in the local newspaper. Reverend Simpson had thought it best that Azalea's marriage not be publicized in Williamsburg. It might make her social life uncomfortable, he said, to be perceived as being "different" from her peers.

The rector's wife began to play the organ, signalling the start of the ceremony, and Azalea entered the sanctuary dressed, not in a real bridal gown, but in her best white poplin.

Glancing around nervously, she took in every detail of the familiar church, which she had attended weekly all her life. Everything now seemed new and different. For one thing, the rector was not perched in his customary place in the carved wooden pulpit, where he could look down on the congregation in their private pews. Instead, he stood at the front altar, as he normally did only for communion.

As the church was nearly empty, the usual rustlings and whisperings of the assembled congregation were strangely absent. The aisle appeared abnormally long as she slowly walked between the high wooden walls of the vacant pews. She hadn't thought she would be nervous, but now...

Christian watched her progress from his position next to the altar and couldn't help thinking how young and defenceless Azalea looked. An unexpected surge of protectiveness welled up in him. He suddenly regretted that he would have to leave her here, in the wilds of this new, untamed country. Of course, she would have her grandfather to watch over her, but still...

When Azalea finally reached the altar, the participants took their places and the rector began his homily. Neither bride nor groom heard much of his explanation of the purpose and responsibilities of marriage. It hardly seemed to apply in their case.

Abruptly, they were repeating the vows, and Azalea heard herself saying, "...until death us do part."

The very permanency of the oath made her tremble. How well did she know Chris, really? Glancing up, she met his eyes and he winked reassuringly. She sighed. Everything would be all right.

At the conclusion of the ceremony Christian hesitated, then kissed his new bride on the forehead. Azalea was slightly disappointed, but chided herself for the feeling. She knew it had been agreed that this would not be a true marriage for some years. Recalling what Clara Banks had told her about her sister's wedding night, she knew she should be relieved.

Then her new father-in-law was hugging her, the rector's wife offering congratulations and there was no more time for relief or regret. She was Mrs. Christian Morely.

Walking home from Jonathan's farewell party, Azalea noticed the unmistakeable signs of autumn in the rosy blush of the dogwood leaves and the prominence of their berries. A few chrysanthemums bloomed in the tangle of weeds by the walls of the old magazine.

She did not pause long to admire such botanical delights this afternoon, for there was already a noticeable nip in the air, and dusk would be coming early. Azalea was going to miss Jonathan. True, they had not been as close this past year, but that was no doubt due mainly to the fact that they had less free time to spend together.

In the six months since her marriage, Azalea felt that she had hardly kept her promise to Christian not to grow up too fast. Everyone was pushing her to learn so many things. She had little time now for horses and gardens —or for romping with Jonathan.

And now her friend was leaving for England, to attend Oxford at his maternal grandfather, Lord Holte's, insistence. Perhaps she'd see him when she went to London in another few years. Wouldn't he be surprised!

For Azalea had reluctantly agreed to keep her marriage secret. Not even Swannee had been told. Although she knew that her friends would treat her differently if they knew, she would dearly have loved to tweak Missy Farmer's so superior nose with the news.

But the worst thing was not being able to confide in Jonathan. But she knew he would never have been able to keep such a plum to himself, no matter how many promises she extracted from him. Perhaps it was just as well she had seen so little of him since the wedding.

She had managed to convince herself that having such a delicious secret more than made up for missing the satisfaction of seeing everybody's reaction to her news. It had helped to keep life interesting in the absence of the rather unconventional pastimes she had previously enjoyed. To think, it had been three months and more since she had so much as climbed a tree!

Azalea sighed to herself as she pushed open the self-closing gate, weighted by an old cannon-ball on a chain, to enter the back gardens. If only the time would pass more quickly. The years stretching ahead of her before she could join Chris in England seemed like an eternity.

He and Lord Glaedon had returned after their trip to Richmond, but had been able to stay for a mere three days before meeting their ship. Wistfully, Azalea wished again that she and Chris could have had more time together.

Perhaps Grandfather could be persuaded that sixteen would be old enough for her to join her husband, she thought, returning to her favourite subject. After all, only two months ago Gwenny Pugh, the postmistress's youngest daughter, had married at sixteen.

With this argument in mind, Azalea skipped up the front porch steps and entered the house. She let the door slam behind her, and at once Millie, the young serving maid who doubled as Cook's assistant, scurried from the parlour, where she had apparently been waiting for her young mistress.

"Oh, miss, thank the good Lord you've come home at last!" she exclaimed in obvious agitation. "The Reverend, he's been asking after you this past hour and more. Fair upset he seems to be! You'd best go to him at once."

"Upset? Do you mean he is angry with me?" Azalea asked in some confusion, unable to think of any scrapes she might have gotten into recently.

"Oh, no, miss!" replied Millie. "I only meant that he seems

disturbed. He got some letter or message or some such, and he's been—"

Without waiting to hear the end of the girl's sentence, Azalea turned and ran to the library, a deep foreboding clutching at her heart.

Opening the door a crack, she cautiously peered inside to see her grandfather sitting before the dying fire, a crumpled paper in his lap. He seemed not to have heard her, but continued to stare unseeing into the flames. Azalea's apprehension increased.

"Grandfather?" she whispered.

The old man slowly turned towards her, and she was shocked at the change in his face. It was as though he had aged ten years in a few hours.

"What is it? What's wrong?" She could feel the blood draining from her face.

"You had better sit down, my dear. I'm afraid I have some very bad news," he said heavily.

He waited while Azalea shakily seated herself across from him.

"I don't know how to prepare you for this, child," he began in a voice devoid of expression. "I have received a letter from Herschel Morely, Howard's eldest son."

She closed her eyes, willing the words to stop, but her grandfather continued inexorably.

"The *Fortitude,* which was carrying his father and brother home to England, never reached port. It was lost in a storm at sea, along with its passengers and crew. No trace has been found of the ship, nor of any survivors. I'm sorry, Azalea."

CHAPTER TWO

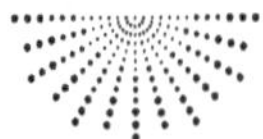

SEPTEMBER 1815

AZALEA CLOSED AND FASTENED THE VALISE CONTAINING THE few clothes and essential toiletries she would need during her voyage. Everything else had already been packed in trunks and sent ahead. The sun was just rising, but in an hour's time a coach would arrive to carry her the forty miles to Hampton, where she would stay the night. The following day, she would board a ship for England.

She sighed as she contemplated the tedious journey before her. The months since her grandfather's death had been spent preparing for the voyage, down to the smallest detail, yet she felt far from prepared mentally. Mechanically, she walked to the window and gazed out over the lawns.

The past six years were almost a blur in her memory. Only a few events stood out clearly in her mind. The most vivid, still, was the day she'd learned of Christian's death at sea. Her grandfather had suffered a seizure two days after receipt of that sad news, brought on, no doubt, by the stress of coping with both his own grief and Azalea's. He never fully recovered his faculties and for his final two years had been entirely bedridden.

Azalea had focused herself completely on his care, though her grandfather had repeatedly expressed concern that such determined devotion, while touching, was an unhealthy escape from reality.

"The world goes on, my dear, and so must your life," he had said. "You cannot hide here with me forever. There is money enough to hire a nurse. An hour or two of your time in the evenings, playing chess or reading, would content me. I would not have you waste your youth at my bedside and then remember me with bitterness because of it when I am gone."

"You know how much you mean to me, Grandfather," she had replied. "It is my own choice to be here. The boys have all gone away to school or are tied up with their farming, and I never did have much in common with other girls and their silly, gossiping ways. I am much happier here with you, believe me."

Eventually, she allowed the persistent Mrs. Swann to share a bit in his nursing, but she used the extra time only to tend her neglected gardens and horses. Azalea had spoken truthfully when she'd said she had little desire for the society of others.

This was still true. Well-meaning neighbours came and went, their sympathy a cloak for curiosity. Especially unwelcome was the frequently asked question, "What will you do now?"

For Azalea's future was foggier than her past, even though her path had been carefully laid for her. Despite his infirmity,

Reverend Simpson had prepared quite thoroughly for his granddaughter's future, she found. When it became clear that he could not linger much longer, he had summoned his lawyer, dictated letters and made certain changes to his will.

The reading of that will was another event that stood out clearly in her mind. Reverend Simpson had left all of his land and possessions to Azalea, which in itself had not surprised her. But the conditions of that legacy did: that she sell the house and land and, with the proceeds, remove herself to England. There she was to establish herself in London and regain her father's inheritance, currently held by her uncle, Lord Kayce.

She had assumed her grandfather's primary motive in stipulating such a course was to prevent her from retreating further from society, but then she read the letters that accompanied the will.

The first must have been written early in his illness, as it was in her grandfather's own hand. It detailed his suspicions of Lord Kayce, citing as evidence various things Azalea's own father had told him years ago. If these suspicions were to be believed, Lord Kayce had forced his elder brother to flee England in order to secure for himself the vast Kayce lands and wealth. Included in the letter was a stern warning to Azalea not to trust her uncle.

The second letter was from a Lady Beauforth, first cousin to Azalea's mother and niece to her grandfather. It was dated quite recently, and was obviously in response to a query the Reverend had sent some months earlier.

My dear Uncle Gregory:

I was delighted to hear from you after so many years. I remember you with affection from my childhood, and Mother always spoke lovingly of you. Of course I would be delighted to offer my young cousin Azalea entree to London Society. She will be wonderful company for my own daughter, Marilyn, whom your Azalea cannot fail to love as dearly as I do. And how exciting to have a young American in our midst! Such a pity that your health will prevent you from accompanying her, but the whirl of London is always more enjoyable for the young, in any event.

I will endeavour to introduce Azalea about without mentioning her American origin, unless her accent should give her away—to avoid any unpleasantness about the recent war, you understand. Of course, I myself have never much regarded politics, nor have most of my friends, so do not worry on that score. Please assure her that she will be delighted with Town life. We shall await Azalea's arrival impatiently.

Your devoted niece, etc.
Alice Beauforth

A postscript to this letter, dictated by her grandfather, informed Azalea that for all of her apparent flightiness, Lady Beauforth was very highly placed in Society and would afford Azalea ample protection while she regained her own fortune — protection he could no longer give her.

Enclosed with the letters were the proofs of Azalea's marriage to Christian, with instructions to use them, if necessary, to enlist the aid of Herschel Morely, the new Lord Glaedon, in her mission.

Azalea had reluctantly answered Lady Beauforth's somewhat disjointed missive, informing her cousin of Reverend

Simpson's death and of her own expected arrival date in England. She had no intention of concealing her nationality, of course, but refrained from mentioning this in her letter.

She also omitted any mention of Lord Kayce, her early marriage, or her plans to gain her inheritance. If her uncle really were dangerous, no good could come of giving him advance warning of her arrival or her existence. And after reading her rambling letter, she did not trust Lady Beauforth to remain silent on any point.

Thus it was a very brief, almost terse, note that Lady Beauforth would have received. No doubt that lady would attribute it to her young cousin's grief, or the influence of having been brought up in the wilds. Azalea could not bring herself to care overmuch which.

She absently fingered the large packet containing a copy of the will, the letters and the marriage lines. On impulse, she opened it again, to glance through the contents. There was the marriage certificate, with signatures of the rector, Dr. Wills, as having performed the ceremony and of Mrs. Wills as witness, as well as a document of consent signed by her grandfather.

Her throat tightened when she saw Christian's signature above her own childish one. Even after so many years, that loss still hurt.

She returned the certificate to the packet and tucked it into a compartment of her valise. Fastening it, she took a final glance around to assure herself that nothing had been forgotten, then turned and closed the door on the echoing chamber that had been her bedroom for most of her nineteen years.

The sound brought Millie, the mulatto servant, out of her own room at the end of the upstairs hallway. "Why, miss! I didn't know you was awake! I never heard a sound in your room all morning. You should have at least called me to help you dress—I could use the practice. Miz Swann says young ladies don't never dress theirselves in Londonengland." Millie's hands fluttered about her as she spoke.

"Yes, Millie, I'll have to get used to that myself, I suppose. But for this morning, I was certain you would have enough to do without helping me to dress. Besides, this gown fastens down the front, so it was no trouble at all for me to do myself." She glanced into her looking glass to make certain her toilette was complete.

For the start of her journey, Azalea was clad in half mourning, her simple dress of deep plum ornamented only by black lace at throat and wrists. Her hair, tied back by a simple black ribbon, now reached nearly to her waist, its colour having deepened over the past few years to a rich auburn. At the same time, her hermitlike existence had caused her youthful tan to fade and her complexion was now of a paleness that she imagined might rival that of any London lady addicted to creams and sunshades.

Her eyes remained the deep grey-green of the Atlantic, but six years had ripened her figure until, at nineteen, Azalea was endowed by nature with the full bust and tiny waist that so many women of her time used padding and corsets to achieve.

"Breakfast is ready, girls!" called Mrs. Swann from the foot of the stairs.

Azalea thought the housekeeper looked younger, somehow. Perhaps it was the excitement of setting out on a journey that had put the sparkle in her eye; that, or the knowledge that she was going back to her homeland and a reunion with her two sisters.

Looking at Mrs. Swann, Azalea felt a small stirring of anticipation in her own breast. Maybe she *had* been cloistered away in this house for too long. Feeling suddenly more optimistic, she went down to breakfast.

The hired coach drew up to the front of the house just as the travellers finished breakfast. In a final flurry, cloaks, hats and gloves were found, and Mrs. Swann ushered the two girls out the door and down to the waiting coach.

American to the core, Azalea had never made much distinction of rank. She felt more as if she were travelling with an older and younger sister than with two servants. This was fortunate, as it made her departure from all she had ever known much less frightening.

With only a brief stop for refreshment at midday, they made good time over the surprisingly well-maintained roads, one of the few benefits of the recent war. They arrived at Hampton just after four o'clock.

Azalea was struck immediately by the unusual appearance of the town, which brought home to her the suffering caused by that second conflict with England, during which Hampton had been burned to the ground. In the intervening year much reconstruction had taken place, but stark, blackened ruins still dominated the scene.

Passing a large cathedral, she saw that some of the original structure remained, its red brick bell tower discolored by smoke, while two wooden wings were obviously newly built. The same combination of charred stone and recent woodwork, still under construction, could be seen throughout the busy town.

She realized how very fortunate they had been in Williamsburg to have escaped the worst ravages of this "Second War of Independence." Even there, though, where no English troops had come, the townspeople had not gone unscathed. Several sons of local farmers and merchants, and even two students she had known, had departed to join the defending army and never returned.

A sudden surge of resentment against the British startled her with its violence. How dared they! Her resolve to openly acknowledge herself an American became stronger, regardless of Cousin Alice or any other squeamish family members.

The coach finally stopped in front of The Republic Inn, a large, partially rebuilt house within sight of the docks. The glass windows and fresh paint proclaimed it a prosperous establishment and a well-maintained one.

Alighting from the coach before the coachman could climb down to assist her, Azalea turned to help Millie and Mrs. Swann descend.

"Let's get inside for a hot meal and a good night's sleep on dry land," Mrs. Swann recommended cheerfully. "We've got quite a day ahead of us tomorrow."

Gazing around the drawing-room of the Beauforth Town house on Curzon Street, Azalea was overcome by depression. She did not doubt that this was one of the finer houses in London, as Sir Matthew Beauforth had possessed a fortune of no little consequence. But the cold formality of the chamber, with its gilt chairs and white upholstery, did nothing to lift her spirits, now weighed down by apprehension, loneliness and fatigue.

Immediately upon her arrival nearly an hour ago, Mrs. Swann and Millie had been ushered off to the servants' quarters by a housekeeper so stiff and fastidiously dressed that Azalea had at first mistaken her for Lady Beauforth.

The butler, Smythe— if possible even more coldly formal than Mrs. Straite (whose name Azalea found peculiarly appropriate) —had shown her into this room with the intimation that Lady Beauforth would see her shortly.

Azalea's stomach growled. She was just wondering whether "shortly" meant something different in England than it had at home when a short, fat, gaudily gowned lady swept into the drawing-room, her bejeweled hands outstretched. An overpowering cloud of violet fragrance enveloped Azalea as the woman advanced.

"You must be little Azalea Clayton! Have you been *very* bored, my dear? I only just finished dressing after my afternoon nap."

Azalea was torn between an urge to laugh at the lady's voice and appearance and a reluctance to breathe in her sickly sweet perfume. Collecting herself, she rose and extended her own hand.

"Lady Beauforth?" she asked uncertainly. After her experience with the housekeeper, she was afraid to jump to conclusions.

"Cousin Alice, my dear, please! Let us not stand on ceremony —we are kin, after all. Was your journey *dreadful?* You'll want to go straight to your room and sleep for *days,* I am certain. I was so sorry to hear about poor Uncle Gregory! You must feel the loss just *dreadfully,* my dear."

Azalea nodded noncommittally, wondering if this could possibly be her cousin's real speaking voice. Surely no one could feign that high-pitched tone indefinitely.

"Lady— Cousin Alice," Azalea said when it appeared that

her hostess had temporarily run out of words, "I want to thank you so much for your willingness to take me in and sponsor me. I hope I won't be obliged to impose upon your kindness for too long."

"Tut, tut, my dear! What is family for? Besides, there is very little generosity in this case, as Uncle Gregory insisted on paying all of your expenses himself."

Azalea winced at this reminder of the terms of her grandfather's will, which she had not been certain Lady Beauforth understood. She was relieved to find that apparently she did, which meant there was no chance of her being mistaken for a charity case.

Meanwhile Lady Beauforth, who was not quite so shatter-brained as she appeared, was making some calculations of her own regarding Azalea. With her air of maturity and grace, her unusual colouring and striking beauty, the girl was bound to cause a stir in the fashionable world of the ton. At first glance, she might not take— that gown was positively dowdy —but in a new wardrobe, with her hair stylishly cut...

"Now, my dear, I absolutely *insist* that you rest until tea," she said firmly. "If you're asleep, we shan't wake you till dinner, or even breakfast, if you prefer." Lady Beauforth needed some time to reorganize her thinking before her darling Marilyn made Azalea's acquaintance. This was not the rough savage they had both expected.

"Thank you, Cousin Alice, I am a bit fatigued. But please do not let me sleep through dinner, or I might well starve before breakfast." Azalea rose with a smile and followed a hovering maidservant out of the room.

As she climbed the curving oak staircase, she was struck again by the elegance of the furnishings she could see from this vantage point. Obviously someone other than Lady Beauforth had been in charge of decorating the house, unless her cousin's eccentricities were limited to matters of dress and speech, which Azalea somehow doubted. Most likely the bulk of it had been done by generations past, or perhaps by hired professionals.

"This here's your room, miss," the young maid said, interrupting Azalea's musings. "Her ladyship let Miss Marilyn choose the room, and she must have thought you'd be most comfortable here." She opened the door to the chamber and stepped aside. "My name's Junie, if you should be needing anything."

Azalea smiled warmly at the girl. "Thank you, Junie. I'm afraid I'm not very good company right now. I'm very tired. We'll have time for a good talk later, I'm sure."

"Of—of course, miss," the girl said, plainly disconcerted. "Will you be needing anything now? Her ladyship said as how I should unpack for you and act as your abigail, if you approve, of course." She smiled tentatively.

"That's very sweet, Junie, but I've already promised Millie, who travelled all the way from America with me, that she should have that post. I hope that won't cause a problem?"

"Oh, no, miss, I don't see how it would," Junie replied, though she looked a bit disappointed. "I'll just tell Mrs. Straite you've brought your own abigail. I'll continue on as upstairs maid. I was promoted just last month," she added proudly, with another shy smile.

Azalea realized that becoming her personal abigail would have represented an even greater promotion and thought she understood the girl's disappointment.

"How wonderful for you," she said warmly. "But I've just

had an idea. Millie is an American, like myself, and has no real experience as a fashionable lady's maid. Do you suppose Mrs. Straite would consent to your training her? Both she and I would be very grateful, I assure you."

Junie's face broke into a delighted smile. "I'll ask her right away, miss! And thank you, miss!" she exclaimed, fairly skipping from the room.

Alone, Azalea finally had an opportunity to look about her room. Even at first glance it was apparent that the furnishings were not quite up to the standard of the rest of the house, though they were still far finer than any she had been used to. Azalea guessed that furniture a little too worn for the finer guest rooms had been put here, but she didn't mind a bit. The room was done in faded shades of green and gold, which she found soothing, and the bed and chairs looked more comfortable than newer ones might be.

Crossing to the window, Azalea caught her first glimpse of the gardens and gasped with delight. What a botanical wonderland! Even in late November, a few chrysanthemums were in bloom, and she could identify several species of ornamental shrubs.

She would explore the gardens as soon as she went back down —well, after some tea, anyway. She was famished —and tired. Removing her shoes, Azalea stretched out on the gold counterpane of the bed and closed her eyes. Just a few minutes rest...

Hunger awakened her several hours later. The sun had set, and Azalea found herself in almost total darkness. For a few moments she imagined she was still in her cabin on the ship, but then was recalled to her surroundings by the distant sound of hooves and carriage wheels from the street.

Rising, she hurried to the window in an effort to determine the hour. The last faint rays of the recently departed sun informed her that there should still be ample time to dress before dinner. How late would that be, here? Swannee had told her that Town meals were later than those in the country, but she hadn't been specific. Perhaps each household kept its own hours.

Fumbling along the top of the dressing-table, Azalea found a branch of candles and lit them from the embers of what that afternoon had been a cheerful fire. Opening the clothes-press in the corner of the chamber, she was pleased to find that the efficient Junie had unpacked and hung her gowns, and had apparently even shaken out the worst of the travel creases.

Selecting her best gown, a deep rust-coloured velvet, she donned it with full knowledge that it would hardly stand comparison with the fashionable creations she had seen in a ladies' periodical on the drawing-room table earlier. Shopping for new clothes would have to be high on her list of things to do.

Her hair was neat, but hardly attractive, drawn severely back from her face and twisted into a knot at the base of her neck. However, this was the only style, other than letting it hang loose, that she was capable of on her own, and she knew that Millie could scarcely have done better. Hairdressing was not one of the girl's strong points.

Feeling very much the dowdy country cousin, Azalea descended the stairs and paused at the bottom, listening for voices that might give her a clue as to where the family was assembled at this hour. A murmur behind the doors of the drawing-room encouraged her to approach.

Entering, she beheld her cousin, still attired in her brilliant rose, yellow and amethyst silks, speaking with a dazzling young lady dressed with impeccable and obviously expensive taste. At Azalea's entrance, the young lady turned wide, blandly interested blue eyes in her direction.

"Awake already, my dear?" Lady Beauforth asked solicitously. "I was going to have Junie check on you in half an hour, when I retired to my room to dress for dinner."

Azalea's imagination faltered at what her ladyship's idea of evening attire might be.

"Did you rest at all?"

"Oh, yes, Cousin Alice, I feel very refreshed. Truth to tell, it was hunger that awakened me, and not knowing the dinner hour here, I thought it best to dress and come down directly."

"How thoughtless of me! Of course, you would not be familiar with our customs yet. Dinner won't be for another hour and more. Marilyn and I were going upstairs to dress in a few more minutes."

Thus recalling Marilyn's presence, Lady Beauforth turned to introduce Azalea to her daughter, whose smile had become rather fixed.

"Marilyn, this is your cousin, Azalea Clayton, of course. Azalea, let me present my daughter, Miss Marilyn Beauforth." This last was said with a flourish, and her ladyship stepped back as if presenting a rare artwork to view.

Azalea was suitably impressed. She could scarcely conceive of a more perfect picture of fashion than the beautiful creature now facing her. Honey-coloured hair was piled artistically atop her graceful head in a style that caused Azalea an unfamiliar twinge of envy. The beautiful creature seemed a shade less than charmed, however.

"Pleased to make your acquaintance, I'm certain, Miss

Clayton," Marilyn said with a slight nod. The formality of her words clashed oddly with her voice—a high, childish lisp that was still a good octave lower than her mother's.

"The honour is mine, Miss Beauforth," replied Azalea, following her cousin's lead. As Marilyn seemed disinclined to pursue the conversation further, Azalea turned back to Lady Beauforth.

"Ma'am, I could not help admiring your gardens from my window earlier. As I am down so early, would it be permissible for me to take a stroll through them before dinner?"

Though expressing surprise that Azalea should wish to walk out in the chill air after dark, Lady Beauforth saw no reason to disallow it, providing she was accompanied by Junie and wore a cloak.

Thanking her cousin with a warmth that drew surprised looks from both ladies, Azalea excused herself.

"Well!" Marilyn exclaimed pettishly as soon as the door had closed behind Azalea. "'Cousin Alice,' is it? And am I to be 'Cousin Marilyn'?" She shuddered delicately. "And her accent! Why, simply to be seen with her—was she really dressed for dinner, do you think? —may well lower me in Society."

Her mama tut-tutted and reassured her, but Marilyn seemed unwilling to clasp her new-found cousin to her bosom as Lady Beauforth had hoped she might.

Meanwhile, oblivious of the conversation within doors, Azalea was enjoying her tour of the gardens immensely. Led by her nose, she had discovered two late-blooming roses of a variety she had never encountered in Virginia.

Azalea appealed to Junie for information about this rare strain. Junie was forced to plead ignorance but, clearly not wanting to disappoint, volunteered to introduce Azalea to the gardener on the morrow.

"He knows every flower and bush in the place, miss, and would dearly love to talk to someone what knows so much as yourself, I know."

"That would be lovely. Thank you, Junie," said Azalea. "But now, I suppose I had best hurry inside to comb my hair before dinner."

"Might I dress it for you, miss? I've been taught how, and even did Miss Marilyn's once, when her abigail was sick," Junie offered eagerly.

"Could you? That's one thing I'm certain Millie cannot do yet. Perhaps you can be my personal hairdresser, as well as Millie's tutor."

When Azalea descended to the dining-room half an hour later, her confidence was bolstered by the knowledge that her hairstyle, at least, rivaled that of her cousin Marilyn. True to her word, Junie knew her business and had arranged Azalea's hair beautifully, with curling tendrils escaping from a high crown to frame her face.

Junie had assured her that with a little more time and a little less hair she could have done even better. After seeing Junie's ability, Azalea had promised to have her hair cut in the morning, even before visiting a dressmaker. She realized that she would need her cousins' advice on these matters, and determined to bring up the subject at dinner.

Proceeding to the place at table indicated by Smythe, Azalea was gratified by the slight widening of Miss Beauforth's eyes, taking it as a compliment to Junie's skill. Lady Beauforth was more outspoken, cheerfully greeting Azalea from her place at the head of the table.

"Why, what a difference that hairstyle makes, my dear! I declare, you look like a new person. Don't you agree, darling?" she asked hopefully, turning toward her daughter.

Marilyn responded with an insincere smile. "Indeed, it makes you look almost English. A definite improvement."

Azalea had to bite her tongue to suppress the angry retort that rose to her lips. If it were not so absurd, she might almost think Marilyn was jealous of her. However, it would not do to antagonize her relatives on her first evening in their home.

"Thank you," she forced herself to say. "I thought perhaps tomorrow I might have it cut as well. Junie tells me it is far too long and thick to be fashionable."

"Junie?" Marilyn looked blank.

"The upstairs maid. It was she who styled my hair." Marilyn's glance slid negligently away to focus on her mother, who had already launched into a stream of advice to Azalea concerning the only hairdressers and modistes worth visiting.

"I vow, you'll be quite a credit to us when you are properly attired," she declared. "We'll have you betrothed by the end of the Season, I doubt not. It is most fortunate that you have come to us now, when we shall have all winter to bring you smack up to the nines."

"Mama, I was just thinking about *my* wedding clothes," Marilyn interrupted with a sidelong glance at Azalea. "I saw a new watered silk yesterday that would do admirably for my travelling dress."

"Are you to be wed soon, Cousin?" asked Azalea politely, to cover her dismay at Lady Beauforth's words. It had not occurred to her that she might be expected to marry. She didn't want another husband, at least not yet. Not after Chris... She hurriedly thrust that memory aside.

"Oh, yes, Marilyn has made *such* a conquest!" gushed Lady Beauforth before her daughter could answer. "And Lord Glaedon, old friend and neighbour that he is, has been *quite* flatteringly insistent on an early wedding date. It will scarce give us time to ready a suitable trousseau."

"No, Glaedon would not be put off till June, but must needs marry me in February," Marilyn tittered. "I must say he has been most attentive of late, as well." Demurely casting her eyes down, Marilyn glanced sideways through her lashes at her cousin, as though to ascertain that she was paying proper attention.

Azalea scarcely noticed. "Lord Glaedon, did you say, ma'am?" she asked in a tight, strained voice. Suddenly, it seemed difficult to breathe. "I—I did not know that you were acquainted with him."

She hardly knew what she was saying, the shock of hearing the name was so great. Of course she had known that if she stayed permanently in England, she would likely encounter Christian's older brother eventually, but she had pushed that thought far to the back of her mind. Suddenly learning that he was a frequent visitor to this very house took her completely off guard.

Struggling to regain her composure, she noticed that her cousins were regarding her rather strangely. "What did you say, ma'am?" Belatedly, she realized that Lady Beauforth had asked her a question.

"I asked how you come to know of Lord Glaedon, my dear. Are you all right? Your colour is quite gone. You are not about to swoon, are you?"

"Oh, no ma'am, I—I'm fine," Azalea answered in a tolerably steady voice. "I was merely startled."

She took a few deep breaths to calm herself before explaining. "The previous Earl, Lord Glaedon's father, was a close friend of my grandfather's, you see. He spoke of Lord Glaedon frequently, and was devastated by the news of his death. It—it is my belief that the shock played a large part in the illness to which he eventually succumbed."

"Oh! Oh, I see," said her ladyship with a nod, her curiosity apparently satisfied. "No wonder mention of the name distressed you. But I do hope you won't mind meeting the present Earl of Glaedon. As he is Marilyn's fiancé, we encounter him frequently in Society, as well as here at home."

Lady Beauforth's tone, while concerned, did not indicate any suspicion that Azalea had told considerably less than the truth. For that, Azalea could only be relieved. She had no intention of acquainting her cousins with the details of her early life. However, she had no reason to believe that Lord Glaedon would be so reticent once he knew who she was. It was even possible he might hold her partially responsible for the deaths of his father and younger brother.

She stifled a sigh. That was one problem she refused to worry about before it materialized.

"No, I'm certain I will be able to encounter his lordship with composure, Cousin Alice," Azalea assured her, hoping she spoke the truth. "It was merely the unexpectedness of hearing his name that overset me for a moment."

Reassured on that point, Lady Beauforth resumed her instructions to the girls on where they were to shop on the morrow, since she would be unable to accompany them.

"I find my uncertain state of health makes it difficult for me to get about. I quite rejoice at the idea of your being able to accompany Marilyn to the shops and functions when I am unable to, Azalea— though of course we are delighted to have you here for your own sake, as well."

This last statement was added almost as an afterthought, and gave Azalea some insight into her cousin's real motive for offering her a home. It also helped to explain the contradictory nature of the letter sent to her grandfather. The thought bothered Azalea very little. She liked to know where she stood with people, and acting as Marilyn's companion made staying here smack even less of accepting charity.

Back in her room, Azalea dismissed Junie for the night after repeating Lady Beauforth's compliments on her hairstyle. Feeling no inclination to sleep, due, no doubt, to her nap earlier, Azalea reviewed her first day in London. In all, she found more to be pleased with than she had expected.

She doubted whether she would ever become truly close to her cousins, but they had treated her cordially enough and she saw no cause for complaint. By the end of the week, she would begin her campaign to regain her inheritance.

Since leaving America, she had thought of little else, regarding it as her grandfather's dying wish. If nothing more, dwelling on it served to distract her from her grief over her grandfather, and yes, over Christian as well. That loss still had the power to cause her pain, even after all this time.

On the passage from America, she had found the very sea a constant reminder of him. She had tried to spend as little time as possible on deck, devoting her days instead to needlework and to Millie, who had been seasick for most of the voyage. Occasionally, however, she had been irresistibly drawn to the railings of the foredeck, where she would gaze out across that beautiful, treacherous expanse, keeping her mind carefully blank.

The only time she allowed herself to think of Christian was in her prayers when, against all reason, she would unfailingly ask for a miracle to bring him back. She had done so every night since learning of his death six years ago.

Staring sightlessly down at the gardens, where wisps of fog trailed across the paths, Azalea deliberately lowered her rigid shield and allowed herself the luxury of remembering.

Immediately, Christian arose vividly in her mind, just as he had appeared the first evening they had met: handsome, care-free and self-assured. The few conversations they had shared replayed themselves word for word, until Azalea glanced over her shoulder, so strongly did she feel his presence.

She stopped her reverie abruptly on arriving at that fatal day that had destroyed her happy dreams and shook her head fiercely, surprised to find her cheeks wet with tears. For she was not really sad.

Instead, she felt oddly cleansed by the memories she had suppressed for so long. It was as if a tight knot within her had become untied, releasing her and allowing a freedom she had forgotten existed.

After six long years, Azalea was finally able to let Christian go, into the past where he now belonged. Suddenly tired, she turned back to the bed and slipped beneath the quilts. With a little sigh, she drifted off to sleep, dreaming of the future, rather than the past.

CHAPTER THREE

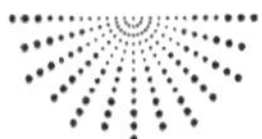

AZALEA DESCENDED AT EIGHT O'CLOCK THE NEXT MORNING
in search of breakfast, only to be informed by a startled maidservant that the ladies were still abed. In fact, the girl stammered, they did not customarily appear before ten o'clock, and
then only after an early evening.

The bright morning sunshine helped to relieve the sombre-
ness of the dining-room, with its dark panelled wainscotting
and beige-and-brown-figured wallpaper, making it bearable if
not cheerful. Still, it was hardly in keeping with her high spirits. Azalea hoped that the sunshine was a good omen for her
first full day in London.

"Could I perhaps have some breakfast in the garden?" she
asked the little maid. "I'm very hungry." She smiled hopefully
at the nervous girl, whose mouth twitched timidly in return.

"Certainly, miss! I'll fetch it at once."

"Or perhaps you could have Millie, the girl I brought with
me, bring it out?" suggested Azalea. "And I'd very much like
to speak with Mrs. Swann, as well, if that can be arranged."

She broadened her smile to disguise her discomfort at dispensing orders. She wondered if she'd ever get used to it.

When Millie and Mrs. Swann joined her in the gardens, they compared notes as Azalea ate. Mrs. Swann related that Mrs. Straite had agreed to keep her on as under-housekeeper and still-room maid until she could find a housekeeping position elsewhere. Though she professed herself content, Azalea noticed she pursed her mouth whenever she spoke of the housekeeper.

"Not to worry, miss," she concluded with a sniff. "I'll stay here as long as you have any need of me."

Azalea knew that it must be galling to her to be relegated to such a position, but was too grateful for her support to say so.

"Have you located your sisters, Swannee?" she asked her old friend with a smile. "Are they still living in London?"

"Drusilla is, I think, for I had a letter from her after I wrote that we might be coming. Margaret moved to Yorkshire some years back, though, so I don't expect I'll be seeing her any time soon."

Azalea nodded and turned to Millie.

The younger girl seemed quite uncomfortable with her prospective position as Azalea's abigail. "Folks do seem to stare at me a bit, Miss Azalea. I never thought much about my looks back home, but here... Couldn't I find some sort of work to do in the kitchens? I've already made friends with the scullery maid and one or two others there."

Her mixed ancestry had caused little comment in Virginia, where free Negroes and mulattos were not uncommon. But for the first time, Azalea realized how noticeable Millie must be in London. She agreed to this arrangement, recognizing that the shy girl might be happier occupying a less-conspicuous position than that of abigail.

With this matter settled to the satisfaction of all concerned, Azalea returned to the house to discover that Lady Beauforth was awake, but had sent word that she would remain in her room until nuncheon.

Marilyn descended half an hour later and asked if Azalea were ready to commence their shopping expedition.

"More than ready," Azalea replied. She had grown a bit bored with no one to talk to and no duties to perform. "I am eager to make myself presentable for London Society. I will appreciate any advice you can spare me, Cousin, for I can see that your taste is flawless." She was determined to do what she could to overcome the young lady's animosity, whatever its cause.

Seemingly gratified by the compliment, Marilyn bestowed a brief, dazzling smile on her cousin and agreed to guide her selections if necessary.

The girls' first stop was at the establishment of Madame Jeannine, the hairdresser Lady Beauforth had proclaimed to be superior to all others. That lady exclaimed over the thickness and rich auburn colour of Azalea's hair as she deftly cut and styled it with rapidly moving scissors and comb.

"A delight to work with, *mademoiselle*," she said more than once during the process.

In a surprisingly short time, she handed Azalea a mirror and invited her to view the result. Azalea gasped with pleasure. Relieved of excess weight, her natural curls had reasserted themselves and framed her face charmingly. The back remained long, though not so heavy, and was piled loosely but artfully on top of her head.

She looked questioningly at Marilyn, who reluctantly admitted that it looked very well. Azalea thanked Madame Jeannine as they took their leave of her with a profuseness that Marilyn appeared to consider slightly ill-bred.

En route to their next destination, the shop of a very fashionable modiste on Bond Street, Azalea couldn't help noticing the unusual level of noise in the streets. She commented on it to her companion.

"What do you mean? I perceive nothing out of the ordinary," said Marilyn in some surprise.

"Why all the shouting, singing, and street shows. And see those *jongleurs* over there? Is some type of fair or festival in Town?"

"No, my dear, it is merely London." Marilyn's breathy voice held amused condescension. "Do you mean to say there are no hawkers or entertainers on the streets in America?" she asked, betraying more interest than she had yet shown in a conversation with her cousin.

"Why, no. At least, not in Williamsburg. The merchants confine their selling to their shops, for the most part, and the public entertainment is to be found in the theatres, or in the town square during summer lay-by festivals. But I find all of this most interesting and exciting," she added quickly, not wishing Marilyn to think her critical of London.

Her cousin merely looked thoughtful, however.

Azalea was entranced by the dazzling array of silks, satins, velvets, muslins and laces paraded before her at Madame Clarisse's exclusive shop. Still, she was not so dazzled that she neglected to enquire about prices before ordering anything to be made up for her. She was secretly shocked by the replies, delivered in an accent that belied *Madame*'s fashionably French name.

It took little of her mathematical training to tell her that her small competence could quickly be consumed by far less than Lady Beauforth's idea of an adequate wardrobe. Nevertheless, she ordered three morning dresses and an evening gown, slightly less elaborate than what the modiste recommended. She also purchased a pair of stockings, some drawing-room slippers and a parasol.

"I believe that will be all for today, thank you. Shall we return home for nuncheon, Cousin?" she enquired brightly, turning to Marilyn.

"All?" repeated Marilyn in obvious disbelief.

Before she could continue, Azalea spoke again. She was not about to mention her lack of funds in front of the sharp-eared modiste, who had shared enough gossip during the past hour to demonstrate how carefully she listened to her customers' chance comments.

"For the present. I find myself quite fatigued, as well as hungry." Luckily Marilyn was not aware of the hearty breakfast she had enjoyed three hours earlier.

"Very well. I must not forget you are new to Town and unaccustomed to the exertions of shopping," said Marilyn pityingly.

Nor do I sleep until ten o'clock, thought Azalea, though she only nodded in reply.

During the carriage ride back to Curzon Street, Marilyn kindly offered to bring her cousin up to date on the current gossip. While she chattered on, Azalea was busy planning an early, discreet visit to the solicitor her grandfather had mentioned. It was obvious her present funds would scarcely last the Season if she were to enter Society as planned.

Why had no one told her London was so expensive? She determined to have a private conference with Lady Beauforth at the earliest opportunity. She thought it might be unwise to mention her problem to Marilyn, who seemed as prone to carrying tales as the modiste had been.

Upon their return, the ladies were informed by Smythe that Lord Glaedon had called in their absence and would look to see them in the Park that afternoon. Azalea was glad they had missed him. She needed a chance to compose herself first, and to decide what sort of enquiries about his family would be appropriate.

She wondered whether Marilyn or her mother had told him of their American cousin's visit. It seemed likely, given the degree of intimacy Marilyn had claimed last night. If so, it seemed odd that he had not mentioned to them the connection between the two families. She finally decided that her best course would be to take her cue from him, and to neither volunteer nor request any information unless he seemed disposed to be friendly.

After the meal, Azalea rang for Junie and asked if it would be possible to speak with Lady Beauforth, as she had not appeared at table. Junie seemed doubtful, but went to enquire. She returned after a moment to say that her ladyship was resting, and then asked how the morning's shopping had gone.

"I can see you took my advice about your hair, miss. It looks lovely!" she declared.

"Thank you, Junie. Perhaps you can advise me again," said Azalea tentatively. It had occurred to her that Lady Beauforth might not entirely welcome the news of her guest's lack of funds.

"Of course, Miss Azalea," said Junie importantly. Plainly, she was enjoying her new role as abigail/adviser to the American girl.

"Well, I seem to have a problem. I hadn't realized London would be so, well, expensive. Can you tell me if there is any way to make over my wardrobe without squandering all I have in the world? I'm afraid Lady Beauforth might not understand. After all, she recommended the modiste I visited today, so she must not consider her prices outrageous. But I don't see how I can possibly purchase one fourth of what my cousin seems to think necessary for the coming Season on what my grandfather left me."

Junie fairly swelled with pride at this evidence of Azalea's reliance on both her judgement and her discretion. "Well, miss, I know there are stalls down in Soho where there are bargains to be had, but it would never do for you to be seen there. I could go for you, with your permission. We're much the same size, and I'm handy enough with a needle to make what changes might be necessary."

"Oh, Junie, would you? That would be famous! But... do you think Lady Beauforth would be angry if she found out?" Azalea suddenly sobered. "I won't allow you to run that risk on my account."

Junie smiled with genuine affection for this unique young lady who actually put concern for an abigail above her own wants. "I'll just be certain she don't find out, that's all," she replied confidently. "You be thinking of a way to account for the new clothes you'll be having shortly, and I'll leave this very moment!"

Impulsively, Azalea hugged the girl, assuring her that she could come up with a plausible story.

When Junie returned, less than an hour before Azalea and Marilyn were to leave for the Park, she brought with her four dresses that rivalled those ordered that morning at Madame Clarisse's.

"There were lots to choose from, miss, but I thought you might need me to help you dress. I can go back tomorrow, if you like." Junie was nearly breathless, making Azalea wonder if she had run part of the way home in order to be back in time to help her new mistress.

Azalea was astonished and delighted when the abigail revealed what the gowns had cost—a mere fraction of the modiste's prices. Junie explained that most of the gowns at the Soho markets had been worn only once or twice, since it was considered bad ton to be seen twice in the same dress, particularly a ball gown.

"Then won't the ladies who originally had these made up recognize them if I wear them in public?" asked Azalea uneasily. That would be a snag in their ingenious plan.

"Not if I make a few little changes —add a ruffle here, remove some artificial flowers there. So many dresses are nearly alike anyway, no one will notice," Junie reassured her. "Now, what will you wear for your drive in the Park?"

Half an hour later, Azalea descended wearing one of the new gowns, hastily basted in at the waist. She felt positively elegant. True, there was a small stain near the hem at the back which there had not been time to remove, but if she remained seated in the carriage, no one should notice it.

Marilyn joined her a few moments later, resplendent in jonquil silk. "We must hurry," she said as they proceeded to the waiting barouche. "Lord Glaedon dislikes to keep his horse standing in the Park." Azalea wondered why Lord Glaedon had not come to fetch them, but refrained from voicing her thoughts. The drive to Hyde Park was short and in the opposite direction from Bond Street, affording her a look at more of Mayfair's imposing homes. The atmosphere here was far quieter than it had been in the shopping district, she noticed.

When they turned into the Park, Azalea had to stifle a gasp. So this was where everyone was! Lady Beauforth had complained last night that London was thin of company, but it seemed to Azalea that a veritable horde of fashionable people were here to take advantage of the fine weather, walking, riding and driving. How on earth did Marilyn intend to find her betrothed in this throng?

As if in answer, the girl at her side waved as a tall man in a dark blue riding coat trotted up on an enormous black gelding. "Lord Glaedon! I trust we have not kept you waiting long?"

"Not at all, my dear," he said smoothly, as he bent over her extended hand. Marilyn simpered prettily for a moment before belatedly recalling her manners.

"This is my cousin, Miss Clayton," she said, and Lord Glaedon turned his attention to Azalea.

As he bowed in acknowledgement, his eyes fastened on her face with an expression of mingled curiosity and bemusement.

Azalea felt similarly bemused, and only just remembered to nod in return. She had expected some slight resemblance to Christian, but the likeness was so striking it left her momentarily speechless. Herschel had the same dark hair and stormy blue-grey eyes as his younger brother. Even his voice was amazingly similar. He could have been Christian himself, risen from the dead.

Suddenly aware that they had been staring at one another, she made a determined effort to pull herself together.

"I'm pleased to make your acquaintance, my lord," she said rather lamely.

As she spoke, his gaze seemed to harden slightly and he hastily withdrew his hand before it could touch hers. He flicked a glance at Marilyn.

"Perhaps I should have warned you that my cousin is newly come from— from America to live with us," she stammered. "Nothing was really settled until she arrived yesterday, so I did not mention it before."

Her cousin seemed almost to be apologizing, Azalea thought indignantly.

"Yes. Quite," was all he said in reply. "Shall we commence our tour of the Park?"

Marilyn assented eagerly and the coachman urged the horses on. Lord Glaedon rode comfortably alongside, listening to his fiancée's chatter, and carefully avoided any glance in Azalea's direction. This afforded her an excellent opportunity to examine him at leisure, though she was careful not to stare, as Marilyn might misinterpret her reasons.

She had been right about the Earl's resemblance to his younger brother, but there were subtle differences that became apparent as she watched him. For one thing, he looked— and acted —far older than Chris would have been if he had lived, though Herschel was only a year or two older than Christian, if her memory served her.

Certainly, his manners were inferior to his brother's. Even his smile had a decidedly cynical twist, exaggerated by a faint scar that traced a line from his left ear to the corner of his mouth. It occasionally gave him a mysterious, almost sinister expression. No, perhaps the resemblance was not so strong after all, she decided.

He obviously had not recognized the name Clayton, but then the marriage had been no certain thing when Chris and his father had set out from England. Perhaps it was not remarkable that Herschel had not been informed of it. His hostility had seemed directed not so much at her as at Americans in general. A holdover from the recent war, perhaps?

Watching him surreptitiously, she also decided that his attitude towards Marilyn was not what it should be. There was no real warmth in his manner, for all her cousin's earlier boasting about his impatient ardour. Of course, her own presence might be inhibiting him somewhat, Azalea supposed, but really, he looked almost bored.

Their circuit of the Park was finished long before Marilyn exhausted her store of gossip.

"May I call upon you tomorrow?" Lord Glaedon asked, almost perfunctorily.

"You know you may, my lord," replied Marilyn, dimpling at him. "We shall look forward to your visit."

He touched his hat to both of them and turned his horse. As he rode away, he began to whistle a lilting Irish tune. Frozen in sudden shock, Azalea was left staring openmouthed at his retreating back.

CHAPTER FOUR

AZALEA TOOK IN NONE OF THE SCENERY DURING THE DRIVE
back to Beauforth House. Fortunately, Marilyn's aimless
chatter did not require anything in the way of a thoughtful
response. At any rate, her cousin seemed to detect nothing
wrong in her manner.

Still trembling from the discovery she had made, Azalea
stared ahead blindly, trying desperately to force her mind to
function. She felt as if her whole world had just been turned
upside down without warning. Blinking rapidly against the
darkness that seemed to be advancing on the edges of her
sight, she nodded vaguely to something her cousin had
said.

Think! Think!

Christian had distinctly told her, once upon a time, that
Herschel not only detested whistling, but that he had never
learned to do it. And that tune—it had been the same one she
had heard Christian whistle in Williamsburg. Azalea herself
had been struck by Lord Glaedon's uncanny resemblance to

the Chris she remembered. *Could* he possibly be her husband? How? *How?*

Clasping her hands tightly together in her lap, Azalea strove to organize her whirling thoughts. That he had not recognized her was patently obvious.

Or... was he merely pretending not to?

She honestly didn't think so. Surely he would have betrayed himself somehow, if only with a flash of awareness at his first sight of her.

And what of Herschel? If Christian was now the Earl of Glaedon, then Herschel must also be dead. She and her grandfather had heard no word of that tragedy, though she doubted anyone would have informed them. But how could Christian possibly have been alive all these years without her knowledge? And could he have changed so much?

The Christian she remembered had been a carefree, easygoing young man with engaging manners, nothing at all like the curt, cynical fellow she had met an hour ago. And he could never have aged that much in only six years. She supposed he could have received that scar in the shipwreck, but how could his whole personality have changed so completely?

What was far more likely was that Herschel had taken up whistling late in life, perhaps even in tribute to the younger brother he had lost. Likely, but... somehow she didn't think so. That sense of familiarity had nagged at her from the first moment she had seen Lord Glaedon. And when she'd heard him whistling, she had known beyond any doubt, for one crystal-clear moment, that he was indeed her Chris.

But without any facts, she realized, her guess was only wild conjecture. She must have the facts.

Would they be common knowledge? If so, Lady Beauforth

could undoubtedly tell her what she so urgently needed to know. She had heard enough at dinner last night to realize that very little of what went on in the fashionable world escaped her ladyship's notice.

The moment she had put off her cloak, Azalea went in search of her hostess.

Glancing up and down the empty upstairs hallway, she decided that the corner room at the far end was most likely Lady Beauforth's, as it was undoubtedly the largest. Before she could reconsider, she walked quickly to the door and knocked, more loudly than she had intended. Her cousin's startled "Yes?" told her that she had guessed correctly.

"It is I, Cousin Alice. Azalea. May I speak to you for a moment?"

"Of course, dear, come in."

Azalea opened the door and found herself in a chamber that bore no resemblance to the tasteful decor of the rest of the house. Cousin Alice's boudoir was a hodgepodge of antique and modern tables, chairs, *étagères*, pillows and ottomans. Incredibly, there was even a stuffed elephant's foot in one corner, with a bright pink cloth on top.

Every colour of the rainbow was present, though red and purple predominated, and every available surface, including the elephant's foot, was crowded with a dizzying variety of ornaments, valuable works of art competing for space with obvious trumpery pieces.

After a moment, Azalea succeeded in locating her cousin among the startling assortment. Dressed in a magenta wrapper, Lady Beauforth reclined on a chaise longue in the centre of the room.

"Yes, dear child, what is it?" she asked, completely at home in her astonishing surroundings. "Is something troubling you?"

With a start, Azalea recalled her purpose. "Not troubling me precisely, Cousin Alice," she began with studied casualness, "but I am curious about something and was hoping that you could enlighten me." Ever eager to be a source of information, Lady Beauforth beamed at her young relative. "Of *course,* dear! I'll be delighted to be of assistance."

"Miss Beauforth and I just encountered Lord Glaedon in the Park. As I, ah, mentioned last night, my grandfather was well acquainted with his father, the fourth Earl. He spoke of the family to me on more than one occasion, and it was my understanding that it was Herschel who was next in the succession?" Azalea could not quite bring herself to say Christian's name. She paused, hoping that Lady Beauforth would take it from there. She was not disappointed.

"Oh, my *dear,* I assumed you knew! It's best you do, I suppose, all things considered. After all, if there were any unpleasantness in that quarter, it's only fair you should know why, don't you think?"

Azalea nodded vaguely, having absolutely no idea what her cousin was talking about.

Lady Beauforth continued. "What I mean to say is that Herschel was killed two years ago in the war— the American war, you understand, not the French. Marilyn was *quite* devastated, I assure you. You may not have known it, but it was planned almost from her infancy that she would marry poor Herschel. Our lands run with theirs, you see.

"At any rate, Christian seems to have taken all Americans in dislike because of his brother's death. Quite understandable, I suppose. Not that it is *your* fault, of course, or anyone else's who wasn't actually in the fighting, but I'm sure you understand."

Azalea was beginning to, though the suddenness of having her suspicion confirmed almost took away her capacity for thought. "But, my lady—" A light tap on the door interrupted her, and Marilyn's abigail entered with a note for Lady Beauforth.

As her cousin read the message, Azalea had time to consider what she had just learned and to be glad of the interruption. She had been on the point of asking how Christian had escaped the shipwreck, a question that would have demanded more explanations than she was ready to give at the moment. There was another matter she could bring up, however.

"Tell my daughter that we'll discuss this at dinner. Perhaps we can contrive to make an appearance at both," said Lady Beauforth to the maid, dismissing her.

She turned her attention back to Azalea. "Now, my dear, where were we? Oh, yes, dear Christian. I pray you'll not take offence at his manner if he should, ah, treat you less than charmingly, now that you know the cause. And I suppose it would be quite proper if you were to make some show of sympathy over poor Herschel, seeing how you know the family, so to speak. But let me tell you the most interesting *on dit*— Oh, was there any other advice you needed?" Lady Beauforth interrupted herself, apparently remembering her current role as social advisor.

"As a matter of fact, Cousin Alice, there is," said Azalea reluctantly. She thought she might have liked to hear that particular *on dit*. "I find myself in need of visiting my grandfather's London solicitor, a Mr. John Timmons, and have no idea how to go about doing so."

"Oh, surely there will be no need to actually visit the man," said Lady Beauforth, clearly disappointed by the mundane request. "Indeed, most solicitors very much dislike women in their offices, I understand. I know dear Sir Matthew's lawyers always called on me here at the house after he went to his reward. Your best course would be to send a message round, asking him to visit you."

Azalea doubted this very much. After all, she was hardly of her cousin's social standing, which would likely make this Mr. Timmons reluctant to take so much time out of his busy schedule to cater to her whims. In addition, if she were to decide to ask his advice about her six-year-old marriage, she had no desire to be overheard by any member of her cousin's household. She decided to confide in Lady Beauforth about the lesser of her problems.

"The truth is, Cousin Alice, I need to speak to him about a rather delicate matter. I find that what my grandfather left me, which seemed so ample in America, will hardly support a London Season and certainly would leave me nothing to live on once it is over. I wish to enquire into the particulars of my paternal grandfather's will, to see if I have any money coming to me from the Kayce estates."

"Oh, my dear, I had no idea! How very dreadful for you, to be sure!" exclaimed Lady Beauforth, struggling up into a sitting position. "I naturally assumed that you were suffi-ciently well set up... but enough of that. Of course, under such circumstances it would be best for you to visit him. He would likely refuse to come to you, anyway, if he knew the truth. But in the meantime, what shall we do for you?" She appeared to be genuinely concerned, perhaps partially out of a fear that she might be expected to finance Azalea's Season herself.

"I shall be fine, Cousin, really," said Azalea quickly, banishing such an uncharitable thought. "Junie has been telling me about some places in Soho—"

"That's *it!*" Lady Beauforth's brow cleared as if by magic. "The very thing, if we are discreet. You wouldn't *believe* how many ladies of the ton shop there—by proxy, of course— because of the nip-farthing allowances their husbands give them. I daresay one or two of Marilyn's old gowns might be altered to fit you as well, as you are neither as plump nor as tall as she."

Azalea was relieved at her cousin's enthusiastic reception of the idea and it emboldened her to continue. "To tell the truth, Cousin Alice, Junie already made a brief trip to Soho for me early this afternoon. The dress I am wearing now came from one of the markets, though we only had time enough to take it in at the waist. She assures me that she can refurbish it to make it even more modish."

Lady Beauforth waved this idea aside and assured her that her own dressmaker could make any necessary alterations, as her taste was exquisite. Relieved of the possibility of having to fund Azalea's comeout herself, she seemed disposed to be generous.

"Now run along, my dear, and I'll have Marilyn's abigail look over her gowns from last Season. We are fortunate that the styles have not changed so very much. I'm certain Mrs. Osgood can bring them bang up to the nines for you." She dismissed Azalea with the most unaffected smile she had yet bestowed on her.

The next morning Junie appeared with a breakfast tray almost the instant Azalea awoke. An envelope rested on the tray next to the cup of chocolate and Azalea picked it up. "What is this?"

"I couldn't say, miss. It was given to me last night by Cartwright, her ladyship's dresser, to bring to you first thing. I set it on your tray so I wouldn't forget." Azalea opened the envelope to find that it contained the direction of Mr. John J. Timmons, Esq., and the information that Lady Beauforth's carriage would convey her there in the course of the morning, if she so wished.

"Why, how kind," Azalea exclaimed. "I'll go directly after breakfast. Junie, do you suppose you could order her lady-ship's carriage to be ready in three-quarters of an hour?"

"It's early yet, miss, but I'll try," answered the abigail doubtfully.

"Don't put the coachman to any trouble. I'll wait until he's had a chance to eat something. There is no real hurry, I suppose." But Azalea could not subdue her eagerness to carry out this errand as quickly as possible, and Junie gave her a most perceptive smile.

"It will be ready inside an hour, miss, for certain," she promised, and left the room with a militant gleam in her eye.

Junie returned in under five minutes to inform her mistress that the carriage could indeed be ready by nine o'clock, or even sooner if she wished.

"Thank you, Junie. You take very good care of me," said Azalea warmly, making the abigail flush with pleasure.

"No more than you deserve, miss," she said brusquely.

"Now, which dress will you wear? I got that stain out of the white one, and hemmed up the blue."

At precisely nine o'clock Azalea descended the front steps to the waiting carriage, wearing a charming morning dress of sky blue. She was accompanied by a smart-looking Junie, who had bought herself a dress at the market yesterday as well, in keeping with her new post as a fashionable lady's maid. She had informed Azalea that young ladies of Quality simply did not go about in public alone, and stubbornly insisted upon coming with her.

Azalea thought it absurd for Junie to waste a whole morning trailing after her as if she were a child, but finally agreed to abide by the social customs of the London ton. Truth be told, she was somewhat nervous about the coming interview and was just as glad to have Junie's company.

Leaning back against the velvet squabs in the elegant carriage, Azalea tried to organize her thoughts for the ordeal ahead. She had brought along every bit of legal documentation she possessed and hoped it would be enough to satisfy Mr. Timmons of the validity of her claims, at least regarding the Kayce estate.

The marriage papers resided in her reticule, separate from the rest. Two days ago she had regarded them as mere sentimental keepsakes, but she now realized that they might well be vitally important, in a legal sense, at least.

The mansions of the elite and fashionable West End had been left behind and they were now travelling through a less attractive part of London. Peering out of the carriage window, Azalea was shocked at the squalor that existed less than ten minutes from the elegant Mayfair neighbourhood where her cousins lived. Nowhere in America had she seen such filth and human degradation.

Slovenly and obviously inebriated women lounged in gloomy doorways, many nursing infants. Azalea saw one woman offer her baby something out of a bottle and she turned to Junie in dismay.

"Look at that woman! Surely she is not giving that poor baby liquor to drink?"

"Like as not, miss," replied the abigail after a brief glance. "In these parts, gin is the lifeblood of the poor folks. No doubt the child would get nearly as drunk on its mother's milk."

"But that's terrible! Why doesn't someone do something?"

Junie looked at her in amazement. "It's her babe, to raise or kill as she sees fit."

Azalea lapsed into silence, feeling immeasurably depressed by the scene of degrading poverty she had just witnessed. In America, at least in the part of it she had known, the poor worked where they could and kept their dignity. If jobs were not to be had, they moved west, where there was farmland for the taking.

A few minutes later her spirits revived somewhat as the scene changed again to what was obviously a business district. Well-dressed merchants and gentlemen moved purposefully along the streets. No women were in evidence. The carriage came to a stop in front of an imposing red brick edifice identified by a brass plate that simply read Law Offices.

Stepping out of the carriage, Azalea told her maid firmly to remain where she was. Though Junie looked as though she would have liked to argue, she obeyed.

Following the directions she had been given, Azalea proceeded to a suite on the second floor of the Law Offices with a door plate reading John J. Timmons, Esq., Barr. Opening the door, she found herself in a plush but rather musty chamber facing an owlish man of indeterminate age seated at an enormous wooden desk.

He looked up from his sheaf of papers with a frown that gave way to blank astonishment as he beheld a lady in these sacred male precincts.

As the man appeared totally bereft of speech, Azalea opened the conversation herself, speaking quickly before she could lose her courage.

"Mr. Timmons? I am Azalea Clayton. I was referred to you by my grandfather, the Reverend Gregory Simpson. I believe you handled his business when he was young, as well as that of his father, Sir Philip Simpson."

She was running out of opening remarks when he finally recovered himself enough to speak.

"Oh, uh... no, ma'am. I mean, I'm not Mr. Timmons at all. I am Peter Greene, his clerk. I—I'll tell him you're here. Miss Clayton, was it?"

Mr. Greene disappeared through a heavy door at the rear of the room, obviously more intimidated by her presence than by the task of informing his employer of it, however unwelcome such information might be.

Looking absently around at the innumerable leather-bound volumes lining the walls and stacked on the floor, Azalea mentally prepared her arguments against the possibility of Mr. Timmons refusing to see her. She had worked herself into a state of imaginary indignation when Mr. Greene reappeared and indicated, mainly by gesture, that she could proceed into the inner sanctum.

The second office was immaculate in comparison to the dusty disorder of the first. An elderly and rather stout gentleman rose to greet her, bowing with old-fashioned courtesy.

"Miss Clayton? I am honoured to make your acquaintance. Pray sit down. In what way may I be of service to you?" His tone was formally polite, but Azalea thought the man looked puzzled, and wondered what garbled account of her connections Mr. Greene had given him.

"Mr. Timmons," she began tentatively, perching on the edge of the overstuffed leather chair opposite the desk, "I believe you knew my grandfather slightly and conducted business for his father, Sir Philip Simpson, before his death."

"Of course, of course," replied the lawyer, now more at ease. "I remember young Gregory well, though I suppose I shouldn't say young exactly, as we are almost of an age. Is he still in Virginia? How is he?"

"He died eight months ago, which is why I am here."

"I am sorry," said Mr. Timmons sincerely. "I remember him as an unusually intelligent man. He went to America to teach at one of the universities, I recollect."

Azalea lost some of her diffidence. "Yes, at the College of William and Mary, in Williamsburg. He became one of their most respected faculty members," she added with unconscious pride.

"And in what circumstances are you left? He was your guardian?" She nodded. "What became of your parents?"

"Both died when I was very young. My mother was his only daughter. My father was Walter Clayton, fifth Baron Kayce. On his death, my grandfather left me everything he had, on the condition that I sell the property and come to

England. I am presently staying with my cousin, Lady Beauforth, in Curzon Street."

"I know of Lady Beauforth," said Mr. Timmons mildly when she paused. "An estimable woman, I believe."

Azalea took a deep breath before continuing. "Grandfather wished me to take steps to reclaim my inheritance. Indeed, I have found that I must do so, as a Season with Lady Beauforth will cost a great deal more than I can presently afford. On my grandfather's recommendation, I would like to engage you as my man of business here in London, if that would be acceptable to you?"

"Why, of course, my child. I thought that was settled already." Mr. Timmons's eyes twinkled with a trace of humour. "It appears you have a measure of your grandfather's independence, and likely his intelligence as well. Otherwise, you wouldn't have come to me."

Gratefully, Azalea pushed the packet of papers across the desk to him. "Here is a summary of the fourth Lord Kayce's will, which was sent to my father on his death. The estate itself, as I understand it, was entailed, but there was a substantial sum that was brought into the family by marriage and that should have come to me at my father's death."

Mr. Timmons opened the packet and began sorting through the papers it contained. "I shall need to look over the original will, of course. It should be filed at Somerset House. I assume your father left none?" Azalea shook her head.

"Not unusual in so young a man. We shall also need indisputable proof of your own identity —ah, here we are. Yes, these will be more than sufficient."

He met her eyes solemnly. "I shall not attempt to deceive you, Miss Clayton. Lord Kayce, your uncle, is a very powerful man. He may very well attempt to counter your claims. After all, he could stand to lose a good deal of money as a result. Have you communicated with him at all?"

"No, I haven't. From certain things my grandfather told me, I thought that might be... unwise. In fact, I'm not sure he's even aware of my existence." Mr. Timmons raised his brows at this and she hurried on. "In any event, I arrived in London only the day before yesterday, and thought it would be prudent to consult with an expert in legal matters before deciding upon any course of action."

"A wise precaution," the lawyer replied noncommittally. "However, as you are under age, Miss Clayton, you will need a guardian —and the most natural person for that role would be your uncle."

Azalea stared at the lawyer in dismay. "But I am perfectly happy with Lady Beauforth, and it was my grandfather's express wish that she act as my guardian. And... suppose Lord Kayce wishes me ill?"

Mr. Timmons blinked.

"Well," she continued more cautiously, "Grandfather once hinted at something like that, though he was sick at the time and I suppose I might have misunderstood him." Here, in the face of the lawyer's skeptical gaze, her grandfather's accusations seemed rather unlikely.

"As to that, I cannot say." Mr. Timmons had retreated into cool professionalism now. "Though I would imagine that any danger from your uncle would be financial rather than physical. But the fact remains that in the normal course of things, Lord Kayce would legally be named your guardian until you come of age or, of course, marry."

At this last word, her head came up. She believed that Mr.

Timmons was a man she could trust and that he had a certain interest in her welfare, if only because of his memories of her grandfather. Decisively, she pulled the remaining papers from her reticule and handed them to the lawyer.

"Perhaps this will make a difference."

Frowning puzzlement gave way to incredulous amazement as the lawyer unfolded and perused the documents. "These appear to be genuine. Why did you say nothing of this before?"

Azalea thought she detected a hint of suspicion behind the kindly brown eyes. She knew instinctively that her only course must be one of total honesty if she were not to lose Mr. Timmons as an ally.

Adhering strictly to the facts, she explained the circumstances of her marriage and subsequent supposed widowhood. She then confided her belief that grief at Howard Morely's death had precipitated her grandfather's decline and eventual demise. Throughout the recital, she kept her voice carefully level, drawing on the control she had cultivated over the past six years.

"It was only yesterday that I discovered that Christian Morely, now Earl of Glaedon, is still alive," she concluded. "I still do not understand how that can be, but I met him myself in Hyde Park."

"I do seem to remember some furor over the Earl, or perhaps it was his brother, a year or two ago," said Mr. Timmons thoughtfully. "I cannot seem to recall the details, but something was in the papers, I believe. However, this would seem to be the answer to both of your problems. Glaedon is not so wealthy as your uncle, but he is quite well situated, I believe."

He turned his keen gaze back to Azalea. "What is it, my dear? Is he unwilling to acknowledge you?" When she did not answer, his brows drew together. "I assure you he can be legally forced to do so. These documents constitute sufficient proof—"

"Not precisely that, Mr. Timmons," Azalea broke in. "At least, I'm not certain that is the case. When I met him yesterday, he seemed not to recognize me, even when we were introduced. As a matter of fact, he was almost rude to me."

Mr. Timmons opened his mouth, but Azalea hurried on. "So, if you don't mind, I'd rather not make these documents public just yet. I want to discover what is going on first. Perhaps it will transpire that I don't care to acknowledge *him!*" she concluded with a defiant lift of her chin.

A half smile played about the old solicitor's mouth, but he seemed compelled to try again. "Understand, my dear lady— or Miss Clayton, if you will—that the resources you would have at your disposal as Countess of Glaedon could make all the difference in the world to your legal battle with Lord Kayce. It is unlikely—"

"Please, Mr. Timmons, can you not understand?" she interrupted urgently. "Lord Glaedon already dislikes Americans. If I were to declare myself his wife now, not only might he not believe me, but it could serve to confirm his negative opinion. I also think it would not be very conducive to my future happiness in marriage. Promise me you will say nothing of this to anyone, at least for the present."

Mr. Timmons regarded her gravely for a long moment, but finally nodded. "Very well, my dear. For the present, though it goes against my better judgement. I shall see what I can manage with the other documents you have given me. And I must recommend that you entrust the marriage papers to me as well, for safe keeping."

"Of course." She leaned forward. "And you won't inform my uncle about my presence in London just yet either, will you?"

He shook his head. "No, though he must be told eventually, of course. I am sure he will be very surprised. But you have given me enough to work on for the present, I believe, without complicating matters further. I shall send word when I have made some progress. My first step will be to obtain your paternal grandfather's will."

Azalea thanked the older man warmly and rose. Nothing of substance had been accomplished yet, but her spirits were higher than they had been half an hour earlier. Merely sharing her dilemma with the capable solicitor was a vast relief, and it was with a renewed lightness in her step that she left Mr. Timmons's offices.

Smiling brilliantly at Mr. Greene simply for the pleasure of watching him stammer in confusion, she tripped out the door and down the stairs to the waiting carriage.

CHAPTER FIVE

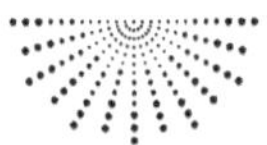

AZALEA'S RELIEF WAS SHORT-LIVED, FOR MARILYN'S greeting upon her return to Beauforth House served to remind her of the difficulties she had yet to overcome.

"Cousin, I thought you would never return! Have you forgotten that my dear Glaedon is to call on us this morning?" she exclaimed as Azalea took off her cloak. "He would find it most odd, even rude, if you were out when he arrived. You would not wish to give him an even lower opinion of Americans, I am sure."

"Oh, heavens no," replied Azalea, but her sarcasm was lost on her cousin.

"I thought not," Marilyn said with a satisfied nod. "And pray try as much as possible to refrain from speaking while he is here," she added. "I saw yesterday how little he liked hearing your accent. Oh! One of my curls is come undone!"

Marilyn hurried upstairs to find her maid before Azalea could respond to her outrageous suggestion. It was probably just as well, she realized belatedly. The retort she'd almost made would not have contributed to cousinly feeling at all. But neither that nor any other consideration would persuade her to apologize for her nationality!

She was still seething when Lord Glaedon was announced a moment later.

"Good day, Miss... Clayton, is it not?" he said as he entered the parlour behind the butler.

"Yes, that's right. Good day, my lord. And how are you this fine morning?" Marilyn's recent caution prompted her to intensify her accent. She was rewarded by a slight tightening around Lord Glaedon's mouth.

"Very well, I thank you," he replied tersely. "Is Lady Beauforth not in?"

"Oh, yes. She and Miss Beauforth should be down at any moment, I should think. They have been kindness itself to me since my arrival from America," Azalea said deliberately. His presence was unsettling, especially now that she knew who he was. But that did not stop her from baiting him. She had to know just how deep his animosity went. And talk of America must surely make him realize who she was—and recall the claim she had upon him.

"You arrived only a few days ago, I believe?" was all he said, however.

"The day before yesterday. And already I am finding that England is vastly different from America."

"I would imagine so," he said before she could elaborate. "We have had the benefit of several more centuries in which to become civilized. But then, our civilization is one thing you colonists fought so hard to free yourselves from, is it not?"

Azalea blinked at this sudden attack. "Indeed—" she began indignantly, but broke off at the sound of Cousin Alice's voice.

"Good afternoon, my lord. I hope you haven't been waiting long," Lady Beauforth called out. She was dressed today in varying shades of bright pink silk. "Ah, but I see Miss Clayton has been here to keep you company. You two met in the Park yesterday, I believe?"

Marilyn came in on her mother's heels with a brilliant smile for Lord Glaedon and a breathless reply to the offhand compliment he made her. Both ladies had eyes only for their gentleman caller, allowing Azalea a chance to compose herself and subdue her sudden anger.

Ringing for tea, Lady Beauforth waved Lord Glaedon into the most ornate —and least comfortable —chair in the room. Marilyn lost no time in seating herself by his right hand while her mother, chattering gaily, moved to his left. Azalea was left to shift for herself.

"Do you still leave for your estates tomorrow, my lord?" asked Marilyn as soon as her mother paused in her recital of the past week's scandals. "I do hope you will return to Town in time for our theatre engagement the week after next."

Her fluttering lashes and shy smiles amused Azalea, for they had plainly been cultivated for his lordship's benefit —or perhaps for the benefit of gentlemen in general. The effect was undeniably attractive and for a moment Azalea toyed with the idea of learning to emulate this behaviour before regretfully deciding that it simply wasn't her style.

Watching Lord Glaedon as he responded to Marilyn's flirtatious sallies, Azalea found it hard to believe that this was the same man she had befriended, married and, yes, even loved, six years ago. This Christian was solemn, almost dour, rather than laughing and carefree, as she remembered him. Could the deaths of his father and brother have wrought such a change in him?

Realizing that she was staring, Azalea pulled her attention back to the conversation, hoping to gain some useful insight into the intricacies of London Society.

"...and Lady Gascombe cut her *dead,* can you imagine?" Lady Beauforth was saying, "Because her sister had become engaged to a merchant! But then, everyone knows what a high stickler Harriet Gascombe is—not that that's a bad thing in itself, of course. But poor Miss Fenworth is lost now, I fear. No one will receive her after that, I daresay."

Despite her intention to listen quietly, Azalea burst in on the conversation. "I cannot believe anyone of sense would hold a young lady responsible for her sister's actions! Surely others have survived worse family connections than a merchant."

Everyone round the tea table started as though one of the chairs had spoken. After a slight, uncomfortable pause, Marilyn tittered and Lady Beauforth answered, "Not after being cut at a public theatre by someone of Lady Gascombe's standing, I assure you, my dear. Though it is possible that her ladyship had another motive for her actions, I admit. It is rumoured that her own daughter and Miss Fenworth are rivals for at least one titled gentleman."

"But how infamous!" exclaimed Azalea, forgetting that her purpose was to learn London customs rather than condemn them. "Surely anyone who knew that would see Lady Gascombe's actions for what they were?"

"Now, now, my dear," Lady Beauforth said soothingly. "Remember, you are new to London and our ways. Marilyn, you must be sure to acquaint Azalea with some of the more notable names before we spring her on Society. We don't want her to offend." Lady Beauforth looked alarmed at the mere possibility of such a *faux pas*.

But Lord Glaedon was looking at Azalea rather strangely. "Azalea?" he repeated when Lady Beauforth fell momentarily silent. "What an unusual name. I believe I once knew someone with that name —as a child, perhaps." He was frowning slightly in concentration.

"My mother named me so, after a flowering shrub native to Virginia," she offered, hoping to jog his memory. Marilyn, however, glared at her.

"Azalea, dear, would you be so kind as to pour out for us?" asked Lady Beauforth hastily, intercepting the glare.

"Yes, they still teach that skill in the colonies, do they not?" said Marilyn with a honeyed smile.

So much for avoiding all mention of my origins, thought Azalea cynically, though her smile of acquiescence matched her cousin's for sweetness.

As she poured, Azalea realized that her own personality was as far removed from what it had been six years ago as Christian's appeared to be. Glancing involuntarily at him at the thought, she found him regarding her intently, his black brows drawn down in a frown.

"Oh! I do beg your pardon, Cousin Alice," Azalea exclaimed as she sloshed a little tea into Lady Beauforth's lap. "The— the pot was hotter than I expected." She cursed her inattention, especially when she saw Marilyn's smirk.

"Mama, your faith appears to have been misplaced," Miss Beauforth commented liltingly. "I suppose I'd best do the honours myself. You'd not wish to risk hot tea on your own person, would you, my lord?" she cooed, fluttering her lashes at the Earl as she wrested the pot from Azalea's hands.

For an instant, Azalea considered deliberately spilling the remainder of the tea over Miss Beauforth. As it was, she resisted just long enough so that when she released it, Marilyn narrowly escaped spilling it herself. Quickly, Azalea turned to Lady Beauforth.

"I'm truly sorry, ma'am. Do allow me to blot that from your gown before it sets." Her irritation towards Marilyn was swallowed by dismay at the sight of the brown rivulets on Cousin Alice's fuchsia day dress. Ineffectually, she dabbed at the stains with her napkin.

"Pray do not regard it, my dear." Lady Beauforth pushed her hands away gently. "Cartwright will have it good as new by morning."

Azalea resumed her seat, trying vainly to control the colour she could feel rising to her face. Perhaps she hadn't grown up so much after all. Another quick glance at the Earl showed that he was studying her again, but now his look was thoughtful rather than forbidding.

She immediately returned her gaze to her lap, but that brief glimpse had done nothing to calm her rapid pulse. Those blue-grey eyes, which had affected her so deeply when she was a girl, had a far stronger and more profound impact on her as a woman.

"Well, this has been delightful," said the Earl before she could think of anything else that might remind him of his time in Virginia, "but I really must be going. I have several matters to attend to before leaving London. I shouldn't have spared even this much time, but I did promise to call."

A polite smile at Marilyn accompanied this statement, and she simpered back at him.

"Very well, if you must," said Lady Beauforth with a slight pout, "but we shall hope to see you at Lady Burnham's card party, if not before. Oh, and Christian, give my regards to your grandmother. It has been an age since we've seen her in Town."

"Of course, my lady. Miss Beauforth, Miss Clayton." Bowing to all of them collectively, he departed.

"Welcome home, my boy!" The Dowager Countess of Glaedon greeted Christian at the door of Glaedon Oaks the next day, unwilling as usual to await him in the parlour. "I have missed you. Do you stay through the Christmas season?"

"I fear not, though I shall return for it," Christian replied. "I have another week's worth of business awaiting me in Town before then."

"To do with your recent betrothal, no doubt." The dowager, undisputed matriarch of the family, put her head on one side as she gazed lovingly up at her grandson. "What is this I hear about a February wedding? Dare I hope that means you are truly smitten with the girl?"

"Come, Grandmother, let us go in by the fire. I am chilled from my long ride."

Though she docilely allowed herself to be led back into the parlour, the dowager did not relinquish her topic so easily. After ringing for a bowl of hot punch, she returned to the attack. "Well? And how goes your courtship of Miss Beauforth?"

Christian blinked. "Courtship? It is done, I imagine, as we are betrothed; Now I have merely to do the pretty by her until the wedding."

His grandmother's face fell noticeably. "So that is the reason for the early date? I had so hoped—"

"Don't be absurd," he said, more sharply than he had intended. "I have known Marilyn Beauforth most of my life, and she is still the vain, silly thing she ever was. I only offered for her because it seemed the honourable thing to do, now that Herschel is gone."

"Goodness, Christian, you were in no way bound by that old promise your father made to Sir Matthew Beauforth! Herschel planned to offer for the girl because he wanted to, I assure you. If you do not care for her there is no need for you to wed her. The family honour will not suffer in the least —or would not have, had you not offered."

Christian shrugged, though in truth his grandmother had hit on the heart of the matter. He had done enough to blacken the family honour already without disregarding old promises. " 'Tis as good a way to ensure the succession as any," he said negligently, "especially as it will unite our two estates."

The dowager frowned. "Christian, I do not like to hear you speak so. I shall be the first to admit that in many, if not most, marriages, love follows later rather than coming before. But I cannot think it proper to enter the married state without *some* degree of affection for one's future spouse."

"I apologize, Grandmother. Miss Beauforth has grown into a diamond of the first water, and I would be blind not to appreciate that fact. Perhaps my admiration of her person will later develop into something stronger, as you suggest. It is not as though I harbour a *tendre* for another."

He paused, suddenly recalling another young lady he had met lately.

From the moment he had first laid eyes on Miss Clayton, something about her had profoundly disturbed him. She was lovely, certainly, even more striking than Miss Beauforth with her unusual colouring, but that was not it—or at least he didn't think so. He'd never been particularly swayed by mere beauty before.

At any rate, Miss Clayton's beauty could hardly make up for her origins. Doubtless it was her accent combined with that beauty that had so unsettled him. That must be why he had allowed himself to be goaded into open criticism of her homeland on the second occasion they'd met.

It hadn't been like him at all, for he had always prided himself on his coolness in uncomfortable situations. His grandmother, not to mention his few friends, would have been amazed had they witnessed his rudeness to Miss Clayton.

Azalea. That's what Lady Beauforth had called her. Again that vague disquiet crept over him, though his lips curved in a smile of their own volition. Such a pretty name. So unusual. He was certain he'd heard it before...

"What? What is it, Christian?" His grandmother's voice recalled him to the present.

Christian shook his head. "Nothing, Grandmother."

There was no point dwelling on it now. Most likely, Lady Beauforth had mentioned the girl's name when she'd told him her cousin would be coming to live with her. He didn't recall her doing so, but it seemed a reasonable explanation. If he *had* known someone of that name before, it would come to him in time.

He swallowed his punch and stood to ring the bell. "I may

as well ride over the grounds with the steward before changing out of my travelling clothes," he said. "There is no point wasting what little daylight remains."

Lady Glaedon watched him go, shaking her head with a mixture of sadness and fondness. She had noticed the preoccupation in her grandson's manner, obvious to one who had raised him as her own from the time his mother had died, shortly after his eighth birthday. She hoped that all would work out well for him. The last few years had not been easy for Christian.

They had not been easy for the dowager, either. She had lost her son and, she had then believed, her favourite grandson to a shipwreck. Then, only four years later, her other grandson, the new Earl, had been lulled in the war in America, in which Herschel had insisted on participating despite his family responsibilities.

Herschel's death had been the final straw. Lady Glaedon had become a virtual recluse, refusing to see anyone but family. Then Christian's miraculous return had restored hope and meaning to her life.

The two of them had always been close, probably closer than would have been possible were she truly his mother. After Christian's arrival back in England, she had reentered Society to some small extent, more for his sake than for her own.

She had been saddened by the singular change in Christian, once so fun loving and easygoing. His experiences, which he refused to discuss with her, had somehow turned him into a taciturn, cynical man. She had become determined to do everything in her power to ensure his happiness, and thereby her own.

To that end, she had tried her hand at some subtle match-making. There were certainly plenty of young ladies to choose from in London. Lord Glaedon's romantic good looks, combined with the air of mystery surrounding his sudden reappearance on the scene, caused feminine hearts to flutter wherever he went.

He had never shown the slightest interest in any of them, however. And then, without warning, he had offered for Miss Beauforth. Lady Glaedon had hoped that he had fallen in love at long last, but plainly that was not the case.

Sighing, she picked up her embroidery. If anyone deserved happiness, Christian did, but she feared he was far from finding it.

The next two weeks were relatively happy ones for Azalea. Since Lord Glaedon had gone from London, she'd been able to push her problems to the back of her mind for the present.

She had the pleasure of seeing Millie comfortably accepted by the staff at Curzon Street as an under kitchen maid. Mrs. Swann, meanwhile, had received a letter from her sister in Yorkshire, inviting her for an extended visit and Azalea convinced her to accept. It had become obvious that Mrs. Swann was unhappy under the supercilious eye of Mrs. Straite and that it was only a matter of time before a confrontation occurred between the two women.

An even greater concern, however was Azalea's fear that Swannee might complicate the situation with Lord Glaedon. Though the housekeeper had never been told of the marriage, Azalea had often suspected that her old friend knew the truth.

There was no knowing what she might do or say if she learned that Christian was still alive. It would be best if Mrs. Swann were out of London until Azalea had a chance to settle the matter for herself.

Though it was long past the autumn Little Season, Azalea made a few acquaintances among the fashionable callers at Lady Beauforth's home. Her wardrobe had grown to an adequate size for a winter in London, although she realized much more would be needed for the spring Season. A dozen bargain gowns had been purchased for refurbishing, and two new outfits were being made up: a riding habit of rich green-and-gold velvet and a ball gown in a pale green satin that Azalea had found irresistible.

Her relationship with her cousins was improving as well. Lady Beauforth had warmed towards her until she no longer felt herself a charity case in the household. And though Marilyn still persisted in holding her at a distance, she, too, showed some signs of thawing.

The two young ladies were in each other's company most mornings. While shopping, receiving and returning calls, Azalea had ample opportunity to observe Miss Beauforth's character. She came to the conclusion that while Marilyn was spoiled, certainly, and had done little to improve her mind, she was not actually malicious or stupid. Azalea hoped that in time they might truly become friends.

One blustery afternoon in early December, she sat in the library writing a letter to a young lady in Williamsburg who had extracted a promise from her to correspond upon her arrival in England. A two-month separation, combined with the stiff formality of the English ladies she had met, caused Azalea to remember Miss Severson with more fondness than she'd ever felt towards her in Virginia. As she was closing her surprisingly affectionate missive, Lady Beauforth bustled into the room, in obvious high spirits.

"Ah, *there* you are, my dear! I have the most *splendid* news! I have just received an invitation to a Christmas ball at Lady Queesley's on Thursday. She is leaving for the country and wishes to give a farewell entertainment. No doubt she feels the need to fortify herself for the dull weeks ahead. I must say I find London, even thin of company, far preferable to rusticating over the holidays. But that is neither here nor there. I vow, I had *quite* given up being able to present you to Society before spring, but this will be a *marvellous* opportunity! This will be your debut, in a manner of speaking, so we must choose your ensemble with care."

This speech left Azalea nearly as breathless as it did Lady Beauforth, but she recovered quickly. She was pleased at the news, partly because of the qualms she had felt over the expensive ball gown she had purchased with the Season still some months away. And, of course, what female could suppress a flutter of pleasure at the prospect of her first ball?

She turned to Lady Beauforth with a smile, her letter forgotten. "Oh, Cousin Alice, how delightful! Are you certain I am invited? I do not recollect ever having met Lady Queesley."

"Yes, she enclosed cards for each of us. Indeed, it would be strange if you were *not* invited, as it is generally known that you are staying with us. And Lady Queesley never does anything shabbily, I assure you," said Lady Beauforth in a tone that quite settled the matter.

"In that case, dear cousin, I can look forward to the ball with all my heart," said Azalea cheerfully. "Will my new green satin be appropriate, do you think?"

"The very thing, my dear! We'll have to see about finding you some matching flowers for your hair. But I must get back upstairs to Marilyn —I promised her I would only be a moment. Oh, I *do* hope dear Glaedon returns in time for this ball...." So saying, Lady Beauforth departed as quickly as she had come, her words trailing behind her.

Azalea's pleasure dimmed abruptly at this reminder of the very real problems she still faced. If Lord Glaedon *were* at the ball, she would have to make some attempt to solve them, though as yet she hadn't a clue how she was to do so. Frowning, she turned back to her letter.

As she dressed for the ball a few nights later, Azalea's thoughts kept straying to Lord Glaedon and the dilemma he represented. He was back in Town, she knew, for Lady Beauforth had announced that tidbit at nuncheon. How her cousin could have discovered the fact so quickly Azalea did not know. Lady Beauforth apparently had her sources.

Still, she refused to let that problem, or the one concerning Lord Kayce, whom she had all but forgotten, completely destroy her enjoyment of the evening ahead. This was to be her first ball, after all. Surely everything would work itself out in time.

Junie put the finishing touches to her hair and invited Azalea to view the result in the long glass on the wardrobe door. "You'll be the belle of the ball, Miss Azalea, that's certain," she announced proudly.

Looking into the mirror, Azalea could almost agree with her. Surely, the exquisitely gowned and coiffed young lady gazing back at her bore no resemblance to the rough provincial she had been a few weeks earlier.

Pale green satin gleamed richly through the overskirt of matching net. The waist was high, just under her full breasts, with a low neckline —so low, in fact, that she had protested to Madame Clarisse, the modiste, only to be assured that she would see many more revealing gowns, and that this one was in the best possible taste for a young girl making her comeout.

Her white throat was adorned by a single strand of small but perfectly matched pearls that had been her mother's, and white flowers wreathed her hair. The colour of the gown intensified the green of her eyes and the deep red of her hair, just as its lines emphasized the best points of her figure. She felt that the overall effect was pleasing and that her appearance, at least, would hardly cause her cousins embarrassment.

She was able to judge their reactions a few moments later when she nervously descended the long staircase. Lady Beauforth's face lit up immediately upon perceiving Azalea above. Her pleased smile quickly allayed any doubts about her approval.

Marilyn's feelings were more difficult to fathom, but Azalea thought she could construe her slight frown and the widening of her blue eyes as an oblique sort of compliment. Marilyn herself was an absolute vision of loveliness in ethereal white.

Azalea had to wonder again how her cousin could be jealous of her—and, more importantly, how she could possibly win Lord Glaedon away from such a beauty. She suppressed a small sigh as they slipped into their wraps and out the door to the waiting carriage.

"What a pleasant evening," she remarked to her cousins, in

an attempt to ignore the trembling in her midsection that seemed to increase as they neared Lady Queesley's mansion. "In Virginia, the December winds are quite bitter, compared to this."

"But I had understood the colonies —er, the United States —to be quite warm. I'm certain Mr. Symes, who was in Charleston several years ago, said that the summers there were unbearably hot, and plagued by insects," said Marilyn, sitting up a little straighter and looking directly at her cousin for the first time since leaving Curzon Street.

Azalea had once or twice before noticed her cousin's interest in her chance comments about America. "Yes, that's true as well," she agreed. "I haven't spent a summer here, of course, but I understand that your climate is not subject to the extremes we experience in the New World. Perhaps the surrounding ocean acts as a buffer to the elements here." She was about to expand on this theory, which Reverend Marston, one of her numerous tutors, had once put forth, but she sensed she was losing the attention of her audience.

"In any event," she went on, "in Virginia we have both extremes. Summer and winter both can be rather unpleasant at times, but spring and autumn are generally delightful, with colours as vivid as the temperatures are pleasant. And we only rarely see fog there."

She continued discussing Virginia's seasons, with more and more frequent questions from Marilyn and an occasional comment from Lady Beauforth. In this manner, the time passed pleasantly for Azalea as the coach inched forward in the long queue before Lady Queesley's doorstep. Finally it was their turn to alight and Azalea's anxiety returned suddenly and in full force.

As if reading her mind, Lady Beauforth gently patted her shoulder and said, "Chin up, my dear. One's first ball is exciting, but can be a bit terrifying also. Just pretend you've done it all before, and don't forget to breathe!"

Lady Queesley greeted Lady Beauforth warmly, exchanging the latest news of some mutual acquaintances, before turning to the two younger ladies.

"Why, Marilyn, I declare you become more beautiful by the day," the Countess exclaimed, in a fair imitation of Lady Beauforth's style. Azalea had noticed that this affected, gushing manner was the rule rather the exception among the older ladies of the ton.

"Your mother must be very proud. It's no wonder you managed to snare the pick of the Season." This last was directed at Lady Beauforth with a knowing smile and the ghost of a wink. "But pray present me to your little American relative! Your niece, did you say?" Lady Queesley's overpowering smile was now turned on Azalea.

"My second cousin, actually, Lydia," returned Lady Beauforth, smiling every bit as broadly as her hostess. "This is Miss Azalea Clayton, lately from Williamsburg, Virginia. Azalea, Lady Queesley."

Azalea dropped a curtsy of the proper depth and murmured that she was honoured to meet her ladyship.

Plainly pleased by the girl's respectful manner, a contrast to Marilyn's bored observance of the proprieties, Lady Queesley offered her opinion that a delightful surprise was in store for the young men lucky enough to be present tonight. She concluded by promising to present her son, Lord Mallows, to the newcomer as soon as she could resign her post by the door.

As the trio progressed into the ballroom, Lady Beauforth whispered, "That is quite a triumph already, my dear! Everyone knows dear Lydia is absurdly protective of her son. She would hardly have made such a promise if she were not vastly taken with you."

Azalea could not help but be gratified by such a compliment, but before she could reply, her attention was claimed by the scene before her. The enormous ballroom glittered with gold and white in the light of what seemed to be thousands of candles in sconces and chandeliers.

As the Beauforth party was announced, a veritable sea of faces turned toward them, and Azalea was seized by an almost overwhelming desire to turn tail and flee. She mastered the impulse quickly, by necessity —her cousins were advancing into the crowd at a steady pace, and she had no wish to be left on her own among this throng of strangers.

"I thought you said everyone was away from London this close to Christmas!" she said to Lady Beauforth, raising her voice slightly to be heard over the collective, well-modulated tones of the guests.

"Oh, they are, my dear!" replied her cousin. "You will see the difference next spring, when the Season has begun. This is a fairly intimate and quite comfortable gathering. I assure you, at a successful ball at the height of the Season, one can scarcely breathe, much less move. Not nearly so pleasant as a small party like this one, in my opinion."

Azalea shook her head and looked around her in disbelief. A small party? She had never in her life seen so many people gathered under one roof.

Marilyn, meanwhile, had already located —or been located by— several admirers and was happily chatting and flirting with no less than four young men at once. As she made no move to introduce any of them to her cousin, Azalea turned away to observe another portion of the crowd.

The sea of faces was beginning to resolve into individuals and Azalea noticed a few people she had met on morning calls with her cousins. Seeing Lady Dinsmore, a young matron she had befriended, a short distance away, she turned to ask Lady Beauforth whether it would be acceptable to approach her alone. Before she had opened her mouth, however, she saw the unmistakable figure of Lord Glaedon coming towards them.

CHAPTER SIX

AZALEA WAS COMPLETELY UNPREPARED FOR THE RIOT OF emotions that assaulted her at her first sight of Lord Glaedon after his absence. She felt now that she must have been blind at their first meeting not to have realized instantly that he was Chris, the Christian Morely she had been so infatuated with in her youth. His height, his colouring, his stance and especially his eyes shouted his identity at her, though he was not even looking her way. In fact, he was making a beeline towards Marilyn.

With a sinking sensation, she watched as he bent over her cousin's hand and neatly extricated her from the knot of admirers, to his apparent amusement and their equally obvious chagrin. He looked almost unbearably handsome to Azalea, his dark blue superfine coat matching his eyes, and the whiteness of his intricately tied cravat emphasizing the near blackness of his carefully disordered hair.

Though she could not hear what was being said, she assumed from Marilyn's flirtatious fan and fluttering lashes that it was complimentary. Azalea's excitement at her first ball suddenly fell rather flat.

Still, determined to enjoy herself as much as possible, she turned her back on Lord Glaedon and made her way over to Lady Dinsmore.

That lady seemed sincerely delighted to renew their brief acquaintance, and they chatted for some minutes about botany and gardening, a shared passion. They debated the likely source of the potted holly bushes that had been placed about the ballroom in the spirit of the season, presenting a considerable hazard to those who carelessly passed too close to them. This led to a comparison of English and American hollies by Azalea, followed by a discussion of other differences between the flora of the two countries.

"I hear that there are countless varieties of wildflowers in America that we never see here. I would love some descriptions," Lady Dinsmore was saying, when a slight "ahem" at her elbow caused Azalea to start and look around.

Their hostess, Lady Queesley, stood there, accompanied by a fair, stout young man who had presumably been the one clearing his throat. Lady Dinsmore discreetly excused herself.

"Miss Clayton, I promised to introduce you to my son," the countess said with a smile. "Viscount Mallows." Lady Queesley gestured grandly toward her treasure. "George, do show Miss Clayton about and introduce her to some of the young people," she added in an audible undertone before fading into the crowd.

Lord Mallows seemed somewhat ill at ease and Azalea concluded that he was unused to being thrust forward by his mother. *Overprotective* was the word Cousin Alice had used, and Azalea suspected that it might be quite accurate. He seemed to be searching almost desperately for something to say, so she broke the awkward silence herself.

"This is a lovely room, my lord. We have nothing to compare with such elegance in Williamsburg, I assure you." There. She had given him an opening, and she hoped he would have the courage to pick it up.

"Will-Williamsburg?" he asked with a slight stammer. "That is in Virginia, is it not?"

"Yes, in the southern part of the state."

"I have a friend from that part of the world," Lord Mallows continued, obviously pleased to have something to say for himself. "I'll introduce you if I can find him. He—he's here somewhere." Whereupon he stood on tiptoe, being only an inch or two taller than Azalea herself, and scanned the room.

"How kind of you!" she exclaimed. "But you needn't search for him this instant, surely." She was rather hoping to have her first public dance with the viscount, since she was certain he wouldn't be too critical of any mistakes she might make. But it was too late. He was already gesturing, quite conspicuously, to someone across the room.

"He's on his way," Lord Mallows said smugly, turning back to Azalea with a smile. It was clear to her that he was extremely eager to escape her presence, but she could not take offence. She suspected that he behaved similarly with all ladies.

"You wanted me, George?" A tall, sandy-haired young man shouldered his way between two imposing dowagers who blocked his path, ignoring their outraged murmurs. "What was so important that you had to summon me from the side of one of the most fascinating ... But who's this?"

His glance fell on Azalea and remained there. "If this is the reason for my summons, I forgive you, George. Might you introduce me to Miss..."

"Jonathan?" gasped Azalea incredulously.

The young man's mouth fell open. "Azalea?" he exclaimed, equally taken aback.

Thrown off his stride by their behaviour, the Viscount tried to steer the conversation back into more conventional channels. "Miss Clayton, I—I'd like to present Mr. Jonathan P-Plummer," he said as quickly as his stammer would allow.

"It *is* you!" she cried. "I knew I could not be mistaken!"

After gazing at one another for a few seconds, both began talking excitedly, almost as if trying to cover the last six years in ten minutes.

"I vow I would never have known you...."

"Yes, when I left your father was well...."

"How are Missy and James and the others...?"

"...with my cousins, in Curzon Street..."

Finally, Lord Mallows's repeated attempts to take his leave brought them back to their surroundings.

"Yes, George, off to the cards with you. I am deeply in your debt," said Jonathan, smiling broadly. Then, turning back to Azalea as if still unable to believe that this exquisite creature was the friend he had romped with in childhood, he bowed and said with mock formality, "Miss Clayton, may I have this dance?"

Still dimpling with the pleasure of finding a friend from home among the cold London ton, Azalea dipped him a flawless half curtsy and replied in the same vein.

"But of course, Mr. Plummer." Then she marred the effect by whispering, "You must not mind if I forget a few of the steps —I have only just learned to dance, and have never done so in public before."

Jonathan chuckled as he led her onto the floor, where the first set was just forming. "I'm glad to see you haven't changed completely, 'Zalea," he said.

The dance began and Azalea had opportunity to discover that Jonathan, at least, knew ail the steps. He was, in fact, a very accomplished dancer and neatly covered her few mistakes. She was relieved to find dancing less of a trial than she had expected, and as the set progressed, her steps became surer. Nor could she be especially conspicuous, she thought, with so many other couples whirling about the floor.

In this last thought, however, Azalea was not quite correct. The two young Americans made a striking couple and drew glances from several quarters, some admiring, some envious and some merely thoughtful. Among the latter was Lord Kayce, who had discovered her identity by chance, having overheard a conversation between two of the envious watchers, a pair of spinsters about to enter their fourth Season.

He had first learned of Azalea's existence less than a week ago, so he saw no immediate need to play the part of the devoted long-lost uncle. No, he was willing to await a more opportune moment for introductions. As he watched Azalea twirl past, her lovely face alight with laughter at some comment her partner had made, his pale brown eyes narrowed thoughtfully.

Lord Glaedon was another thoughtful observer, watching the pair speculatively and trying, still unsuccessfully, to remember who the girl reminded him of. She had continued to thrust her way into his thoughts frequently during the past two weeks, sometimes at the most inopportune of times. She was the primary reason he had neglected to call at Beauforth House upon his return to Town yesterday, in fact.

He could not deny that she was very beautiful, but he was certain now that that was not the reason behind her disturbing effect on him. It was almost as if she were trying to tell him something —not in words, but by her very presence. Shaking his head to clear it of such thoughts, he turned back to Marilyn, who had apparently not noticed his momentary defection and continued her avid recital of Miss Belgrave's most recent fall from grace.

Suddenly, her manner irritated him. It occurred to him that Miss Beauforth's conversation consisted almost entirely of gossip. Though he had been about to ask her for another dance, he now chose not to intervene when young Smallwood stepped up and requested the honour. Christian glanced around as the couples took their places and, seeing no sign of the disturbing American beauty, retired to the balcony to think.

Meanwhile, Azalea was having a better time than she would have thought possible a scant half hour before. Jonathan had introduced her to his circle of friends, a lively group of young people, and several of the gentlemen were already vying for her attention.

Never having flirted before, Azalea was surprised to discover how easy and amusing it was, with no expectations raised on either side. She had essentially cut herself off from Society for the past six years, but now, surrounded by the light banter of her new acquaintances, she found herself opening up.

Returning breathless and smiling from the exertions of a country dance with Lord Soames, Azalea suddenly found herself face to face with Lord Glaedon. Still in high spirits, she mastered the sudden shyness that threatened and dropped a quick curtsy, saying brightly, "How nice to see you again, my lord. I trust you are enjoying the evening?" Marilyn was nowhere to be seen.

"Indeed, yes, Miss Clayton," replied the Earl gravely. "I was hoping to persuade you to stand up with me for the next dance in order to increase that enjoyment."

He spoke so stiffly that Azalea was tempted to refuse, but realized that this might be a perfect opportunity to untangle some of the mystery surrounding him.

"Of course, my lord," she answered, after only the briefest pause.

Then, to her consternation, the orchestra proceeded to strike up a waltz. Chiding herself for her alarm, she told herself that this would make it that much easier to engage him in conversation.

Still, Azalea was glad that it was not her first waltz of the evening, otherwise nervousness would have been sure to make her stumble. At his first touch, a light, perfectly proper clasp on her waist and hand, she had to struggle to keep her features composed.

His palm seemed to burn against the small of her back, while his hand meshed with hers as no other gentleman's had. After the first shock, however, she floated almost effortlessly in his arms.

His nearness, his touch, made her throat dry and took away her capacity for thought, and it began to appear that they would pass the entire dance without a word. Determined that this not be the case, Azalea had just steeled herself to ask her partner if he had ever been to America, when he caught her off guard with a question of his own.

"Is it possible that we have met before, Miss Clayton? I felt when I first saw you that day in the Park that you reminded me of someone, and I have been unable to shake the impression." He spoke warily, as though expecting a rebuff.

"It is possible, of course, my lord," she answered, seizing the opening. "Have you ever been to Virginia?"

Lord Glaedon stiffened. "I fear not, Miss Clayton. I intended to visit it at one time, but the ship foundered in the crossing and my father, I regret to say, died at sea. I could never bring myself to repeat the trip."

His tone was cold and emotionless, but Azalea was moved regardless. She remembered how close he and his father had been and realized that this must be one more grudge Christian bore against Americans. For the moment, she ignored his baffling assertion that the shipwreck had taken place on the outward voyage.

"I am sorry, my lord. I, too, once lost a loved one at sea." How, she wondered, would he respond to that? But not even a flicker indicated that he was aware of her intent.

"The sea, at least, takes life without motive or malice," Lord Glaedon replied after a moment. "So much cannot be said of people who kill and degrade their fellow human beings. Tell me, Miss Clayton, as an American, what are your views on slavery? Do you consider it a 'sad necessity,' as I hear is the fashionable view among your countrymen?"

Although his sudden change of topic surprised her, Azalea answered without hesitation, for this was a subject near to her heart.

"Slavery is 'necessary' only to the rich, my lord, so that they can remain so. Money is a paltry excuse for turning humans into possessions, and I am confident that the majority of Americans —voting Americans —feel the same way, and that the days of that reprehensible institution are numbered." She spoke with conviction, but Lord Glaedon's expression was cynical.

"How touching, to be sure," he said. "But I'll wager you're not above eating the sugar or wearing the cotton that slave labourers have gathered. And how willing would you be, I wonder, to forgo any part of your personal comfort to change that institution? I have heard such high-sounding words from Americans before, but it would seem that words are all they are. Something must be fundamentally wrong with the citizens of a nation that would condone such inhumanity."

Azalea was struck momentarily speechless. She felt as strongly about the matter as he did and knew full well that many of her countrymen were hypocrites on the subject. But she was furious that he should so deliberately choose to doubt her sincerity.

The music had stopped, but he continued to look down at her, waiting sardonically for her answer.

"You asked for my opinion and I gave it, my lord," said Azalea with deceptive sweetness. "I see it was not the opinion you expected or wished to hear. Obviously, you would rather mock me than believe me sincere, since to do that would be to admit that all Americans are not the heartless villains you wish to think us. What of your countrymen who must serve in the Royal Navy against their will? I don't believe America has a monopoly on inhumanity. Or on hypocrisy and deceit."

With that parting shot, Azalea turned and left him without a backward glance.

Luckily, the next dance was a cotillion and afforded little chance for conversation with her partner. As Azalea focused on the intricate steps of the dance, her temper cooled somewhat, though she still deeply resented Lord Glaedon's assumption that she shared the mercenary motives of the worst of her countrymen.

Looking around at the outrageously expensive splendour of the ballroom, she suddenly felt a desire to laugh. Obviously wealth, and especially the ostentatious display of it, was at least as important to the English ton as to any American! By the end of the dance, she found she was looking forward to crossing swords with Lord Glaedon again.

Christian watched Azalea as she flounced away, struck less by her words than by the sweet seductiveness of her hips as they moved beneath the green satin of her gown. He had intended to discover more about her during that dance, in an attempt to allay the disquiet he felt in her presence. Instead, he had again been drawn into an attack on her homeland.

As she danced the cotillion with another admirer, Christian was forced to admit that he was far more drawn than repelled by Miss Clayton. Not that it mattered, of course. He had already committed his future to Miss Beauforth and nothing could change that. After the mess he had already made of his life, he owed it to his family to marry her, a woman of fortune and impeccable breeding. The marriage would bring to fruition the honourable plans of his father and brother, now dead.

But for the first time since his betrothal, those ringing,

lofty arguments sounded hollow. Whatever his feelings, however, he would stand by his given word. To do otherwise would be unworthy of the name he bore, a name he had damaged enough. Rapping out an oath under his breath, he went in search of his fiancée to secure her for the supper dance.

On her way in to supper with Jonathan and a group of his friends, Azalea came face to face with Lord Glaedon once again. Marilyn clung to one of his arms and Lady Beauforth rested a hand on the other.

After one brief glance at the Earl, Azalea turned quickly to her cousins. "Ma'am, may I present a very old friend of mine from Williamsburg? Jonathan Plummer, Lady Beauforth, Miss Beauforth... and Lord Glaedon." She did not hesitate quite long enough to be rude.

Glaedon's nod, however, was curt. "Servant, Plummer. Miss Beauforth, my lady, I'll go ahead to reserve a table."

Azalea nearly gaped at his retreating back, but before she could exclaim at his incivility, Lady Beauforth spoke.

"Mr. Plummer, how charming to meet you. You knew our Azalea in America then?"

Marilyn had looked as though she were about to follow Lord Glaedon's example, but at the sound of Jonathan's voice, she hesitated.

"The pleasure is all mine, Lady Beauforth. Yes, I lived in Williamsburg until my grandfather, Lord Holte, insisted I attend Oxford. As he was footing the bills, my father sent me off with his blessing. Since finishing, I have found several reasons to prolong my stay in England." This was said with a lingering look at Marilyn, who fluttered her lashes in return.

"You must come to call on us in Curzon Street, Mr. Plummer," insisted Lady Beauforth, all smiles.

Azalea's estimation of Jonathan's social standing rose precipitously at this unusual mark of distinction. She knew by now that her cousins were considered "high sticklers" and were very particular about who they deigned to name their friends.

She said as much to Jonathan as they proceeded to the supper table where a few of his friends were already assembled.

"Yes, I don't often invoke Grandfather's name like that, but I wanted to be sure of seeing you often. I thought it would be more convenient if I were allowed to run tame at Beauforth House. What can you tell me of your fair cousin?" He glanced over to where the young lady in question sat at a nearby table.

He appeared vaguely disappointed when she informed him that Marilyn was betrothed to Lord Glaedon. "Ah, well, I can but dream," he said philosophically.

Just in time, Azalea stopped herself from hinting that the marriage would not take place at all if she had any say in the matter. Even after several years' separation, she found it hard to be guarded with Jonathan. Instead, she followed his glance, to find Lord Glaedon's eyes on her, his expression unreadable.

Turning away hastily, she said, "Pray do not get your hopes up, Jonathan. Even were the match broken off, I can't think Miss Beauforth would care for life in the colonies."

This drew a general chuckle from Jonathan's set, and a lively discussion of the relative rigours of fashionable life in America and England ensued.

At the other table, Christian continued to regard Miss Clayton for a moment, admiring the way her green eyes flashed and sparkled as she laughed with her young American friend. Turning back to Miss Beauforth, he was struck anew at the contrast between his betrothed and her colonial cousin.

Though Azalea was the elder by a year, a fact which Marilyn had brought to his attention three times now, she gave an impression of youthful innocence that Miss Beauforth singularly lacked. While Miss Clayton seemed completely unaware of her physical charms, his fiancée made full use of her own with a sophistication that would have done credit to a woman twice her age.

"You must try the ham, my lord," cooed Marilyn at that moment, leaning far forward to afford him a tantalizing glimpse of cleavage. "It is sliced so thin it nigh melts in your mouth." She smiled seductively as she licked the corners of her full lips.

With an effort, he smiled back. "I'm sure it is delicious."

She tittered and batted her eyes, and he realized that she took his words as a veiled compliment, when in fact they had been no more than inattention. Mentally, he shrugged. What did it matter, as long as she was content?

Though he strove to attend to the conversation between Miss Beauforth and her mother, Christian was keenly aware of the laughter from Miss Clayton's table. Much as it irked him to admit it, he rather wished he were there instead.

Azalea reflected on the events of the evening with a measure of satisfaction during the carriage ride back to Curzon Street.

After supper, she had been engaged for every dance, and not just with members of Jonathan's youthful set.

Several titled gentlemen, including Lord Chilton, a dandified marquess, had also vied for her attention.

She had not seen Lord Glaedon again after supper; from something Marilyn said to her mother, she gathered that he had taken his leave early, a circumstance that had disappointed both her cousins. For herself, she felt it was just as well, as she wanted to prepare a few unanswerable arguments before speaking to him again.

Her plan had not gone especially well, she had to admit. She had intended to fascinate Lord Glaedon, to get him talking about himself, to discover what lay behind his refusal to acknowledge her. Instead, she had fallen to arguing politics with the man.

Far from charming him away from Marilyn, it appeared she had only deepened his dislike of her. Nor was she any closer to solving the mystery of his escape from the shipwreck. Even more alarming, she found that she was more strongly attracted to him than ever.

But even had she found him repugnant, she could not allow him to go through with his intended marriage to Marilyn. Perhaps something *had* happened to make him forget their wedding. Something to do with the shipwreck, perhaps?

Whatever the case, she would not be party to the crime of bigamy by standing by silently. She owed it to Lady Beauforth, not to mention Marilyn and Christian, to prevent such a thing. And somehow she would, even if it meant alienating Lord Glaedon forever by pressing her claim. But first she would try other, more subtle means.

No, she could not regret attending the ball. Everything had

been new to her, and Jonathan and his friends had been more than pleasant. She had discovered that she could dance without embarrassing herself, and had made dozens of acquaintances. In fact, she had enjoyed every moment —even her argument with Lord Glaedon. Especially her argument with Lord Glaedon.

All in all, she thought, as the carriage rolled to a stop before the Beauforth Town house, it had been a satisfactory first ball.

So why didn't she feel more satisfied?

CHAPTER SEVEN

WHEN SHE AWOKE THE NEXT MORNING FROM A DEEP, dreamless sleep, Azalea was amazed at the lateness of the hour. Why, it must be near eleven o'clock! She could not remember ever having slept so late in her life. Junie had apparently been at the keyhole, for she entered mere seconds after Azalea stirred.

"Well, miss, I trust you slept well after your grand night?" she asked with a smile, setting a tray of toast and chocolate on the bedside stand.

"Like a stone, Junie, thank you," Azalea answered. "I must have been more tired than I realized."

"'Twas the excitement, Miss Azalea, as much as the dancing, I'll warrant. A first ball will do that to a body, so I hear. Now, have a bite to eat, and I'll be back in a few minutes to help you dress. You're certain to have some morning callers within the half hour, or I miss my guess. Didn't I say you'd be a sure success?" she asked smugly as she left the room, leaving

Azalea to marvel at the speed of the below-stairs gossip network.

Descending to the front parlour some twenty minutes later in a flattering new gown of fine peach wool, Azalea saw that Junie had been correct, as usual. Her hostesses were already entertaining no fewer than five callers, four of whom were among Azalea's admirers from the previous evening.

The fifth was a middle-aged gentleman unknown to her. Several bouquets of hothouse flowers reposed in vases about the room, she noted with pleasure. She could hardly wait to examine them, as she was certain at least one of the varieties represented was unfamiliar to her. Right now, though, she must greet the guests.

Every gentleman present rose at her entrance, and Lady Beauforth turned to beam at her. Marilyn, who had been enjoying the undivided attention of the visitors in her cousin's absence, offered a smile that was a tinge less welcoming.

Azalea nodded to each of the gentlemen in turn, with a light comment to each about last night's ball. Mr. Gresham, she noticed, seemed content to resume his flirtation with Marilyn after greeting her, but the others, including Lord Chilton, were flatteringly attentive, clustering about her as she took her seat. Before conversation could resume, however, Lady Beauforth drew her attention to the older gentleman at her side.

"My dear Azalea," she exclaimed, "let me present your uncle, Lord Kayce. I collect that you did not make his acquaintance last night, though he was in attendance, were you not, sir?"

"I was indeed, my lady," Lord Kayce returned in an affectedly nasal tone as he bowed in Azalea's direction. "There was such a flock about my young niece, however, that I forbore to intrude the presence of a stodgy old man like myself on her obvious enjoyment." A pleasant smile accompanied this remark, and Azalea felt her shock at his identity giving way to surprise at his manner.

Lord Kayce was thin, slightly over middle height, and possessed an expressive, if not a handsome, countenance. He was dressed in the absolute height of elegance, with a froth of rich, cream-coloured lace at his throat and wrists setting off the deep green of his embroidered waistcoat and matching jacket. His hair, which he wore tied back with a green ribbon in an old-fashioned style, had apparently been the same deep auburn as his niece's in his youth, though now it was heavily threaded with grey. Azalea couldn't help thinking that this was what her father might have looked like had he still been alive. The thought warred with her misgivings.

"I wish you had approached me, my lord. Surely you don't think me such a pleasure seeker that I would regret time spent with my nearest kinsman!" she said, the warmth in her tone not entirely feigned.

"You reassure me, my dear," he replied. "But please, no more 'my lording.' As you remind me, we are the only members left of the Clayton family, so it must be Uncle Simon." He was all affability, apparently eager to welcome her both to England and into his life. He certainly did not resemble the calculating, ruthless mercenary her grandfather had led her to expect.

"Of course. And you must call me Azalea." She wished she had the courage to ask him outright what he meant to do about her share of her father's estate. Could Grandfather have been mistaken about him?

As they chatted of America and of Azalea's impressions of

London for a few minutes, Azalea found herself unwillingly drawn to her new-found kinsman, although his effeminate way of speaking and gesturing with his hands reminded her of Lord Chilton. Her uncle was not a member of the dandy set, however —one had only to look at his clothing, which was far more subdued than Lord Chilton's, to ascertain that.

Though distracting, the affectedness of his manner along with his self-deprecating air only served to make him appear that much more harmless. The unworthy thought occurred to Azalea that this might be the reason for its cultivation.

"I really must be going, but I do trust we shall see each other often, my dear child," said Kayce, rising smoothly after a glance at his pocket watch. "Perhaps, once the Season is under way in the spring, we can collaborate on a comeout ball for our young relative," he suggested lightly to Lady Beauforth as he took his leave.

"Of course, if you would care to, my lord," she answered, simpering as fulsomely as Marilyn did with the younger gentlemen.

"We'll discuss it at some future date," he assured her. "Oh, and I pray you will allow me to send round a token of my affection, my dear," he said to Azalea. With another warm smile for his niece, he bowed smoothly and departed.

Before he was out of the room, Azalea's gallants returned to their various assaults on her heart, and she was soon laughing at their outrageous flattery. Her enjoyment of the moment was only marred by the absence of one particular gentleman, but she refused to dwell on it just then.

"*Well*, my dear, I would say that your social position is assured now that Lord Kayce has decided to recognize you," Lady Beauforth said as the last of their callers departed. "He is incredibly wealthy, as well as influential among the ton. With his patronage and, of course, my own, which is not inconsequential, I assure you, you are sure to take next Season. We'll have you married to a lord or I miss my guess!"

"But why should he not recognize me, Cousin Alice?" asked Azalea choosing to ignore Lady Beauforth's increasingly frequent references to finding her a husband. "The family connection cannot be doubted, so would he not look foolish to ignore it?"

"Foolish? Kayce?" Lady Beauforth was plainly shocked. "Nothing of the sort, my dear! It is scarcely possible for a man of his standing to look foolish, whatever the circumstances. Had he decided to ignore the connection, you would have stood in grave danger of being cut on the mere notion that he must have some reason for not acknowledging you. I am very happy for you that it will not come to that! "

"But why should he do such a thing?" Azalea persisted suspiciously. "He *seemed* a most pleasant man. I concluded from his manner that he became aware of my presence in London only last night, else he would have called sooner."

"Yes, he did say that, didn't he?" Lady Beauforth looked thoughtful. "Normally, absolutely *nothing* goes on in London of which Lord Kayce is unaware. I'd have expected him to know of your presence the day of your arrival, or the day after at the very latest. Perhaps he has merely been deciding what to do. Your success last night may have clinched the matter for him. If you are going to take, he will certainly want some of the credit, and would not wish to look foolish by ignoring his niece when she becomes a Toast next spring," she concluded, blithely unaware, as always, that she had contradicted herself.

Azalea was accustomed to Cousin Alice's confusing

speeches and had learned by now not to take her every utterance at face value. It could not be denied, however, that Lady Beauforth was nearly as well-informed as she claimed Lord Kayce was. Thus, Azalea could not lightly dismiss everything she had said, especially given her grandfather's warnings. But could her uncle—or anyone —really be capable of such duplicity?

Perhaps so. She recalled a time when her cousins had encountered on the street two ladies they apparently despised, judging by previous conversations. To watch that meeting, one would have thought it a reunion of the dearest of friends.

The English, she reminded herself, were not nearly so open as Americans, so it might be possible that her uncle would conceal any dislike of herself that he might feel. She would go slowly with him, and make more of an effort to discover his true feelings. After all, she could hardly judge his character accurately on the basis of a single fifteen-minute interview.

"Secure that line!" bellowed the captain, his black hair dripping with sea water. "Furl the main topsail!"

"This looks like a bad blow." Christian's father sounded concerned.

Suddenly, flowers were everywhere. Apple blossoms. Daisies. A soft breeze was blowing. What was everyone worried about? he wondered.

"My God, Chris!" His father's face was white. The sky behind him had gone from blue to leaden, an odd, yellowish grey.

"Man overboard!" shouted the captain, red hair and beard now whipping in the gale. Chris turned to see a crate of chickens wash

over the rail, then another. The brown-and-white birds squawked in terror, their feathers flying, then they were gone.

"That was a close one!" His father's voice again.

Christian awoke with a start, sweat beading his brow. The bed linens were damp around him.

"Damn," he muttered. It had been so many months since he'd last had that nightmare, he had begun to hope he was finally free of it.

Still shaken, he rose to light the oil lamp on the desk, determined this time to write it down while it was fresh in his mind. Before he could dip his pen, however, it was gone— again. All that remained was a vague memory of wind and waves, and his father's voice. It always happened like this. Somehow, he was certain that if he could just remember it long enough to commit it to paper, the dreams would cease plaguing him. But he never could.

Fiercely, he scoured his memory, but all that came to him were more recent recollections. Port cities in the tropics, nights of celebration so decadent they made the amusements offered in London seem like nursery games by comparison. Quickly, he thrust the distasteful memories from his mind.

That was before, he told himself. When he hadn't known any better. He was not like that now, and would never be again. Now he was head of the Morely family, sixth Earl of Glaedon. No one must ever know how he'd stained the proud name he bore. He would forget it himself. He must.

Christian pulled out some papers he had brought with him from Glaedon Oaks and read through them until his eyes began to grow heavy. The day was well advanced when he finally awoke again.

Feeling remarkably refreshed, he rang for his valet. He

had been remiss since his return to Town. It was time he paid a social call at Lady Beauforth's. He was, after all, betrothed to her daughter. It was not Marilyn's face, however, that arose before him as he tied his cravat. Humming cheerfully for a reason he refused to examine, he picked up his hat and gloves and strode purposefully into the chill December afternoon.

Azalea and her cousins were just sitting down to tea when Smythe entered stiffly, announcing, "Mr. Plummer," in his formal, slightly bored tone. Jonathan strolled in nearly on his heels, encompassing the three ladies with his engaging smile and offering a vivid contrast to the starchy butler.

"So good to see you again, Lady Beauforth, Miss Beauforth, Azalea. I trust I'm not intruding? I had planned to come this morning, but I'm afraid I didn't feel quite the thing. Fully recovered now, though, I assure you." He sat next to Marilyn and helped himself to three buttered scones in proof of his words.

"Of course you're not intruding, dear boy," gushed Lady Beauforth as her daughter nodded in agreement. "We're delighted to see you again! As you are such an old friend of Azalea's you must regard us as family and drop in whenever the fancy strikes you."

Jonathan merely nodded, his mouth too full to allow any audible reply.

"How is Lord Holte?" Lady Beauforth continued, without regard to her guest's inability to answer. "I don't remember if you said whether you were staying with him in Town or have your own lodgings, as you young gentlemen so often do these days."

With the assistance of a judicious sip of tea, Jonathan managed to swallow. "Grandfather is still in Essex at present, so I am perforce in lodgings. I plan to join him at Bitters for Christmas and try to persuade him to accompany me back to Town in the spring, as this will be my last Season for some time to come."

"Do you go abroad, then, sir?" asked Marilyn. Azalea thought she detected a trace of disappointment in her cousin's voice.

"Not precisely, Miss Beauforth. I return to my home in Virginia next summer. Father is not as young as he once was, and he has been hinting in his letters that he could use my help, particularly at harvest time. Filial duty, or guilt, if you will, is finally getting the better of me."

"How very responsible of you!" exclaimed Marilyn warmly. "Dear Azalea has been telling me a bit about America, and I'm certain you must have even more exciting stories to tell of life there," she added, to Azalea's surprise. "What is it you will be helping your father to harvest?"

"Apples, mostly," replied Jonathan, then proceeded to describe his father's orchards and the surrounding countryside in some detail.

Azalea took little part in the discussion, content to watch with some amusement the conversation between her cousin and her erstwhile best friend. Marilyn leaned toward him, asking question after question, appearing genuinely fascinated by the topic. In fact, she was so absorbed in the conversation that she scarcely flirted at all.

Without her assumed airs, she appeared even more attractive than usual, Azalea thought. Her fine blue eyes sparkled, and as she leaned forward she displayed an eagerness that seemed genuine rather than contrived.

Azalea did not mind Marilyn's monopolization of her old friend —on the contrary, she was delighted. For all of Jonathan's outrageous compliments the night before, Azalea knew he would never see her as more than a little sister grown up. And at least one of her problems would be closer to a solution if Marilyn were to form an attachment for Jonathan, in lieu of Lord Glaedon.

As if on cue, Smythe entered the parlour to announce his lordship. Marilyn looked up with a brilliant smile, her affections obviously not yet engaged to the point of whistling an earl and his fortune down the wind.

Azalea felt her heart beat faster as she stole a glimpse at him, looking handsome as ever in a rust-coloured coat and fawn buckskins, then quickly turned her attention back to her plate.

"My lord, how good of you to call," Lady Beauforth exclaimed delightedly. "Pray take a seat while I ring for a fresh pot of tea." After only the briefest hesitation, Lord Glaedon seated himself in the remaining empty chair, which happened to be next to Azalea.

"How do you do, my lord," she murmured, not quite meeting his eyes. She was remembering their rather heated "discussion" last night and was suddenly embarrassed. How forward he must think her! And then there was that hint she had thrown out about his deceitfulness, perhaps undeserved.

Or perhaps not. She stiffened her spine and raised her head to attend to the conversation.

Marilyn was enthusiastically recounting one of the anecdotes Jonathan had just shared, apparently forgetting for the moment the Earl's dislike of America and its inhabitants. He did not seem especially put out, however, listening with polite interest as she concluded and Jonathan took up the story where she had left off.

Marilyn's unusual animation did not escape Christian's notice any more than it had escaped Azalea's, and he was just as able to make a shrewd guess as to its cause. He was surprised to realize that the idea did not disturb him in the least. Instead, he was aware of a distinct sense of relief that it was Marilyn and not her cousin who drew Mr. Plummer here.

Clearly he had not engaged Miss Beauforth's affections to the extent she had led him to believe. Of a certainty, he had never been able to evoke the animation of spirits she was evincing now at the rustic tales of this colonial.

To be fair, the fellow seemed likable enough, and did tell a good story. But who was he? Plummer? Christian couldn't remember ever having heard the name before last night. A friend of Miss Clayton's, Lady Beauforth had said.

He listened more closely to the conversation in hopes of discovering more about him—and, perhaps, about the intriguing, maddening Miss Clayton as well. Though she sat in silence beside him, he was profoundly aware of her nearness.

"So you see," Plummer was saying, "my grandfather had to be obeyed, even if it meant travelling halfway around the world for my education when there was a perfectly adequate, probably superior, university within walking distance of my home."

"And what school might that be?" asked Christian, raising one brow sceptically. He seriously doubted that any "higher education" the colonies had to offer could compare to Cambridge or Oxford.

"Why, the College of William and Mary, of course!" the other man answered with some surprise. "like Azalea, I am from Williamsburg," he said carefully. "We both grew up practically in the shadow of the College. It so dominated our lives that it is difficult to remember that there are those, especially here across the Atlantic, who may be unaware of its very existence." He regarded Christian rather strangely.

"No, not quite that, I assure you. As a matter of fact, my father had a very close friend who, I believe, was a professor at that school."

Mr. Plummer glanced at Miss Clayton, who seemed completely absorbed in examining the lace edging of her sleeve. "Who might that have been, my lord?" he asked after a moment. "I knew several of the faculty, and I believe Azalea was well acquainted with nearly all of them through her grandfather, who also taught there."

Christian turned to the young woman at his side, but she still did not look up. Lady Beauforth began hastily to clear her throat, apparently preparatory to changing the subject, but Christian answered the question without hesitation.

"A Reverend Gregory Simpson," he said. "He teaches, or taught, mathematics, I believe."

"Well, if it ain't a small world!" exclaimed Mr. Plummer. He looked again at Miss Clayton, who this time was moved to speak.

"He was my grandfather, my lord," she said quietly, meeting Christian's eyes for the first time since his arrival. "He died last spring, which is why I find myself in England. I—I knew of his friendship with the late Earl, but there seemed no opportunity, or reason, to mention it before this." She looked as though she were about to say more, but then decided against it.

"I'm sorry, Miss Clayton," he said sincerely. "Believe me, I had no wish to distress you with painful recollections."

He continued to regard her intently for a moment and was startled to see her colour rise. His own body began to stir in response and his pulse quickened.

Christian had done his best to put Miss Clayton from his mind since last night's ball, and he'd thought he'd succeeded. But now, in her presence, he found himself more disturbed by her face and voice as ever. It was almost as though a part of him, deeply buried, was linked to a similar part of her. It made no sense.

At this point, Lady Beauforth broke in with an observation on the decorations used at the Queesley's ball and Jonathan joined in determinedly, giving both Azalea and Christian a chance to reflect while appearing politely interested in the conversation.

Azalea had known it was inevitable that the bond between their two families would come out in conversation sooner or later. She had even hoped for an opportunity to bring it up so that she could watch Lord Glaedon's expression for evidence of deception.

His face had told her precisely nothing.

He seemed genuinely sorry for her loss, and had betrayed not the slightest consciousness at the disclosure. For a moment, there *had* been something else in his eyes, a warmth that went beyond sympathy, but then it was gone.

Now he merely looked thoughtful. Either Lord Glaedon was such an accomplished actor that he could give Edmund

Keane a run for his money, or he honestly had no recollection of his weeks in Virginia.

Or I'm losing my mind, and the marriage never took place.

No! She had the papers to prove it.

Christian, meanwhile, was every bit as preoccupied as the girl sitting beside him.

Had his father mentioned Simpson's granddaughter? Was that why her name seemed familiar to him? It seemed the most probable explanation yet. He recalled that their disastrous trip to America was to have included a visit to Simpson's home, and she would likely have been mentioned in that context, though she could have been little more than a child at the time.

But what of that elusive familiarity? Was it possible that Reverend Simpson had sent a likeness of the girl to his father and that he himself had seen it years ago? He could not remember such a thing among the old Earl's belongings. He resolved to go through them more carefully when he was next at Glaedon Oaks. He had to discover why she affected him so strongly.

When Lady Beauforth had exhausted the subject of last night's decorations and began criticizing the refreshments served, Lord Glaedon rose and rather absently took his leave.

Azalea was not sorry to see him go. She tried to enter more fully into the discussion so that her companions would not notice her distraction, but Jonathan seemed well aware of the constraint in his friend's manner. He shot several significant looks her way, particularly when Lady Beauforth mentioned Lord Kayce's visit, making Azalea wonder if he knew something about her uncle.

When Jonathan rose to leave, she quickly asked him to

accompany her to the library to see a letter she had just received from a mutual friend in Williamsburg. He acceded willingly and to her relief, neither of her cousins seemed inclined to join them.

His first words when they were alone, however, had nothing to do with Lord Kayce. "Say, 'Zalea, that fellow who just left, Lord Glaedon —isn't he the one who came to visit you in Williamsburg? I thought for certain it was when I first saw him, but then when he started talking, I wasn't so sure."

Azalea froze. She had totally forgotten that brief meeting with Jonathan all those years ago. Swiftly, she made a decision. "No, that was his brother, who died in the recent war. I'm told they looked very much alike."

To her relief, Jonathan appeared to accept her fabrication. She hated to lie, but she was completely unprepared to offer an explanation for Lord Glaedon's memory lapse, especially since she herself did not know what had caused it. Before he could ask any more questions, she changed the subject.

"Tell me, Jonathan, what do you know of my uncle, Lord Kayce? You looked startled, even displeased, when Lady Beauforth mentioned him." Azalea realized that a man was more likely to have accurate information than even the best-informed female, and Jonathan moved in circles that would allow him to hear more than Mr. Timmons might ever discover.

Jonathan looked uncomfortable. "I'll admit I have heard a few unpleasant things about him. Kayce has a reputation as a hard man, for all that soft front he puts on. And there are rumours that, well, cast doubt on his integrity."

"Rumors?" Azalea asked sharply. "Have you specifics?"

"Nothing's been proven, mind you," Jonathan replied. "But

poor Jim Sykes challenged him to a duel last year over some business deal where he claimed Kayce cheated him, and was found dead— killed by footpads, it was said— before the meeting ever took place. My guess is Kayce didn't want to risk his precious person any more than his honour. Don't trust him, Azalea."

"Thank you, Jonathan, I won't. Don't bruit it about just yet that he is my uncle, please. And let me know if you hear anything that you think I should know."

She wished suddenly that she could ask him about Lord Glaedon, too. No doubt Jonathan could find out what sort of reputation he had and perhaps other things about him, as well. But she could not, not without giving explanations that she was not yet ready to give.

Preoccupied with such thoughts, she bade him farewell.

"Mr. Plummer seems a fine young man," declared Lady Beauforth when Jonathan had gone.

"Did you not say he was but a year older than yourself?" asked Marilyn. "He seems far older, somehow. Doubtless due to his life in the wilds of America." A smile played about her lips.

"And grandson to Lord Holte!" continued her mother. "Why did you never tell us before last night that you were acquainted with such an eligible gentleman, Azalea?"

"Eligible, ma'am?" asked Azalea, startled to hear Jonathan mentioned in those terms.

"Oh, quite!" Lady Beauforth assured her. "And he seems greatly taken with you, I notice. I doubt not with a little encouragement, he could be brought to make you an offer."

Marilyn's delicate brows drew down in a quick frown, but Azalea almost choked on a laugh. "An offer? From Jonathan? I assure you, ma'am, that he regards me with nothing more than brotherly affection. Why, we practically grew up together!"

Immediately, Marilyn's expression cleared. "Yes, Mama, you speak foolishness, surely," she said with something suspiciously like relief.

Azalea did not hear Lady Beauforth's reply, for she was struck by the sudden realization that some gentleman might very well make her an offer if she continued to go on as she had last night, flirting and accepting dances as though she were in fact seeking a husband. It would not at all do to forget, amid the excitement of making new friends in London, that she was already a married woman.

She would be more careful from now on, she vowed, and not encourage any such expectations. On no account would she risk breaking some poor man's heart. She knew only too well how that felt.

CHAPTER EIGHT

"I'M SORRY, MY LORD. I HAVE LOOKED INTO EVERY POINT OF law that could be even remotely relevant to our case, but there is nothing we can do. The girl's claim cannot be doubted. Timmons, her man of business, has all the necessary proofs."

"Yes, yes, you told me that before. That's why I called on her today." Lord Kayce eyed his fat solicitor with disfavour. "I pay you an exorbitant fee to protect my interests, Mr. Greely. Those interests are now threatened by a mere slip of a girl—a girl whose existence you somehow failed to apprise me of until last month. I must wonder whether you are worth your keep after all."

The lawyer mopped his brow with an already damp handkerchief. "My lord, her claim against the Kayce estates is insignificant in comparison to the total. Your interests—"

"That is not the point," snapped Kayce. "Why was I never informed that my fool of a brother had offspring? Is that not the sort of thing I employ you for? I dislike surprises, Mr. Greely."

"It is usual that such heirs make application to the estate upon the decease of the holder, my lord. I have no idea why Miss Clayton or her representatives never wrote to us after your brother's death. Naturally, I assumed—"

"I do not pay you to assume. What we must do now is figure a way out of this predicament. While the money involved may represent but a fraction of my holdings, I would prefer not to lose that particular acreage. If you recall, I had made certain arrangements that might be an, ah, embarrassment if they came to light."

Mr. Greely paled visibly. "The right of way. I had forgotten, my lord. And if your niece contests the property, there will certainly be a full investigation." He appeared to think hard for a moment. "I cannot think she will care overmuch whether she receives the land itself, my lord. Perhaps she can be bought off. If you were to offer her a fair price for the acreage, she'd likely take it, particularly if she is as short of funds as you say."

Kayce nodded slowly. "Perhaps. She would not be sending her maid to buy gowns for her in Soho were she well-fixed."

Heartened, the lawyer went on eagerly. "She must surely be grateful for the way you have increased her inheritance over the years. It may even be possible to induce her to accept the original value rather than what it is worth now. That seems only fair. The extent of the Kayce holdings, to include her small piece of it, is solely to your credit. You had little enough to work with when your father died."

That much was true. Though he had successfully forced his elder brother, Walter, to leave England permanently after their father's death, Simon had still struggled to bring profit out of the estates. The fourth Baron's gaming and spendthrift ways had all but depleted his resources. Simon had succeeded beyond anyone's expectations. He rather regretted that his father, who had always favoured Walter, could not have lived to see it.

Word of Walter's death had changed nothing for Simon, except that he could now claim the title he had already felt entitled to by his brother's long absence. The fact that he had precipitated that absence himself was yet another matter he preferred not come to light. Not even Greely knew of it.

With the entire fortune indisputably his, Kayce had redoubled his efforts accordingly, with spectacular results. Until last week, it had never occurred to him that his unmourned brother might have left anything behind beyond the estates and title.

Today Simon Clayton, sixth Baron Kayce, was one of the wealthiest men in England —and one of the most feared. His reputation for ruthlessness was well deserved; he had let no foolish considerations of compassion or even the the law to stand in the way of his advancement. He lived for the power that came with great wealth —and now found himself in the position of losing a galling amount to this upstart niece, unless she could somehow be disposed of.

"It would be well if we could possess ourselves of those proofs you mentioned. Timmons, you said?"

"Yes, at the Law Offices," Mr. Greely confirmed.

Kayce nodded absently, his agile mind toying with the options. "I had thought a discreet accident might be necessary —indeed, certain arrangements have already been made that may bear fruit. But now I am entertaining other ideas. My niece is actually quite a beauty, I have discovered. I almost hate to see such a commodity go to waste if I could possibly turn it to my advantage."

"Of course!" exclaimed Mr. Greely, struggling to sit up straighter in the overstuffed library chair. "Miss Clayton is but twenty years old!"

Kayce began to smile. "Precisely. Who more appropriate for the role of guardian than her closest living relative? And as her guardian, it would be up to me to say where she weds."

"If the girl is as attractive as you say, you might get two or three times the price of her inheritance in a marriage settlement," said the solicitor.

"That and more, I should say." Kayce lapsed into thought. "Yes, that will do nicely, I think. Greely, ring for my valet. I believe a few discreet enquiries are in order."

Two afternoons later Azalea was still wrestling with her options, along with her latest attempt at embroidery. The Beauforth ladies were gossiping with Lady Mountheath and her acid-tongued daughters, who seemed to take an unholy glee in the shredding of reputations. Azalea had therefore retreated to needlework to avoid embarrassing her cousins with another outburst.

English ladies appeared to consider needlework an absolutely necessary accomplishment for any woman with pretensions to quality, so Azalea had spent several fruitless hours since her arrival in London trying to master that feminine art. After much frustrating effort, she had finally reached a point where she could appear to be occupying herself with a canvas, so long as the observer did not examine her rather unusual designs too closely.

At length, Lady Mountheath took herself and her daughters off, just in time for Lady Beauforth and Marilyn to go upstairs to change for dinner. Azalea was debating whether to follow them when Smythe announced a Mr. Greely, identifying him as Lord Kayce's man of business. Azalea put her embroidery aside most willingly to receive him.

Mr. Greely was only a slight improvement over embroidery, unfortunately; Azalea disliked him on sight, and his obsequious manner set her teeth on edge. He was dressed quietly and expensively, as one might expect of Lord Kayce's personal aide, but his hair and nails were considerably less than clean and he seemed unable to meet her gaze directly.

"My dear Miss Clayton," he said silkily, "it is such an honour to make your acquaintance. Lord Kayce's only living relative —you can have no idea how overjoyed he was to learn of your existence."

Was it her imagination or did she detect a note of irony in the man's voice? Entirely likely, given the circumstances, Azalea thought. And this man must know her uncle's mind as well as any person could.

"Thank you, Mr. Greely," was all she said, but her attention sharpened to catch any accidental information the solicitor might let drop by word or tone.

"Your uncle means to call on you again in the very near future, but in the meantime he has sent me to take care of some pressing legal matters and to advance you a few hundred pounds on your inheritance." Mr. Greely beamed, obviously expecting the girl to be overwhelmed by Lord Kayce's generosity.

While surprised and pleased that she was to receive such a sum so promptly, Azalea knew that it represented but a tiny fraction of what was rightfully hers. Still, it implied that Lord Kayce did not intend to dispute her claims after all.

"Has Mr. Timmons spoken with my uncle then?" she asked.

Mr. Greely blinked, but answered quickly. "I have seen Mr. Timmons myself, actually. After our discussions, he and your uncle agree that it will be best for all concerned if Lord Kayce is named your guardian without delay. That way your uncle will be in a position to smooth your entry into London Society." He smiled his oily smile again.

Azalea suspected that Mr. Greely, and most likely her uncle as well, thought her an empty-headed miss who would believe whatever they chose to tell her. She saw no reason at present to disabuse them of that notion. In fact, she might be able to use it to her advantage.

"Must I go to live with my uncle then?" she asked with wide-eyed innocence.

"Oh, I doubt it, Miss Clayton. Your uncle said nothing of your removal to his house." Mr. Greely looked almost alarmed at the suggestion.

After a few more pleasantries, Mr. Greely produced several documents requiring her signature, which Azalea glanced over with assumed bewilderment.

Lord Kayce had apparently arranged for her to receive a generous allowance, she saw, for which she could only be grateful. The document making him her guardian, however, was cleverly worded to sound as though she were merely allowing her uncle to oversee her affairs, while in reality she would be giving him complete authority over her person and property. This contract might possibly be binding even should Lord Kayce's guardianship cease— which she now began to hope it might do very soon.

To sign it was obviously out of the question, but she had no wish to arouse Mr. Greely's suspicions. She put on her sweetest smile.

"I'd love to oblige you, Mr. Greely, but I did promise my grandfather that I would let Mr. Timmons look over any papers before I signed them. As it was practically his dying wish, I would feel just terrible if I disregarded it. Surely you understand?" Azalea allowed a quaver to enter her voice as she spoke of her grandfather, then held her breath, afraid that she might have overplayed her role of sorrowing innocent.

She need not have feared. After a slight hesitation, Mr. Greely returned her smile indulgently. "Of course I understand, Miss Clayton. It sounds as though your grandfather was a wise and prudent man. I will just take these papers to Mr. Timmons myself in the morning. He can bring them here for you to sign once he has, er, approved them."

Azalea rather doubted that Mr. Timmons would see this precise document, as no lawyer worth the name would let his client sign it, but she merely smiled and thanked Mr. Greely for his understanding.

"Before I leave, Miss Clayton, I would like to present you with a gift from your uncle. It is his way of welcoming you to England and to the family. If you would accompany me outside?"

Azalea was wary after reading those documents, nor was Mr. Greely himself a man to inspire trust, but she could think of no gracious way to refuse. Once on the steps, however, her wariness evaporated.

Held by a groom just beyond the front railings was the daintiest, most beautiful bay mare she had ever seen.

"Is she for me?" Azalea gasped, turning to Mr. Greely with her face aglow.

That mercenary gentleman blinked, as though momentarily dazzled. "Indeed she is. A small token of your uncle's affection," he said with the closest thing to a genuine smile she had yet seen from him.

"Has she a name?" asked Azalea, her gaze quickly returning to the lovely animal.

"You may name her what you wish. Lord Kayce will be pleased that you approve of her," replied Mr. Greely blandly.

"Oh, yes! Yes, I do!" Azalea's eyes never left the mare. "Please convey to him my most heartfelt thanks!"

"I'll do that, Miss Clayton. Good day." Mr. Greely descended the steps to the waiting carriage, but Azalea barely noticed his departure. Slowly she approached the waiting mare, still unable to believe that this beautiful creature was really hers. Her uncle was obviously a skilled judge of horse-flesh, whatever else he might be.

"I shall name you Virginia —Ginny for short," said Azalea softly, stroking the mare's black, velvety nose. Her problems were by no means solved, but she allowed them to slip from her mind for the moment. It appeared that there were to be some advantages to her connection with Lord Kayce after all.

From what Lady Beauforth had said after her uncle's visit, Azalea suspected that this development would please her cousins.

~

"Gracious!" exclaimed Lady Beauforth, when Azalea made her announcement during dinner. "I wonder... I mean, how wonderful for you, my dear! And you are certain he means for you to remain with us?"

"That is what Mr. Greely implied, though of course none of the details have been worked out as of yet. I think I would prefer to remain here —if you don't mind, that is, Cousin Alice," she concluded hastily. She realized that she would be more than a little sorry to leave this household, which was beginning to feel like home.

"Mind?" cried Lady Beauforth, plainly touched by the plea in Azalea's voice. "My dear, I would be most distressed to have it any other way. Already you are almost a second daughter to me, and I am certain Marilyn quite regards you as a sister."

Surprisingly, a tight smile and nod from Miss Beauforth acknowledged the sentiment. This response, slight as it was, encouraged Azalea.

"Thank you," she said warmly to her cousins. "Thank you both. As I barely know my uncle as yet, I would very much rather stay here in familiar surroundings with those I have grown to care for." She realized as she spoke that this was only a slight exaggeration, and was gratified by the glow her words produced on Lady Beauforth's countenance.

"I'll let you know instantly, of course, when I have more information," she continued, thrusting back a sudden pang of conscience at her concealment of one particular fact that would by comparison eclipse this latest news. "Perhaps when my uncle calls in a day or two he can give us the details of the arrangement."

To divert her thoughts, Azalea mentioned the generous allowance her uncle meant to give her, a topic of great interest to both of her cousins. That subject dominated their conversation for the remainder of the meal.

Azalea was up at first light the next morning, eager to try the paces of her new mare. It would be her first ride in London — and on her very own horse!

She dressed quickly in the new green-and-gold velvet riding habit she had purchased in case such an opportunity arose, and descended to the kitchen before Junie had even begun her vigil at the keyhole. Cook readily acceded to her request for a sweet roll for herself and some sugar for Ginny, and Azalea proceeded to the stables with her mouth and pockets full.

She breathed deeply as she entered the stables, revelling in the almost-forgotten scent. Why had she not spent time here before this?

Tom, the head groom, noticed her at that moment and hurried forward with a broad smile. "You'll be wanting to see the new arrival, I don't doubt, Miss Azalea."

"Indeed I will, Tom," she replied, returning his smile. "And I'd like to take her out for a turn in the Park before breakfast as well, if you would be so kind as to have her saddled."

"I thought you might, miss. She'll be ready in a trice and I'll accompany you myself."

Azalea started to protest that he need not go to that trouble, but stopped when she saw the set of his jaw. Junie was not the only one determined to see that she stayed within the bounds of propriety, it seemed. She could not be vexed, however, for she knew that they were only trying to protect her from unpleasant gossip —and perhaps from more physical harm.

While Tom cinched the beautiful sidesaddle that had been

delivered with the mare, Azalea introduced herself to Ginny and fed her the lump of sugar she had brought. Her soft voice and gentle, non-threatening movements quickly overcame the little mare's initial shyness, and by the time Tom handed her into the saddle, they were becoming friends.

"A trifle skittish she is, miss, and a bit spirited for a lady's mount, I thought. You ride well, though, I take it?" asked Tom, observing her easy seat with appreciation.

"It has been a few months, and I'll no doubt be sore later, but I'll have no trouble handling her, Tom. Thank you for your concern." The groom mounted a roan gelding and they headed for the Park at a brisk trot.

As they entered the gates, Azalea looked around in delight. There had been a frost during the night, and the grass and trees were lightly glazed with white. The fairyland effect, temporary though it might be, almost made up for the lack of foliage and flowers.

Few people were about; a pair of grooms exercised their masters' horses and a few vendors were setting up their carts for the day's business. The cold air fairly sparkled in the sun, and Azalea could see her breath when she spoke to Tom. She trotted onto the bridle-path and urged her new mount to a canter more brisk than she would have dared had the Park been more crowded.

Rounding a turn past a clump of evergreens, Azalea saw a gentleman approaching on a large black stallion at a pace even quicker than her own. As he rapidly drew closer, she realized with a strange lurch of her heart that the rider was Lord Glaedon.

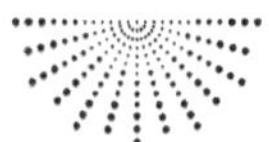

CHAPTER NINE

"MISS CLAYTON!" Lord Glaedon exclaimed, with every appearance of pleasure. "I did not know you were in the habit of riding before breakfast. Might I join you? It is rare to see a lady abroad so early." He pulled up when his horse drew even with hers.

"So I have discovered, my lord;" Azalea replied, wondering if he could hear the hammering of her heart. "I have always been an early riser, and here I am frequently hard-pressed to find anything to do before the household is awake." She noticed that Tom had dropped back out of earshot, though he kept her well within view.

"You have taken to riding to relieve your boredom?" Lord Glaedon asked with a hint of his usual sardonic manner.

"As a matter of fact, this is my first ride since coming to London. I have only just acquired this mare and was anxious to try her paces."

"She's quite a little beauty," said Lord Glaedon appreciatively, casting a knowing eye over the horse. "Did you choose her yourself?"

"Actually, no," replied Azalea, reluctant to mention Lord Kayce. "But I doubt I could have done any better if I had." Reaching forward, she patted the mare on her beautifully arched neck. "She has the cleanest lines I've ever seen, and in Virginia I had the chance to see some absolutely prime animals, I can assure you."

Azalea glanced quickly at the Earl, watching again for any flicker of recognition or anger at her mention of America. Again she detected nothing. His eyes were still on the mare.

"Yes, I had heard that there were some exceptional breeding farms in the New World," he said after a moment. "Perhaps someday I'll attempt the trip again."

A fleeting expression of pain crossed his handsome face, but Azalea thought that only natural considering his loss on the last crossing. She was almost— *almost*— convinced that he truly had no memory of his time in Virginia.

"That stallion is a fine example of horseflesh as well," she said, in an attempt to change the subject. She had no wish to antagonize him—at least not right now.

"Yes, Sultan is my pride and joy. And I did choose him myself," said Lord Glaedon with the first twinkle she had seen in his eyes since she first met him again in London. She felt a flutter of response deep within her.

"I would never have suspected otherwise, with your knowledge of horses," she returned with a tentative smile.

She vividly remembered how enthusiastic he had been on the subject of horses six years ago. Perhaps if she could keep him on that topic, some spark of their old friendship, along with a glimmer of memory, might be rekindled.

"And how did you know of that, may I ask? Is it such common knowledge?" asked Lord Glaedon, with a surprised lift of his brows.

Azalea swallowed, but covered her momentary confusion quickly, replying lightly, "But of course, my lord. You must know that any gallant such as yourself is much discussed among the ladies."

"Perhaps," he said skeptically. "But I would not have thought my judgement of horseflesh one of the topics to interest them."

"Oh, anything to do with you is, I assure you. Shall we ride on?" she asked hurriedly, anxious for a chance to gather her scattered wits before she betrayed herself further.

"Certainly," responded the Earl, obediently turning his horse.

As they cantered along the bridle-path, Azalea felt her confusion give way once again to the exultant pleasure of riding. She had missed it so! Though neither spoke for several minutes, their spirits seemed somehow in tune. Azalea found it unexpectedly pleasant to share this favourite pastime with another enthusiast, even under such awkward circumstances.

As they drew near to the Park gates once again, Azalea finally broke their companionable silence. "I don't suppose you would care to race, my lord?" she asked hopefully. For the moment, her intention of pricking his memory had been forgotten in the exhilaration of riding.

"I would dearly love to," he replied, "but it would certainly be frowned on if we were seen, and I have no desire to be barred from riding in Hyde Park. A pity."

He was smiling down at Azalea as he spoke, and she felt her heart beating faster than the exercise could account for.

"A pity indeed," she said wistfully, slanting a glance up at him. "I remember how I used to race across the fields back home with none to see or criticize. Here, I feel I am constantly being observed —and judged." She recalled with a rush of homesickness the lovely flowered fields and woodlands of Virginia and the solitary rides she used to enjoy there.

"Observed, perhaps," agreed Lord Glaedon with an appreciative glance at her face and figure. "But I cannot imagine anyone criticizing your riding. You are quite an accomplished horsewoman. In fact..." He glanced about them. "Is that groom of yours to be trusted?"

"What do you mean, my lord?" asked Azalea curiously.

"This area of the Park appears to be deserted, except for ourselves. Perhaps we might manage a very *brief* gallop, if you are game."

He sent her a mischievous look, reminding her forcefully of the Chris she had known in Williamsburg. Her heart seemed to stop for a moment.

She grinned back at him. "Of course I am game." With that, she flicked the reins and sent Ginny off at a thundering pace.

After a startled instant, Lord Glaedon followed, catching up fairly easily. "I did not mean this to be a race, you know," he called out.

But Azalea scarcely heard him. When her mare lurched into a gallop, she had felt something slightly amiss, and now the feeling intensified. Her saddle was slipping!

Alarmed, she pulled back on the reins, realizing only then that Ginny had managed to take the bit between her teeth. Ears back, the mare was fully into the spirit of the race, apparently unaware of her mistress's difficulty.

Locked into the sidesaddle as she was, Azalea realized that

she could be badly hurt if the cinch gave way completely. Transferring the reins to one hand, she desperately tried to extricate her knee from around the horn so that she could leap off if necessary. Before she could manage it, however, the saddle made a sickening slip sideways.

"I've got you!" Lord Glaedon, leaning over as he drove his own horse up against hers, grabbed her around the waist.

Ginny responded by shying violently, then half rearing. Lord Glaedon was on the ground by now, however, and pulled Azalea away from her.

"Th-thank you!" she stammered. "I have no idea what got into her!"

The mare was becoming calmer now, though she still skittered away from Sultan when he tossed his head in her direction.

"You said you obtained her only yesterday," Lord Glaedon reminded her. "I suspect she is not as thoroughly broken to riding as you were led to believe." His arms remained around her as he spoke, giving Azalea a warm sense of security that she ached to prolong. But already the groom was upon them, and at his first words, Lord Glaedon released her.

"Good God, Miss! What happened? I told you that mare was too spirited for a lady."

Azalea tried to subdue the trembling that started the moment she was out of Lord Glaedon's grasp. "Nonsense, Tom," she said briskly, to hide the emotions assaulting her. "She merely needs a bit of work. I'd have been fine had the saddle not slipped."

"Slipped? Why, I cinched it myself!" Effortlessly, the groom captured the mare and examined the saddle, which had slid around to her side. "Why, look here," he said after a moment.

"This part ain't even leather. It's some sort of cloth, and it's stretched out. Pretty shoddy way to make a saddle, if you ask me."

Shaken though she was, Azalea felt a nasty suspicion leap into her mind. "The saddle came with the mare, did it not?" She still did not name her uncle. If Lord Kayce had an unsavoury reputation, as Jonathan had implied, she did not want Lord Glaedon to learn of the connection just yet.

Tom was nodding. "Aye. Looks fancy enough, too." He fingered the girth. "I think I can tighten this up enough to get you home, miss, but I'll replace the cinch before you ride out again."

"I should say the entire saddle should be disposed of," said Lord Glaedon firmly. "And I don't recommend you attempt another gallop on that mare for quite some time, Miss Clayton. You should probably hold her to a trot, until you know her temperament better."

Reluctantly, Azalea agreed. "It is just as well that our gallop was cut short, I suppose, as I will probably be sore enough tomorrow as it is," she added, with an attempt at lightness.

"My dear Miss Clayton! I had quite forgotten that this was your first ride in some time. I am doubly at fault for suggesting that damned gallop." Lord Glaedon's eyes were concerned again and Azalea felt warmth flow through her.

"Pray do not blame yourself, my lord. I was enjoying myself immensely and had no wish to stop."

"Still, if you wish to minimize your discomfort, I recommend you walk for a bit before returning home. Trust me, I speak from experience," he concluded wryly.

She smiled. "Very well. It will take Tom a few minutes to see to that strap, anyway."

Christian felt a tremor go through him in response to that smile. Doubtless it was simply reaction to the excitement they had been through, he chided himself. Casting about for a safe topic, he recalled that his father had known Miss Clayton's grandfather.

"I was surprised to learn of the connection between our families," he began as they strolled down the path.

His companion coughed delicately. If he didn't know better, he might have thought she was disguising a chuckle. "My—my grandfather spoke of your father often. I believe they served together in India in their youth," she said.

"So you did not share my surprise. I rather received that impression at the time." Lovely, thick-fringed green eyes watched him expectantly, giving Christian the odd feeling that he was somehow disappointing her.

"You might have told me earlier, you know," he said, more severely than he had intended. What did she want from him?

At his words, she frowned, and he discovered that even her frown was charming.

"And how was I to know that you were ignorant of their friendship? For all I knew, you might have been perfectly aware of who I was but had decided not to recognize the connection."

Christian was taken aback. "What reason could I possibly have for snubbing the granddaughter of my father's closest friend?"

"That is best known to yourself, my lord," she returned primly.

"Come, Miss Clayton, let us cry friends." Suddenly, it seemed imperative that she forgive him. "Now that you know it was mere ignorance on my part, surely you cannot hold my earlier behaviour against me."

Azalea looked thoughtful. "I think I can," she said after a moment. "You were rude to me on the mere grounds of my nationality, which is not something you could reasonably expect me to be responsible for, even if it were cause for shame. Which it is not!" She flashed a speaking glance up at him.

Increasingly bewitched by her, Christian fought valiantly against a smile. He nodded. "You are right, of course, and I humbly beg your pardon."

She regarded him steadily, and he felt his pulse accelerate. He would not look away, however, and after a brief silence she nodded in turn.

"Very well," she said. "If you will consent to learn a little about America before you condemn us out of hand, I think we could even become friends." Her look challenged him now.

"You drive a hard bargain, Miss Clayton, as I think you know," said Christian half-seriously. "Very well, I agree to learn more about America in general and Virginia in particular, if you will be my tutor." He was finding Miss Clayton more delightful with every word that passed her lips, though her beauty was already alluring enough. She seemed both intelligent and naive —a combination he found totally enchanting and quite irresistible.

Azalea regarded him suspiciously. Was he flirting with her? She could not account for the sudden change in his attitude, unless it were merely the discovery that she was Gregory Simpson's granddaughter.

Such old obligations, she thought, must have more hold on Lord Glaedon than she would have imagined. It was probably all tied up in that unfathomable male code of honour.

"Well, Miss Clayton? Have we a bargain?" he prompted when she did not immediately speak.

"Certainly, my lord," she replied decisively. "How can I refuse, when it was I who demanded your further education? What would you like to know?"

"Everything, of course," he said laughingly. "But you can begin by telling me more about the excellent horseflesh you claim to have seen there."

This was a topic with which Azalea was completely at home. She proceeded to describe the breeding programs of some of the landowners of her acquaintance, as well as those of the more famous Virginia horse farms.

As she pursued the topic, she realized that she was repeating almost word for word much of what she had told this same man six years ago. Noticing his occasional slight frowns, she could not help but wonder whether he remembered at least parts of that prior conversation. Then another possibility occurred to her.

"I fear this has become quite a lecture, my lord. I do tend to run on when discussing a subject that interests me, and I have no wish to bore you."

"Bore me? With talk of horses? Impossible! If I seemed distracted, it was merely that I was considering ways of implementing these American innovations in my own stables. Pray continue," he said with every appearance of sincerity.

Azalea thought this explanation likely enough and resumed her "lecture."

In fact, Christian had been less than candid. He was certainly not bored; he suspected that Miss Clayton could discuss Greek history without losing his attention. But he was feeling the oddest sensation of having been here before —of having heard these same words spoken in that same voice.

Flashes of sunlit fields and apple blossoms arose in his mind, and suddenly he was reminded of his nightmares. He realized that Azalea had stopped speaking, and he looked at her questioningly.

"My lord, I must get back," she said with an apologetic smile. "I will likely be missed as it is. At any rate, you have heard most of what I can remember at the moment about Virginia's best-known stables."

"Very well, Miss Clayton," said Christian reluctantly. He found he was very much loath to let her go. "I shall look for you to continue my lessons very soon."

They returned to the horses, where Tom had finished his repairs, and Christian helped Azalea to remount. Retaining her hand for a moment, he brushed her gloved fingertips with his lips. Then, without a word, he swung up into his own saddle and rode off.

Azalea gazed after him until she suddenly remembered Tom's presence. Almost guiltily, she removed her hand from her cheek, where it had unaccountably strayed, and turned thoughtfully towards the gates.

On re-entering Beauforth House, Azalea was extremely relieved to encounter neither of her cousins. The details of her outing would be sure to cause some awkwardness.

If asked directly about her ride, she would mention the meeting with Lord Glaedon, of course. Otherwise, her cousins might very well discover it from Tom, or even the Earl himself, and would think her reticence suspicious. Somehow, though, she rather doubted that Lord Glaedon would mention it.

Still, she was glad that her resolve to be truthful was not to be immediately put to the test. Reaching her bedchamber undetected, Azalea quietly opened the door, only to be confronted by a reproachful Junie.

"Thank heaven you're back, miss! It's 'most ten o'clock, and I was near frantic, not knowing where you'd gone off to! I didn't dare ask anyone, for you know how servants gossip," she said self-righteously, "but if her ladyship had asked for you there'd have been the devil to pay, and no mistake."

"Oh, nonsense, Junie." Azalea laughed to cover her alarm. "I only went riding in the Park to try out my new mare. Tom accompanied me, so everything was perfectly proper. Cook knew where I was also. If you had asked him, you could have spared yourself your mother-hen worrying."

She knew Junie genuinely cared about her, but it did get tiresome now and again to be treated as though she were an ignorant child.

"Well, that's all right then, miss," said Junie, only slightly mollified. "I don't suppose you've breakfasted yet?"

"No, not really. Could you bring me up a tray? I'd like to change before going back down."

By the time Junie returned, Azalea was clad in a fashionable powder blue cambric gown and had taken the pins from her hair in an attempt to rearrange it. She gratefully allowed Junie to take over that task, then proceeded to do full justice to the ample breakfast provided. By now it was nearly eleven o'clock, and she was scarcely surprised when she was summoned downstairs to greet a caller.

She entered the parlour to discover Lord Kayce engaged in desultory conversation with her cousins. The sight of her uncle immediately recalled to her mind her earlier suspicions about the saddle, but in retrospect, she decided they were rather absurd.

Upon Azalea's entrance, Lady Beauforth immediately made excuses to both Azalea and her uncle, saying that she and Marilyn were expected at Madame Clarisse's shop, where they were to meet Lady Silverton and her two daughters. Without giving her own daughter a chance to speak, she bustled her out the door, leaving Azalea alone with Lord Kayce.

"It is good to see you again, my lord," Azalea said cautiously.

"The pleasure is entirely mine, my dear, I assure you. And have you forgotten so soon that I am to be Uncle Simon?" He was dressed as elegantly as before, his exquisitely tailored maroon jacket opening over a matching waistcoat richly embroidered with silver. "Now that I am officially your guardian, I thought a personal visit in order."

"Is it completely settled then, Uncle Simon?" asked Azalea, surprised that she had not heard from Mr. Timmons.

"But for a few legal formalities." He airily waved those aside. "I came to assure you that I have all well in hand regarding your future."

"My—my future?" asked Azalea.

"Certainly. As my ward, your future is my concern, and I did not wish you to spend a moment worrying your pretty head over it."

Lord Kayce was smiling benignly, almost smugly, Azalea thought, and her uneasiness grew.

"I am to remain in this house for the present, am I not, Uncle?"

"Of course," he replied reassuringly, having apparently

noticed her anxiety in spite of her effort to conceal it. Her uncle was far more astute than his man of business, Azalea realized.

"It would be inappropriate for you to reside with me, unless a suitable female companion could be found for you," he continued, "and, as Lady Beauforth is willing to house you and act as chaperon, the need does not arise. However, I would like to ask a favour of you while we are on that subject."

"Yes?" Her most immediate concern had been allayed, but she still did not wholly trust him. Was he going to ask her again to sign those documents? How could she refuse a second time?

"I shall be having a small dinner party Friday evening and I would be honoured if you would consent to act as hostess. I am anxious to show off my new-found niece to a few of my oldest friends. Will you be so kind as to do this for me?"

"Of course, Uncle Simon, I would be delighted to." Azalea was relieved by this apparently innocent request after what she had feared. "What time shall I be ready?"

"I'll send a carriage for you at seven-thirty," said Lord Kayce with barely concealed satisfaction. "Are you happy with the mount I purchased for you?" he asked then, neatly changing the subject before she could question him further.

"Oh, she's marvellous," exclaimed Azalea. "Did not your Mr. Greely convey my thanks? I rode her this morning, and her paces are like silk, though her manners are just the slightest bit rough, I fear. We nearly had a mishap. But I have no doubt she will improve with training." She couldn't quite bring herself to mention the saddle, though she watched him closely as she spoke.

"Indeed! My apologies, in that case. I assure you she came highly recommended." Was it her imagination, or did she detect a certain wariness in his expression?

"No apology necessary, Uncle Simon, I assure you. She's a splendid animal, really."

He smiled thinly. "I am happy that she pleases you. And now, I really must be going. I'll see you a few days hence." Lord Kayce rose smoothly, executed a graceful half bow and departed.

Perhaps he really did mean well, she thought hopefully after he was gone. Still, she would call on Mr. Timmons in a few days if she had not heard from him, to see whether Mr. Greely had indeed brought him those documents.

A little over an hour later Lady Beauforth and Marilyn returned, accompanied by Jonathan Plummer, who, Marilyn said, they had encountered upon leaving Madame Clarisse's shop. Naturally, they had invited him for nuncheon, knowing what a good friend of Azalea's he was.

Watching Marilyn's rapt expression when she looked at Jonathan, Azalea doubted whether this last consideration had actually carried much weight, but she was happy to see her old playmate in any event. She carefully observed both his behaviour and Marilyn's, and was able to conclude that her hopes in that direction were not completely unfounded. There was obviously a fair degree of attraction on both sides.

Nuncheon was a lively meal, with Jonathan and Lady Beauforth carrying the bulk of the conversation, though by no means excluding the others. As before, Azalea noticed that

Marilyn's speech was far less affected when she spoke to Jonathan.

Between anecdotes, Azalea managed to relate Lord Kayce's invitation. Jonathan's look of concern reminded her of his earlier cautions, and after the meal she again contrived to have a brief moment alone with him.

"I fear you may have been quite right about my uncle," she told him without preamble as they lingered in the dining-room after her cousins had proceeded to the parlour. "He seems uncommonly anxious to be made my guardian, and now I have reason to suspect he may actually wish me ill." She related the story of that morning's mishap, omitting, however, any mention of Lord Glaedon.

Jonathan nodded grimly. "You never were anyone's fool, 'Zalea," he said. "You look so much like the other London belles now, I had dashed near forgotten how sharp you can be. Just as well you are, though, with the likes of Kayce to deal with."

"I'm beginning to realize that. I'll be careful, though, I promise you. Should I refuse his invitation to dinner, do you think?"

Jonathan thought for a moment. "No, it should be all right. He'll hardly try to harm you in front of a crowd, and it will be well known to your cousins that you are in his company. My advice is to play along —for now— but to keep your eyes open."

"That's precisely what I had intended to do," she agreed.

Lady Beauforth called to them from the parlour then, querying about their tardiness.

"Don't forget, 'Zalea —if you need a friend, I'm always

here," Jonathan whispered hastily as he turned towards the door. "At least until summer."

"Thank you, Jonathan. I'll remember."

But with Jonathan's cautions added to her original suspicions, she was beginning to suspect that she would need more than a friend, or even a lawyer, to deal with Lord Kayce.

She would need a husband.

CHAPTER TEN

THE NEXT MORNING AZALEA AGAIN ROSE EARLY. SHE HAD decided to make a regular habit of riding before breakfast, for she could tell that even in the few weeks she'd been living in London, her physical condition had deteriorated. In spite of her soreness yesterday, she had more of the energy she had always taken for granted back in Virginia.

She would not admit to herself that the hope of seeing Lord Glaedon played any part in this virtuous resolution. Still, she could not suppress the feeling that had buoyed her since yesterday morning. Surely he had shown something beyond simple courtesy towards her. What that was exactly, she didn't quite dare to speculate —not yet.

Her sore backside distracted her for most of the brief ride to the park, but as she neared the entrance, she finally allowed herself to consciously wonder whether Lord Glaedon would be there. Before she could summon the willpower to banish the fearful, hopeful, question, it was answered. He was waiting just outside the gates. If she had any doubts about whether he was expecting her, they were erased at once by his cheerful wave, along with his greeting.

"Miss Clayton! I was hoping you intended to repeat your morning ride, though I must admit I rather feared you would be too sore to do so." He grinned as she attempted to find a position in the saddle that would cause her less discomfort. "You have a new saddle, I see."

"Yes. I *am* a bit stiff, as you are obviously aware —and I think it most ungallant of you to mention it, my lord. But after being deprived of riding for so long, it would take more than a passing ache to keep me from it." She returned his grin, both delighted and relieved to find him not only present, but still amiably disposed towards her.

"I was counting on that, actually," he said. "I propose a brief trot this morning, followed by a lengthier stroll. That should set you up admirably and relieve your, ah, stiffness somewhat."

Azalea knew he was teasing her for downplaying her soreness, but found that she really didn't mind. "Very well, my lord," she said crisply, to conceal her conflicting emotions, and immediately sent Ginny into a brisk trot.

Lord Glaedon kept pace with her on his beautiful black and they rode, as yesterday, in silence for a few minutes. Before the horses could become winded, the Earl pulled up and motioned for Azalea to do the same.

"I said brief, and I meant it," he explained to her questioning look. "Trust me. You still have the ride back, and I wouldn't wish you to be unable to dance at Lady Sunham's rout tonight."

"And how did you know—" Azalea stopped when she saw the amusement in his face. Of course he would have been invited. There were so few entertainments at this time of year that Lady Beauforth could not bear to forgo any of them —as he well knew. And he had told her to trust him. Did he mean more by that than it appeared?

"Thank you for your consideration, my lord," she concluded with a false sweetness that she sincerely hoped did not deceive him.

He pointedly ignored her comment and helped her to dismount. At the touch of his hand on hers, a tingle went through her. She could not bring herself to meet his eyes, so she had no idea whether he was likewise affected.

As her feet touched the ground, Azalea realized that even that very brief ride had affected her insulted muscles more than she would have believed —though she was careful not to let her expression betray as much to her companion. He seemed to read her thoughts, however, and pointedly accepted her thanks with a maddening "I-told-you-so" air.

After walking for a few moments, Azalea found both her soreness and her confusion over her physical response to Lord Glaedon easing somewhat. At the same time, her curiosity reasserted itself. When he broke the silence to suggest that she continue his instruction about the New World, she suddenly thought of a way to satisfy it, at least in part.

"Before I begin, my lord, perhaps it would be helpful if you could give me some idea of what you already know about America. That way I shall not run the risk of boring you by repeating information you are acquainted with."

She held her breath, half expecting either a set-down for her prying or another tirade on the shortcomings of her countrymen. Either would be a serious blow to her hopes. But she received neither. Instead, Lord Glaedon looked thoughtful.

"Several years ago I intended to learn quite a lot about your country," he said slowly, intently regarding a pair of wrens pecking hopefully at the frozen ground. "I read about its colonization and its rebellion against the King, and I have to admit I rather admired the colonists for the stand they took. In many ways, their cause was just."

He rubbed the back of his neck with one hand. "When I set sail with my father six years ago, I was looking forward to seeing that vast country for myself and forming my own opinions of the land and its people. Our stay was to have been brief, but I had already half formed the idea of returning to make my fortune there if I liked what I saw. I was not then the heir, of course, but the younger son."

He glanced at her briefly, with a slight smile that made her heart pound. Surely he was about to mention their marriage now?

But he turned and fixed his gaze on the wrens again as he continued. "During the first week or two of the voyage, I spoke often with the captain— Taylor, I think his name was, or was it Whitten? I never can seem to remember. Anyway, I spoke often to him about his experiences in the colonies. He had some fascinating stories to tell. I was young enough then to become easily carried away by his tales of battling the elements and carving out one's own destiny. All too soon, however, I was given a chance to battle the elements myself — and to lose."

The Earl seemed to forget Azalea's presence completely as he relived the frightful events on the ship. "A storm blew up suddenly. I remember the wind, the flapping sails, and Captain Taylor's assurance that it would be a brief blow. He sent my father and me below, but before I could reach the hatch, I was hit on the head by a falling spar."

He closed his eyes briefly. "The next thing I remember is being hauled aboard a different ship, half-dead, to be told by a crewman I didn't recognize that he and I were the only survivors of the wreckage. He was the one who always referred to the captain as Whitten. But I'm almost certain that the name was Taylor."

Christian's brow furrowed in an effort to recall exactly what had happened, and Azalea realized she was holding her breath. Slowly, she let it escape. She was beginning to understand.

"Of course, at the time, I couldn't even remember my own name," he went on, "and certainly no one else knew it. I didn't know where I was from or where I was bound, so when the captain of this ship, a merchantman heading for Jamaica, asked if I wanted to join his crew, I had no reason to refuse.

"That captain's name was Farris, of that I'm certain. I served aboard his ship for three months, and unfortunately, I can remember every grisly moment of it. Farris was a slaver, I discovered, and a ruthless one at that—if there is any other kind. No one dared to criticize his running of the ship. Twice, I recall, crewmen who spoke out against his treatment of the 'cargo' were flogged to death, then thrown overboard. I realized even then that I was playing the coward by saying nothing, but I assuaged my conscience with the conviction that dead heroes benefit no one."

Azalea pressed her lips tightly together. She wanted to reassure him, to comfort him, but was afraid that if she spoke he would recall her presence and stop his outpouring of memories. She wondered whether this might be the first time he had related them to anyone since his return.

Oblivious to her struggle, he continued. "In Jamaica, I was able to join the crew of another merchantman, this one Dutch, which didn't depend on human misery for its profits. I remained aboard the *Hyacinth* for nearly four years. Though my life there was far better than it had been aboard the slaver, I behaved as a common sailor —both aboard ship and in port. I knew no better, I suppose, but some of the things I did during those years..."

He stopped and swallowed before going on. "During that time my memory began to return in bits and flashes. One morning I awoke knowing, for the first time, who I was and where I lived. As soon as I could contrive it, I returned to England.

"In my absence, Herschel had gone to fight in America, against our grandmother's pleading. He apparently felt that it was his duty to represent the family on the battlefield, as I was not available to go. Word came only a month before my return that he'd been killed in Upper Canada, at the Battle of the Thames."

Though Azalea's eyes filled as she listened, his own remained dry. He spoke dispassionately, as though telling of events that had happened to someone else.

"I had already realized that my father must have perished in the shipwreck four years earlier. I was Earl of Glaedon, and had been for some months, though the title had erroneously passed to a cousin, as I was presumed dead. However, I had no difficulty proving my identity, and my title and inheritance were restored. Much happiness they have brought me." Sudden bitterness spilled over into his voice.

"One can make one's own happiness, don't you think?" asked Azalea softly, hoping to draw him out of his melancholy mood. Quickly, she brushed her tears away.

Her words seemed to bring Lord Glaedon back to the present with a start. He stared at her for a moment and then his gaze hardened.

"So you see, Miss Clayton, I have good reason to detest Americans. Not only did they cause my brother's death and, inadvertently, my father's, but I have seen the horrors of their abominable slave trade personally —the horrors 'innocent' colonists, like yourself, try so hard to ignore. Perhaps I know all that is necessary about America, after all. Good day, Miss Clayton." Turning on his heel, the Earl walked quickly back to his waiting horse and departed without a backward glance.

Azalea stood as though rooted to the spot, staring after his retreating form. His abrupt return to the hostile manner that had marked their first meetings had startled her, but she was ready to forgive him after hearing his reasons.

What shocked her more was the certain knowledge that he had never intended to deceive her. He was as trustworthy as she had wanted to believe him. And most disturbing of all was the fact that, in spite of everything, she still loved him with all her heart.

Azalea had very little time to reflect on these unsettling discoveries, as she and Marilyn spent all of the morning and much of the afternoon combing the various shops for just the right ribbons, gloves and other accessories to set off the gowns they planned to wear to Lady Sunham's that evening.

In spite of the distracting thoughts that would not be dismissed, Azalea could not help enjoying their outing. With a substantial amount of spending money in her reticule, she was free to indulge her tastes without regard to price, a luxury she feared she could become quite accustomed to, given half a chance.

She and Marilyn were dealing more pleasantly with one another than they had ever done, almost like the sisters Lady Beauforth enjoyed likening them to. But when her cousin mentioned that blue was Lord Glaedon's favourite colour, as she purchased a spray of artificial flowers in that hue, it cast a brief shadow over Azalea's enjoyment.

The comment served to remind her that she had come no closer to preventing the marriage that was due to take place in only two months' time. Lord Glaedon's sudden change in attitude toward her this morning made her hopes of a reconciliation, leading to a full disclosure, even less likely.

She had hoped to somehow win him away from Marilyn before attempting to explain about their marriage. Now it appeared doubtful that she would have that chance. But she would have to tell him soon, whatever his feelings towards her— especially now that she knew he was indeed ignorant of the true state of affairs. Too many people would be hurt if she remained silent.

The gathering at Lady Sunham's elegant Town house was noticeably smaller than the one at Lady Queesley's had been. Christmas was only two weeks away now, and even the most citified families were leaving daily for their country estates in order to spend the holidays in the traditional manner.

This was to be a musical evening, with a noted soprano engaged to delight the assembled guests, as well as a young Italian gentleman said to be worth listening to on the pianoforte. Dancing was to follow later.

As Lord Glaedon had implied that he would attend, Azalea discreetly scanned the room for him upon her arrival, but without success. She moved to take a seat next to Lady Dinsmore, wondering unhappily whether he had changed his mind in order to avoid encountering her. Could he possibly believe she would hold him to his promise of a dance after the way they had parted?

Azalea decided that it was just as well he was not here, for most likely they would only quarrel again. No, it would be better if they did not meet again until his temper had had time to cool. Then she might have a chance of arranging to speak with him privately.

Her thoughts were so busily engaged in convincing herself she was glad Lord Glaedon had chosen to stay away that she missed most of the soprano's performance.

"Not quite the quality we were promised, don't you agree?" The question was spoken so close to her ear that it made her start.

Glancing in some confusion at Lord Glaedon sitting behind her, and wondering how long he had been there, she replied rather at random that she had enjoyed the selection very much.

"Gammon," he whispered back. "I've been watching you, and you were hardly giving Signorina Devita your undivided attention. If you can tear yourself away from this riveting performance, I'd like to talk to you."

A few people in their immediate vicinity were glancing curiously at them by this time, and Azalea felt it would be wiser to accompany his lordship than to continue any discussion here. She rose and stepped past an elderly lady in purple crepe with a murmured apology.

Out of the corner of her eye Azalea saw Marilyn watching them but decided she could not worry about that just now. She was struggling with the decision she had made earlier in the day—to tell Lord Glaedon the truth no matter what. Perhaps this would be an opportunity to do so. Her heart began beating uncomfortably fast.

As they left the room, she whispered, "After this morning, I had expected you would avoid me like the plague."

Lord Glaedon merely led her into the supper-room with a light hand on her elbow.

In point of fact, that was exactly what Christian had intended for about fifteen minutes after he left Miss Clayton in the Park. His emotions had been in such a turmoil that he could almost believe she had in fact bewitched him with her charming smile and those sparkling green eyes. She had betrayed him, somehow, into disclosing details of his past that he had deliberately buried two years ago. He had even momentarily blamed her for the sudden resurgence of grief he had felt at the double loss of his father and brother.

As his temper had cooled, however, he was able to sort through his conflicting feelings. In reality, he had confided in Miss Clayton simply because it seemed somehow the right thing to do. In just two days— two mornings, really —a closeness had sprung up between them that he found both comforting and alarming.

Talking to her seemed almost like talking to himself. He knew, somehow, that anything he told her would be kept in the strictest confidence. That he trusted her was in itself astonishing to a man who had been cynical to the point of bitterness since his return to England two years ago.

What he felt went even beyond trust, however. There was also that recurring feeling of familiarity, that he had known this girl before. He was now almost certain that she had figured in the disturbing dreams that had plagued him at intervals since the shipwreck.

Was fate drawing them together? While not a particularly religious man, Christian had actually taken to prayer occasionally since his experience in hopes of being imparted insight about —or simply relief from— those dreams. Was this girl an answer to his prayer? He felt as if he were on the edge of some blinding revelation, and he was unsure whether to stave it off or welcome it with open arms.

Miss Clayton attracted him on a far more basic level as well. When he had first seen her in the Park this morning, he had been seized by a wild desire to take her in his arms. His brief anger had saved him from that folly, at least.

After much thought, he had decided to return home to his estates to search through his father's papers in hopes of finding some clue about her. He wasn't sure what he expected to discover, but he had an inexplicable conviction that some answer would be revealed there.

But first he needed to mend his fences with this most extraordinary young lady. And what then? Not only was he betrothed, but he shrank from the very idea of thrusting himself, with his despicable past, on Miss Clayton's sweet innocence. He did not pause to wonder why he'd had no similar reservations with regard to Miss Beauforth.

"You wished to say something, my lord?" prompted Azalea, when Christian made no move to speak immediately.

"Yes, Miss Clayton," he responded, collecting his thoughts. "First, and most importantly, I humbly beg your forgiveness for my unpardonably rude behaviour this morning. Is it too much to hope that we may put the incident behind us?"

The mute appeal in his eyes caused Azalea's heart to dance. "I have forgotten it already, my lord," she said breathlessly, hoping he would not notice the flush she could feel mounting in her cheeks.

His sudden smile at her words was so dazzling that she felt almost faint, though whether from relief or some other emotion, she could not be sure.

"Secondly," the Earl continued, "I wished to take leave of you, as I am going into the country tomorrow and will probably not return until after the first of the year. Family Christmas and all that. I did not want to depart with any ill will between us."

Azalea felt a surge of disappointment that he would be leaving, almost, but not quite, undermining the joy imparted by his previous words. She simply *must* tell him the truth before he left. By the time he returned, the wedding would be little more than a month away.

"I shall miss riding with you in the Park, my lord," she said, knowing she must sound forward. But she would have to be more forward still if she was to stop him from marrying Marilyn. She would have to tell him that she was his wife. Desperately, she tried to form the words that would sound so unbelievable to him.

"I, too," replied Christian before she could speak. "I hope we may resume the practice when I return."

He felt a sudden resurgence of the temptation that had assailed him that morning, now stronger than ever. With her so near, his senses fairly swam at the thought of his lips upon hers.

Azalea's eyes locked with his for an instant as she swayed ever so slightly forward, then were quickly veiled by those glorious lashes. "I—I hope so also." She looked back up at him then and spoke in a stronger tone. "Lord Glaedon, I—"

"Well!" Marilyn Beauforth's voice interrupted them.

Christian stepped hastily away from Azalea, for he'd been standing closer than was strictly proper. She looked guilty, too, cheeks suffused with colour.

"And what topic, pray tell, can be so fascinating that you two must steal away from that wonderful performance to discuss it?" his fiancée enquired in a shrill tone.

Not for the first time Christian wondered whether it was solely patriotism that had driven Herschel away from England before formally betrothing himself to Miss Beauforth. "I was merely apologizing to Miss Clayton, my dear," he replied smoothly. "In the past I have been less than cordial to your cousin, and I did not wish to leave London with any ill feeling on that score." That much was true, he told himself.

Marilyn's demeanour changed immediately. "How thoughtful of you, my lord, to attempt to overcome your very natural aversion to an American for my sake!" She simpered up at him in a way that he found more irritating than usual.

"Yes, quite," he said shortly, torn between annoyance at her phrasing and guilt over what his thoughts had been a moment ago. He noticed that Azalea did not meet his eyes.

"Well, then, shall we return for the remainder of the performance now?" Marilyn asked brightly.

"No, I fear I must prepare for my departure tomorrow. I came tonight so that I might take my leave. Pray give my regards to your mother, Miss Beauforth."

"I will. And now, if you will excuse me, I would prefer not to miss any more of the performance." Marilyn hurried away to resume her seat, which Christian had noticed earlier was quite near to that of Mr. Plummer.

"Good evening, Miss Clayton," he said to Azalea as she turned to follow her cousin. "I must admit that I scarcely regret missing the remainder of that soprano's offerings," he added lightly, wishing to see her smile once more. "I hope for your sake that the pianist is of better calibre."

She flashed him the smile he'd hoped for. "Thank you, my lord. I—" she glanced over her shoulder to where Marilyn had paused to wait for her "—I hope you have a safe journey and a pleasant holiday season," she said quickly, then hurried away.

Christian watched her thoughtfully for a moment before heading for the door. There was no denying that Miss Azalea Clayton attracted him, in more ways than he cared to admit. But it was an attraction he would have to subdue ruthlessly. He had entered into his betrothal with Miss Beauforth for the sake of his family's honour. If he were to cry off, or worse, to betray his promised wife, that would be more dishonourable than if he had never made the offer at all.

He still mourned his father and brother, but now, for the first time, he cursed the tangle they had left behind. Was his whole life to be lived fulfilling plans they had made? Scowling darkly, he left the house, too preoccupied with his thoughts to notice the thin, shadowy figure that ducked into a doorway as he approached his carriage.

Azalea, meanwhile, returned thoughtfully to the music-room. Later, she could not have said whether the pianist lived up to Lord Glaedon's hopes or not, for she attended to his performance even less than she had to the soprano's.

She had failed in her intention to tell him the truth, but she could not manage to feel depressed as she thought over their brief conversation. Surely she had not imagined the warmth in his eyes as he had looked at her? Nor his coolness towards Marilyn.

Azalea felt badly for her cousin. While she no longer believed that Marilyn actually loved Lord Glaedon, she could not doubt that the proud young lady would be hurt when the truth came out. Marilyn, she'd come to realize, had as few close female friends as Azalea herself had. She had felt that the two of them were coming to terms, but this matter was likely to destroy their budding friendship entirely. Surely there must be a way to avoid that.

During the dancing and late supper that followed the recital, Azalea attempted to shake off her pensive mood. When she did manage to notice her surroundings somewhat, it was to realize that Jonathan seemed to be dividing his time fairly equally between herself and her cousin, though his manner with her could hardly be mistaken for anything but that of an old friend.

He appeared to be more smitten with Marilyn each time he saw her, and it was increasingly clear that his feelings were returned to some degree. Azalea allowed herself a small hope.

However, on the carriage ride home, Azalea's hope became

fainter. It was clear that Marilyn had not forsworn Lord Glaedon and his wealth for the sake of the intriguing American —at least not yet.

"I still think it odd that Lord Glaedon should have felt it necessary to take particular leave of you, Cousin," she said. "It would have been more seemly had he asked me to convey his apology for him. How vexing that he could not stay for the dancing after all."

Azalea couldn't resist saying, "You seemed to have no lack of admirers, Marilyn. I noticed that Mr. Plummer enjoyed your company exceedingly this evening." She had the satisfaction of seeing her cousin start, then look noticeably guilty.

"He is a very good dancer, and his conversation is always interesting," was Miss Beauforth's only reply before she lapsed into silence.

Lady Beauforth, whom Azalea had assumed to be dozing in her corner of the carriage, sat up a little at her daughter's words and directed a penetrating gaze in her direction. Plainly, Azalea was not the only one who had noticed Marilyn's apparent preference for Mr. Plummer. She hoped that Lady Beauforth's silence on the matter meant that she did not find the discovery distressing.

For Azalea herself, it seemed the only possible solution to the problem of how she was to prevent Marilyn's marriage to Lord Glaedon without losing her friendship. If that preference could be encouraged to the point where Marilyn herself might cry off from their betrothal, then half of Azalea's problem would be solved.

On this happy thought, Azalea settled back in her seat to doze for the remainder of the drive home.

CHAPTER ELEVEN

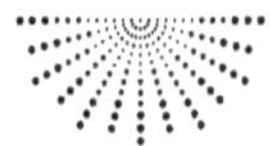

THE NEXT MORNING AZALEA SLEPT LATE, PARTLY DUE TO HER late night but also because she felt no particular inclination to ride. With Lord Glaedon gone from London, her virtuous plan of taking exercise in the Park every day seemed rather tedious. Thus, it was near noon when she and her cousins finally broke their fast, all together in the breakfast-parlour for a change.

They were just rising from the table when a footman delivered a large parcel for Azalea. It was from Lord Kayce. Distracted for a moment from her apathy, she rose to take the package to her bedchamber to open, but was forestalled by Lady Beauforth.

"Why, how curious!" her cousin exclaimed. "What do you suppose it is, Azalea?"

"I don't know, Cousin Alice, but we can certainly find out." She proceeded to remove the paper right there so that Lady Beauforth's curiosity might be assuaged immediately.

A moment later Azalea was startled by a flash of gold within the box and held up the gift for her cousins' inspection.

It was a gown —but what a gown! Designed in the height of fashion, it was of a light, sheer material that seemed to have been spun of incredibly fine gold thread. Its overskirt of gossamer net was liberally sprinkled with tiny topazes, and several tiers of outrageously expensive gold lace graced the hem.

The three ladies gasped in unison. "Straight from Paris, without a doubt!" Lady Beauforth was the first to catch her breath. "My dear, you will look positively divine in it!"

"It should suit your colouring admirably," added Marilyn with more than a touch of envy in her voice.

"I—I've never seen such a fabric before." Azalea finally found her voice. "It doesn't seem quite real. Why should my uncle give me such a gown?" She was genuinely bewildered.

"Did he enclose a card?" asked Marilyn practically.

Azalea looked into the box. "Yes, here it is. And a matching fan, as well. Oh! He wishes me to wear it Friday night. It seems rather... extravagant for a private dinner party, though, don't you think?" She directed her question to Lady Beauforth.

"Oh, certainly you must wear it, my dear," that lady advised. "He obviously sent it for just that purpose —and why not? I should say it means that, as your new guardian, he intends to do well by you."

Azalea could well believe that Lord Kayce wished the world to think this, but it did not allay her uneasiness. During the past two days she had nearly forgotten her worries about her uncle, so absorbed had she been by her other problem. Now her anxiety rushed back.

Still, as long as she could decipher his motives and plan her next move to counter his, she should be all right. But exactly what gambit was this dinner party a part of?

"Try it on, my dear," Lady Beauforth insisted, breaking into her thoughts. "Let us see if it fits, so that we can make any necessary alterations."

Nodding absently, Azalea replaced the gown carefully in its box and carried it upstairs.

"Why do you frown so, miss?" asked Junie curiously as Azalea gazed into the mirror a short time later. "Why, you look like a golden goddess in that gown! True, it's two or three inches too long, but that's easy enough to fix."

It was not the length that was bothering Azalea, however. The tissue-thin fabric clung to her figure seductively, even over the cotton chemise she had insisted on wearing underneath. The bright gold set off her colouring just as Marilyn had predicted, emphasizing the rich auburn of her hair and the creamy whiteness of her throat and bosom.

And that was the problem: entirely too much of her bosom was displayed. She was conscious of a sudden wish that Lord Glaedon could see her like this. If he had looked at her with admiration and warmth last night when she wore her demure blue silk, how might he react to her in this gown? Sternly, she pushed such indecent thoughts from her mind.

Since coming to London, Azalea had already managed to overcome modesty to the extent of wearing the evening gowns Lady Beauforth had deemed appropriate for a girl her age, though even some of those had seemed rather risqué to her less-than-sophisticated tastes. But this gown was positively obscene. Another half an inch and she would fall right out of the top of it!

For some reason, it seemed that her uncle wanted her to project the image of a golden seductress, but she would not oblige him willingly. Azalea surveyed the gown thoughtfully for a moment.

"All right, Junie, help me out of this while I tell you what alterations will need to be made," she said. "Removing the bottom flounce should make it just the right length, but it seems a shame to waste so much of that beautiful lace, don't you think?"

Junie nodded. "I thought maybe an arrangement for your hair—" she began, but her mistress waved her to silence.

"No, I have a better idea," said Azalea. "I want you to work it into a ruffle for the neckline."

Junie looked doubtful. "Are you sure, miss? Them things really aren't in style anymore, you know, though I'll grant you, the top of this gown is a bit revealing, even by this year's standards."

"And much too revealing by mine," said Azalea decisively. "Fashionable or not, if my uncle wants to see me in this gown, it will be with ruffles above as well as below. Can you do it, do you think?"

"Oh, certainly, miss, as long as you're sure that is what you want."

"It is," Azalea stated firmly.

Gathering up the gown, Junie departed to make the desired changes.

Two nights later, as Junie put the finishing touches to her hair, Azalea examined her reflection in the glass with far more satisfaction. The dress still clung to her body in a way that emphasized her curves, but the neckline met with her complete approval.

Junie had done a masterful job of sewing the gold lace from the bottom flounce around the top of the gown, making a ruffle that lined the front, shoulders and back, with an extra layer worked into the area just above her breasts. Azalea didn't see how anyone would guess the gown had not been originally designed this way, as the total effect was charmingly artistic. Perhaps she would create a new fashion.

Pulling on her long, fawn-coloured gloves and picking up the gold fan Lord Kayce had sent with the gown, Azalea rose to go.

"Junie, as always, you have done wonders with my hair. And I say again, if you should ever tire of being a ladies' maid, you can make your way quite well as a designer of gowns. Madame Clarisse herself could not have done better, I am certain."

Junie beamed with pleasure as her mistress left the room.

Before going out to Lord Kayce's carriage, which had just driven up, Azalea stepped into the parlour to take leave of her cousins. Marilyn's eyes widened as she took in the splendour of her country cousin's attire, and Lady Beauforth, after looking hard at the gown, exclaimed, "You're as lovely in that gown as I thought you'd be, my dear! But I thought... no, perhaps I was wrong. At any rate, you look charming."

It seemed but a few moments later that the coachman was helping her to descend from the carriage in front of Lord Kayce's imposing Town residence. Looking up at the uninviting facade, Azalea hoped it was his own acquisition rather than a family property and was conscious of renewed gratitude that he had never suggested she come to live with him here.

Gas lamps burned brightly on either side of the impressive entrance, but far from denoting hospitality, they merely served to illumine a particularly evil-looking gargoyle that leered down from over the front door. Azalea tried not to look at it as she mounted the steps.

The door opened as she reached it, and she was announced by a cadaverous-looking butler with a startlingly deep voice. As her uncle came forward to greet her, Azalea had a moment to notice that the interior of the house was scarcely more inviting than the exterior had been. The furnishings were undeniably expensive and even quite tasteful, but the gas lighting that Lord Kayce evidently preferred to candlelight threw everything into weird relief.

"My dear, I am so happy to welcome you to my home," said Kayce with a smile. "The guests have only just arrived, and I wish to introduce you to them, if you will accompany me."

Azalea thought he frowned quickly as he noticed her gown, but he had already turned away before she could be certain. She wondered why the other guests should be present already, since she was purportedly here to act as hostess, but followed her uncle without a word. They advanced into an elegant and expensively furnished drawing-room, also eerily gaslit, and three men of about her uncle's age rose to their feet.

"My niece and ward, Miss Azalea Clayton," announced Lord Kayce with a flourish. "My dear, allow me to present Mr. Fienton, Lord Drowling, and Lord Carfax," he said, indicating each gentleman in turn.

Azalea curtsied deeply, as was proper, but did not miss the

speculation in their eyes. "I am honoured to make your acquaintance, my lords," she said politely in her soft, musical voice.

All three gentlemen stepped forward, but Lord Drowling was the quickest, eagerly seizing her hand to bestow a lingering kiss upon it. He was tall and coarsely handsome, with thick brown hair only slightly grey at the temples, and full, sensuous lips. His dark eyes burned as they met and held her own.

"The honour is all upon our side, I assure you, Miss Clayton," he said with a smile that was little less than a leer. "I had no idea the New World bred such rare and exotic flowers. Kayce is to be congratulated."

The suggestive tone in which this fulsome compliment was delivered, coupled with the man's frankly assessing gaze, made Azalea drop her eyes in confusion. The small amount of flirting she had done had not prepared her for this. When Lord Drowling showed no inclination to release her hand, despite a slight effort on her part to free it, she glanced somewhat desperately at her uncle.

Lord Kayce intervened smoothly. "Come, Drowling, you must not monopolize my niece tonight. She is here to act as hostess, and courtesy demands that she entertain you all equally."

Though she wondered about her uncle's meaning, Azalea was relieved that his words prompted Lord Drowling to release her.

Mr. Fienton and Lord Carfax were now able to pay their respects. Both of them looked at her in a way that seemed calculated to unsettle her, though neither went quite so far as Drowling had done.

"When do you expect the other guests?" Azalea asked her uncle, devoutly hoping that there would be a few ladies among them.

"There are to be no other guests. I am sure I intimated to you that this was to be a small dinner party, so that you could meet a few of my closest... friends." His smile somehow failed to reassure her. "In fact, as we are all here, let us go in to dinner. My dear?"

Lord Kayce held out his arm and Azalea placed her fingers upon it, trying to stifle her misgivings. She was relieved, at any rate, that Lord Drowling was not to take her in to dinner, and hoped that he would not be seated by her at table.

This hope, at least, was answered, though by the time the second course was served, she thought that she might have preferred his conversation to his ogling, as he was placed directly across from her. She was seated at her uncle's right, with Mr. Fienton on her other side and Lord Carfax opposite him. They were in the smaller dining-room, as Lord Kayce had felt this more appropriate for such a small gathering.

Azalea barely participated in the conversation, feeling out of place in what seemed more like a business meeting than a dinner party. Mr. Fienton, a slight, mousy-looking man with fair hair and watery blue eyes, managed to engage her in conversation about America for a few minutes, but he seemed less interested in her replies than in her cleavage. She found his refusal to meet her eyes both irritating and disconcerting.

She still had not exchanged more than an initial greeting with Lord Carfax, but felt no inclination to further that acquaintance. He appeared to be the oldest of the group, probably well into his fifties, with heavy black brows and a cold, almost sinister directness to his gaze.

Whenever Azalea chanced to encounter his eyes, he regarded her with an intensity that disturbed her, though not in the same way as the knowing leer of Lord Drowling. She felt that Lord Carfax, rather, was trying to see inside her, to read her very thoughts and perhaps control them. She knew these to be mere fancies, but she could not quite dismiss them.

When Lord Glaedon sent admiring glances her way, she recalled, she had felt excited, even flattered. But the expressions of her uncle's friends made her feel soiled.

Thankfully, the meal ended at last, and Azalea began to cast about for some plausible excuse to leave early. As it happened, Lord Kayce himself provided her escape, saying that he was to meet a friend at White's that evening and would be obliged to turn them all out within the hour.

"But I have scarce had a chance to exchange two words with your charming niece, Kayce," protested Lord Drowling. "And I am sure my companions share my eagerness to know her better."

He stepped to her side as he spoke and allowed his fingertips to brush her upper arm, where it was bare between her glove and shoulder ruffle. It took all of Azalea's control not to shrink away from the man.

"Really, Kayce, Drowling is right. It is most inhospitable of you to end the evening so early," drawled Mr. Fienton in his high-pitched monotone. "Can't you send a note round to White's saying you've been detained?"

"I'm afraid not," replied their host. "But I'm certain you will have ample opportunity in future to speak with my niece, as she is permanently fixed in England and will remain in London at least through the Season."

"Might I offer you my escort home, ma'am?" Lord Carfax

stepped forward as he spoke, his deep voice holding the same determined intensity as his gaze.

Before she could reply, her uncle answered for her with a smooth refusal, saying that he had already arranged to return his niece to her home on his way to White's.

"If any of you would care to meet me there in, say, two hours, we might have a game of cards or some quiet conversation," he concluded. At these words, all three gentlemen looked thoughtful and agreed to see him later.

Azalea was so relieved that she need not endure being alone in a carriage with Lord Carfax that she scarcely noticed this exchange.

Graciously taking leave of her uncle's guests at the front entrance, she stepped into Lord Kayce's carriage with a sigh that she hoped he did not hear. She had not really expected to enjoy the evening, but it had been far more uncomfortable than she had anticipated. She thanked heaven it was over.

Now that they were alone, she half expected Lord Kayce to make some comment on her alterations to the gown, but he did not. "What think you of my friends, my dear?" he asked as the coachman whipped up the horses. "They all seemed much taken with you."

"I am most flattered, of course, Uncle Simon," she replied carefully, not wanting to offend him. "However, I was rather at a loss to understand why you wished me to be there at all. No other ladies were present."

"Why, to present you to those most eligible gentlemen, of course," he replied silkily. "I said that your future was my concern, did I not? Thus it falls to me to find you a suitable husband."

With difficulty Azalea suppressed a gasp of dismay. "I—I

am sorry, Uncle Simon, if I gave you the impression that I wished for your help in that matter. It is most unnecessary, I assure you."

"Nonsense, nonsense," he said affably. "You do not wish to end up a spinster, I am certain. As I'm your guardian, it is plainly my responsibility to ensure that you make an advantageous marriage."

Azalea bit her lip. Did she dare tell her uncle the truth? She did not trust him a whit, but even he could scarcely have an existing marriage set aside for whatever ends he had in mind. Still, it seemed wrong to tell this man, whom she neither liked nor trusted, before telling Lord Glaedon himself. Besides, she had no idea just how ruthless Lord Kayce might be. Perhaps by telling him she might be putting Christian at some risk.

Making a quick decision, she said with assumed casualness, "That reminds me, Uncle, that I have not yet heard from Mr. Timmons on the matter of your guardianship of me. I believe I shall call on him Monday. I have certain other matters to discuss with him as well."

Lord Kayce darted a quick look at her. "What might... that is, of course, my dear. No doubt he will have the papers ready for your signature."

Just then, the carriage pulled up before Beauforth House and Kayce escorted Azalea to the door, though he declined to come inside. She heard the clatter of his departure with relief as she stepped into the house.

Azalea would no doubt have felt less relieved had she been able to look in at White's later.

"Well, Kayce, I must admit you told no more than the truth when you described your new-found niece," said Lord Drowling, as he settled into a chair next to the Baron. "If anything, you didn't do her justice. It would seem a waste to find a form and face like that on such an innocent, if one did not imagine the delights of instructing her. But I assume such a privilege won't come cheaply?"

"I think you know what I would want in exchange, Drowling. You have been holding that duel of my brother's over my head for more than twenty years."

"Ah, but it was such a, er, profitable investment for me, you see," replied Drowling with a smile. "Though I admit I had thought its worth to be nearly exhausted... until now. No doubt your dear niece would be most interested to learn how her father was deceived. Perhaps she would even be grateful enough to bestow her hand on me willingly."

Kayce snorted. "When she has every young buck in London panting after her? Not likely. No, if you want her, you must work through me. And do not forget that any son of hers would become my heir. But let us not be hasty. Here come Carfax and Fienton. I would like to hear what each of them has in mind, as well."

"With the charming Azalea to go to the highest bidder, I perceive," said Drowling, with a cynical twist to his smile. "That golden Aphrodite may well be worth what you ask. I shall think on it." Rising, the Viscount nodded a greeting to the two approaching gentlemen and went in search of a game of whist.

~

Directly after breakfast Monday morning, Azalea made good on her promise to call on Mr. Timmons. She had already decided to ask for her marriage proofs back, so that she would have them on hand when Lord Glaedon returned in a few weeks. She still hoped that she could manage to convince him of the truth without them, but time was running out. Better to have the evidence in case she needed it.

She left Junie in the carriage and ascended confidently to the attorney's offices. Her confidence received a setback a moment later, however, when she saw the sign on the door of Mr. Timmons's chambers: Closed Until Further Notice.

Perplexed, she lingered in the empty hallway, biting her lower lip. Could the lawyer have left Town for the holidays? Surely he would have sent a message, at least, as his work on her behalf was by no means done.

Half-heartedly, she reached out to try the doorknob and was surprised when it turned easily in her grasp. She pushed the door open and gasped in astonishment at the scene that greeted her.

The outer office had been far from immaculate before, but it was now in a state of complete chaos. Papers were everywhere, books lay open upon the floor and one large wooden cabinet had been overturned and broken. She stepped further into the room, torn between curiosity and a growing sense of misgiving.

Suddenly, Mr. Greene stood up from behind his desk, where he had apparently taken cover at her entrance, causing her to start violently.

"Oh, Miss Clayton, it is you!" he exclaimed in obvious relief. "I thought they might have returned."

"Who?" asked Azalea, as soon as her heart resumed beating. She was still shaken, but determined to find out what she could. "Whatever has happened here? Where is Mr. Timmons?" She looked about her, half expecting the lawyer to emerge from his inner office at the sound of her voice.

"He's laid up at home, senseless," replied Mr. Greene, seemingly agitated out of his shyness by recent events.

"Senseless? What has happened to him? Is he injured?" asked Azalea in alarm, her concern for the old gentleman temporarily overshadowing her own problems.

"Set upon by footpads last night, miss, not two blocks from here," said Mr. Greene, shaking his head as if he still could not believe it. "They took what little money he had, and his keys, and beat him badly. Left him for dead, or so the Runners think."

"So the same footpads are the ones who did this, also, I presume," Azalea concluded, gesturing about the office. "What do you suppose they were after?" Her mind had already jumped to an ugly suspicion, but she had no intention of voicing it without any evidence to support it. At least not yet.

"After?" asked Mr. Greene in surprise. Apparently he had not yet thought that far into the matter. "Why, money, I suppose. What else?"

"Come, Mr. Greene, even a common footpad would hardly expect to find much money in a solicitor's office, and I rather doubt these were common footpads. It seems obvious to me that they attacked poor Mr. Timmons primarily for the keys to these rooms, and that they were looking for something specific here. Do not tell me that the Bow Street Runners had no similar theory?"

"No, miss," replied Mr. Greene, beginning to return to his usual flustered manner. "At least, I don't think so. No, no they couldn't have, for they didn't know the office had been ransacked. I just found out two hours ago when I came to put the sign on the door."

Perhaps to cover his embarrassment for not having thought of that obvious explanation himself, Mr. Greene turned away to resume the thankless task of straightening up.

"They certainly must be told, and immediately," said Azalea decisively. "Will you do so, Mr. Greene, or shall I?"

The clerk gaped at her. "You, miss? Why ever would you want to involve yourself in this business? No, they will be back later today, and I shall tell them then —or, rather, show them. I'll hardly have the place cleaned up by then." He looked around hopelessly.

"Perhaps you should leave everything as it is until they've seen it," she suggested. Mr. Greene's face brightened noticeably. "Meanwhile, I don't suppose there is any chance you might know where Mr. Timmons kept certain documents I left with him?"

The clerk's face clouded again. "No, miss, I'm sorry. Nothing is in its proper place, as far as I have been able to tell, and Mr. Timmons's personal office is in worse shape than this one. That is where he kept the most important papers."

She had feared that would be the case. "Well, if you should find any papers connected with me, please send me a message or, better, the papers themselves," she said, but without much hope.

"Yes, miss, I'll certainly do that," promised Mr. Greene, appearing more optimistic than she was.

Thinking furiously, Azalea left the office. *Could* Kayce have been behind this? Had he somehow suspected her marriage to

Lord Glaedon? That seemed unlikely, as the only person in London she had told was Mr. Timmons.

No, it seemed more probable that Kayce had been after the proofs of her identity if, in fact, he was responsible. Without those, she would have a difficult, if not impossible, time establishing any claim to her inheritance. Her uncle might be planning to declare her a fraud if she refused to go along with his plans. Of course, if he now had all the papers, he would know that marriage to one of his cronies was out of the question—wouldn't he?

Still deep in thought, she descended to the carriage.

CHAPTER TWELVE

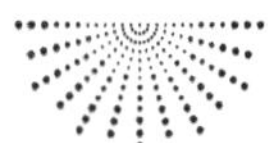

CHRISTMAS WAS NEARLY UPON THEM. AZALEA WAS GLAD that Lady Beauforth felt disposed to make little of the holiday season, since her own heart wasn't in it. She had called on Mr. Timmons at his home the previous afternoon, only to be told by his wife that the doctor had expressly forbidden visitors. Mrs. Timmons had agreed to convey a message as soon as her husband was on the mend, and Azalea tried to be satisfied with that.

Marilyn, however, was not nearly so willing to forgo Christmas festivities as her mother and Azalea seemed to be. At the breakfast table she bemoaned the scarcity of parties and routs in Town at this season, complaining that this was certain to be the dullest Christmas she had ever spent. Her mother's reluctant suggestion that they might go to their country estate for the holidays was quickly rejected.

"Maple Park is bound to be even duller than Town," Marilyn declared with a pretty pout. "If we could but give a party or, better, a ball of our own, it might serve to divert me."

"With Lord Glaedon in the country? People might think it odd, my dear. Besides, with Town so thin of company, who would we invite?"

Such discussions were diverted, however, by the arrival of a letter a short time later.

"Who is it from, my dearest?" asked Lady Beauforth, always eager for news of any kind.

"Mary Trentham," answered her daughter somewhat absently, as she was still perusing the contents of her letter. "Oh! She invites me to Alder House for the holidays! She mentions some of those to be present, and... oh, Mother, do say I may go! It will be ever so much more festive than staying here."

Marilyn's pout had been magically transformed into a radiant smile. Lady Beauforth could not be expected to deny her angel any treat that could bring her such happiness.

"Of course you must go, darling. It will be just the thing for you. It has been putting me about dreadfully to see you so in the doldrums. Do you suppose Miss Trentham could be prevailed upon to extend the invitation to include your cousin, as well?" she asked as an afterthought. She glanced guiltily at Azalea.

Marilyn looked distractedly at her in turn. "What? Oh. I suppose I could write to Mary, but there is so little time...." It was obvious she had no thought to spare for her cousin just then.

"No, please, do not go to any such trouble," Azalea insisted. "I assure you that I have not the least desire to go. I shall be perfectly happy to stay here, catching up on my reading, which I have sadly neglected, and keeping dear Cousin Alice company through the holidays."

Her smile at Lady Beauforth during this last remark was perfectly genuine. Azalea did not wish to risk being away from London when Mr. Timmons recovered —or when Lord Glaedon returned.

Marilyn required no convincing whatsoever. "Well, then, since that is settled, I shall write at once to tell dear, dear Mary that I shall be there." She was out the breakfast-room door before she had finished speaking, and a moment later Azalea could hear her calling out to one of the footmen for a newly mended pen.

The rest of that day and the next passed in a whirl of preparation for Marilyn's visit. Azalea helped with enthusiasm, glad to have her cousin in such happy spirits for a change. Running out to the shops to find just the right shade of ribbon or a fan to go with the gowns being packed provided a welcome distraction to her own problems.

The night before her departure, Marilyn surprised Azalea by coming to her bedchamber. "Cousin, I have a favour to ask," she said with unwonted diffidence.

"Of course," exclaimed Azalea, warming to the welcome change in her cousin's manner. "How may I help you?"

Marilyn hesitated for a moment, then met her eyes with a rather sheepish smile. "Your gold dress —the one Lord Kayce gave you. Do you suppose... that is, could I borrow it for the house party?" she finished her request in a rush.

Struggling between amazement and amusement, Azalea was careful to let neither show on her face. She realized that it must be very difficult for Marilyn, who had always been accustomed to having everything she wished, to actually beg a favour of her country cousin. And lending clothes seemed so... so sisterly.

At this thought, Azalea smiled broadly. "Of course. I had no plans to wear it again any time soon."

She opened her clothes-press and removed the shimmering gold gown. In truth, after the evening she now associated with this dress, she had no intention of ever wearing it again.

"Feel free to make any necessary alterations," she said cheerfully. "I expect it will look better on you, anyway."

Marilyn thanked her graciously. "You don't think it will make me too... all one colour?" she asked suddenly, as she turned to leave the room.

"Oh, no!" Azalea assured her. "You'll look like spun gold, I'm certain."

Marilyn smiled. "Jonathan —your friend, Mr. Plummer — once said something like that. I thought he might recall it if he saw me in this dress."

"Oh, is he to be there?" asked Azalea. Suddenly, Marilyn's careful preparations took on new meaning.

"Yes, but pray do not say anything to Mama about it. I—I wouldn't wish her to worry."

Azalea assured her that she saw no reason to mention the fact to Lady Beauforth. Thanking her again, Marilyn left to finally complete her packing.

The coach drew up to the door directly after breakfast the next day. Marilyn's maid and Tom, the head groom, were to accompany her, and her ladyship had managed to convince herself that her greatest treasure would be safe in their care. Still, Lady Beauforth could not suppress a tear or two at their parting, as this would be the first time in Marilyn's eighteen years that mother and daughter would be separated by any distance, even if it was to be for only a fortnight.

"Are you certain you don't wish to come, too?" Marilyn asked Azalea impulsively as she was turning to climb into the waiting coach.

Though extremely gratified, Azalea shook her head firmly. "No, I really would prefer to stay here and Cousin Alice is rather counting on my company, I flatter myself. But thank you for asking."

Marilyn's smile was as genuine as her cousin's. "I shall see you in a fortnight, then. If anything interesting should occur in my absence, you must write to tell me all about it." With that, the door was closed and the coachman whipped up the team.

Azalea and Lady Beauforth were left standing by the railings. Azalea perceived her cousin's melancholy at once and quickly guided her back into the house to divert her with a humorous tale she had overheard at one of the shops yesterday and saved for exactly this occasion.

Yuletide passed as uneventfully as Marilyn had foretold. Virtually all of their acquaintances had taken advantage of the unusually good travelling conditions to visit family or friends in the country. Azalea, far from bemoaning the lack of diversion, welcomed this respite when she might read, write, ride and, most of all, think to her heart's content.

Christmas passed without any word from Mr. Timmons, and Azalea reluctantly realized that she would have to solve her problems without his assistance. And she must do it soon.

Marilyn's and Lord Glaedon's wedding loomed less than six weeks away.

It was always possible that Jonathan and Marilyn might come to some understanding while at Miss Trentham's house party, but she could not count on that. No, when Lord Glaedon returned to Town, she would do everything possible to *make* him remember.

Failing that, she must try to charm him away from her cousin. Without the marriage papers to back up her claim, it was the only solution she could think of.

One morning only a few days after Christmas, while Azalea was reading aloud to Lady Beauforth in the drawing-room, Lord Drowling was announced. Azalea tried to quell her instinctive dismay as Lady Beauforth rose to greet him effusively.

"Why, Lord Drowling! What an honour, to be sure! I suppose I may construe your call as a compliment to my dear Azalea?"

"Indeed, my lady. As she may have told you, I made her acquaintance at the home of her uncle two weeks ago. Since then, I have been unable to think of anything else. I am but this moment returned from my estates and wished to pay my respects immediately." Though he spoke to Lady Beauforth, his eyes caressed Azalea possessively as he spoke.

"How kind of you, my lord." Azalea kept her voice cool.

"Ah, kindness has nothing to do with it, my vision," he replied, seating himself in the chair closest to her. "My very sanity demanded that I come."

He seemed to devour her with his eyes, and Azalea felt her skin crawl. While his manner in front of Lady Beauforth was more restrained than it had been at Lord Kayce's house,

Azalea was more than relieved that he kept his visit brief. After only ten minutes he took his leave with one last, lingering look that made her feel unclean.

Before she could convey her opinion of him to her cousin, however, Lady Beauforth began to express her admiration of his lordship's person, as well as his many and well-known worldly advantages.

"This is a greater conquest than you can realize, my dear," she concluded after a lengthy and glowing recital of Lord Drowling's assets. "I can tell you that I would have been more than pleased to welcome his attentions towards Marilyn, if he had ever shown the slightest inclination to bestow them. He's as rich as Croesus!"

She fanned herself rapidly before continuing. "But he has never been at all in the petticoat line. At least not with, well..." She tittered self-consciously, her florid cheeks pinkening.

Azalea understood quite well what her cousin had left unsaid, but she remained silent, not wishing to encourage Lady Beauforth in this flight of fancy.

"In point of truth," continued her cousin after a moment, "I've never heard of him calling on *any* eligible girl before. I suppose it could be in deference to Lord Kayce, for I hear they are as thick as thieves."

A singularly apt analogy, Azalea thought.

"But even so, he seemed quite taken with you. Why did you not mention his presence at Kayce's dinner party before now?"

Azalea replied distractedly that she had not thought it of any importance, and thereafter excused herself, saying she wanted to finish writing a letter before nuncheon. She was wondering how she would be able to prevent any further attentions from Lord Drowling, since it was clear he would have Lady Beauforth's unqualified support. Cousin Alice would no doubt do all in her power to throw them together at every opportunity.

She prayed that Lord Glaedon would return to London soon.

The Earl, meanwhile, was making the most of his time in the country, though not as his relations there had expected. In fact, his grandmother considered his behaviour to border on inhospitable.

For Christian spent every moment that could be spared from his duties as host in his father's private library, going through musty old papers and letters, searching for the Lord only knew what.

When Lady Glaedon confronted him, demanding to know what could be so important that it caused him to neglect his guests, he merely replied that he had become curious about his father's youth and was endeavouring to learn more of his deceased parent through his letters.

The dowager pointed out that any personal letters he found were likely to have been written *to* the late Earl rather than *by* him, but her grandson's attention had already wandered back to the pile of papers on the table before him. She gave it up for the time being and returned to their guests, to attempt to compensate for their host's lack of attentiveness.

Christian's persistent research was yielding rewards, however. On leaving London nearly a fortnight before, his emotions had been a turmoil of guilt and longing. He was firm, though, in his intention of carefully examining his father's papers in the hopes of learning something —anything —about Miss Azalea Clayton.

He knew that the late Earl had corresponded with the girl's grandfather regularly over the years, and it was to Reverend Simpson's letters that he directed his attention. There were more of these than he had expected, and what he was learning from their perusal surprised him even more.

Christian had known that the two men had served together in India. He found now that their friendship had begun years before that, when both his father and Gregory Simpson were mere boys at Eton.

Judging by the language in the letters, there was virtually nothing they did not confide to one another. Their separation when Gregory left for America was felt keenly by both. These early letters gave Christian a great deal of insight into Azalea's heritage, on the maternal side, at least.

Adele Simpson, Azalea's mother, had, by her fond father's account, been a spectacular beauty. Fully appreciating what she had bequeathed to her daughter in the way of looks, Christian saw no reason to doubt his word. Gregory lamented the fact that there were no young men even remotely worthy of his daughter in the small college town to which he had removed, and feared that she might become attached to some penniless student or, worse, a farmer's son.

Reverend Simpson, it appeared, had not quite embraced his new country's rejection of class distinctions.

Then Walter Clayton, eldest son and heir of Lord Kayce, had appeared on the scene. He and Adele were immediately drawn to one another, though she was only sixteen at the time. While he fully approved of such a connection, as well as the young man himself, Gregory was unwilling to allow his daughter to marry at so young an age. Finally, however, he had been persuaded to a formal betrothal.

Due to his father's illness, Walter had returned to England shortly thereafter, but had promised to return for Adele. Reading ahead two years, Christian found that Walter, by then the new Lord Kayce, had kept his promise; he and Adele were married in 1791.

At that point, Walter elected to remain in America rather than take his new bride back to England as originally planned, leaving his estates in the hands of his younger brother. This development surprised Reverend Simpson, who hazarded a guess or two as to its cause. He did not openly question it, however, since he was grateful that his only child was not to be removed across the Atlantic.

Reading between the lines, Christian was able to infer that Kayce gradually became infected by the republican spirit of the newly liberated colonies, a turn of events of which his father-in-law did not entirely approve, it appeared.

Sporadic news of the couple occurred in the letters of the next few years, as the Claytons had resettled in the near-wilderness west of Richmond to try their fortunes. Two still-births were reported, then Azalea's birth in November of 1795. Gregory travelled west to see his new granddaughter in the spring of 1796 and sent a letter to the Earl a few months later singing her praises.

Christian began to read the closely written pages more carefully from that point on, grateful that his father had chosen to retain all of his personal correspondence, though not according to any particular system. It had taken him several days to find and then chronologically order all of Reverend Simpson's letters.

Herschel's name, and his own, had been frequently mentioned, mainly in regard to enquiries after their health and activities. The third letter after the one detailing the remarkable cleverness and beauty of five-month-old Azalea, however, mentioned what was apparently a years-old dream of both men—to someday unite their families through the marriage of their offspring.

Gregory pointed out that, as Howard had been so disobliging as to marry much later in life than himself, that dream, if it were ever to be fulfilled, would have to be through his darling Azalea or some future daughter of Adele's. His tone was less than serious, but Christian was much struck by this revelation nonetheless.

There was to be no future daughter. When Azalea was barely two years old, Walter was killed by a fall while hunting, and Adele returned to Williamsburg with her baby daughter.

News of Azalea was now liberally strewn throughout every letter, and Christian read the accounts of her childhood escapades with an absorption he found hard to explain. So caught up in her history did he become that he was actually moved to tears at the account of Adele's death and her five-year-old daughter's uncomprehending grief.

Wiping his eyes, Christian glanced around the library, glad that his grandmother had not chosen this moment to remind him, yet again, of what was expected of the host at a family gathering.

As it happened, that perceptive lady had not believed for a moment in Christian's sudden acquisition of a passion for family history. She had discovered, through an investigation quickly and surreptitiously conducted during one of his brief absences from the library, that his attention seemed focused on a collection of letters from one Gregory Simpson of Williamsburg, Virginia.

Lady Glaedon's curiosity was thoroughly aroused but, as Christian himself seemed disinclined to be communicative, she had to content herself with supposition. For lack of a better confidante, she broached the subject to her daughter, Lady Constance Highton, one evening when they were alone.

"Connie, I've been meaning to ask you if you've noticed anything... odd... in Christian's manner since he arrived home."

Lady Constance, a handsome, middle-aged matron, considered carefully before answering. "Well, Mama, he has been quite as correct in his bearing towards me as ever, though I will admit I have seen less of him than usual this Christmas."

The dowager regarded her daughter with some impatience. She knew that Constance's understanding was not absolutely of the first order, but she felt a need to discuss her concerns with someone and she was unwilling to share them with anyone less closely connected to Christian.

"I was not discussing his politeness, Connie," she continued carefully after a moment. "I meant that he has seemed rather... distracted of late."

"Oh! Yes, now that you mention it, I do remember that just this afternoon at nuncheon I had to speak to him twice before he would answer my question regarding the advisability of new draperies in my small salon at the London house. Mr. Highton favours cream, you see, but I have always felt that the blue and buff we have there now more appropriately reflect—"

"Yes, of course, Connie, we went over all that earlier, if you recall," the dowager broke in, forestalling yet another complete cataloguing of the furnishings of her daughter's small salon. "But we were discussing Christian. If I were to hazard a guess, I would say his manner almost resembles that of a young man in love. However, much as I have wished for just that, I fear there must be another explanation."

"But why? Miss Beauforth is quite lovely." Lady Constance frowned vaguely. "I must agree that if she has captured his heart, 'twould be no bad thing. But even if she has not, it is not quite the thing to be in love with one's spouse, anyway. No doubt they will deal perfectly well together."

"Yes, yes, you are right, of course." The dowager lapsed into discontented silence. Not even to Constance would she voice her suspicion that Christian's preoccupation had nothing whatsoever to do with Miss Beauforth. Nor would she confide that she, herself, would be more pleased than dismayed if that proved to be true.

If he had truly fallen in love with someone else, she doubted she could bring herself to criticize his choice, if only Christian were happy. And she doubted he would ever be truly happy with Marilyn Beauforth. But would he cry off his betrothal, even for love? Not for the first time she mentally cursed that male code of honour with which all the men in her family had been afflicted, often to their detriment.

If her guess were correct, who might the lucky girl be? Could she possibly have some connection to those musty old letters from America? It seemed unlikely.

"Well," she said briskly, bringing her thoughts back to the present, "I suppose the most I can hope is that he will confide in me. Pray don't mention this conversation to Christian," she cautioned her daughter. "I am only guessing, after all, and it is certain that he would not appreciate any interference on our part."

Even as his grandmother and aunt discussed him, Christian was immersed in his self-appointed research once again. He had been charmed by Reverend Simpson's accounts of Azalea's early childhood antics as well as impressed by the evidence he offered of his granddaughter's exceptional abilities. Christian began to understand why the girl was so able to hold her own in the few arguments they had had; her unusual intelligence had been augmented by an excellent education.

He read of her fascination with botany, which had become evident by the time she was six years old, and seemed to be the child's way of retaining some contact with her departed mother. Her other absorbing interest appeared to be horses, and he recalled with some amusement the near-lecture she had given him on that topic their first morning in the Park. They had more in common than he had ever realized.

Irresistibly, he remembered again her sweet curves, her lustrous green eyes. He had tried to forget, but he might as well have tried to stop his heart from beating. The very thought of her, even after a fortnight's absence, still had the power to stir his blood.

Now more than ever, he bitterly regretted his betrothal to Miss Beauforth, made for the sake of maintaining the family honour.

Finally, only two letters remained. Christian had forced himself to read all of them sequentially, although the temptation had been great to open the last letter at the outset. It had been received by his father only a month before their ill-fated voyage to the New World.

Christian had already discovered that for some years his

father had taken a discreet interest in Azalea's English inheritance and the Kayce estates, at her grandfather's request. Some problems had apparently arisen, and in the second-to-last letter Reverend Simpson implied strongly that Kayce was not to be trusted. He also mentioned his own failing health, agreeing that the "steps" Lord Glaedon had recommended might be necessary after all.

The letter concluded with a reference to "what would be best for the youngsters," which made Christian reach for the final envelope in hopes that this curious "problem" and his father's "solution" would be discussed more fully.

The last letter opened with the assurance that Simpson and his granddaughter would be honoured by a visit from Glaedon and his son, Christian, if the Earl would only name the time. Reading further, Christian's interest turned to amazement as he realized what the purport of this visit was to be: no less than his own marriage to Azalea Clayton.

"I recommend that the young people be allowed to meet and form some sort of opinion of each other before any commitment be made," Simpson had written. "It is up to you whether you wish to discuss our plan with Christian in advance. Knowing Azalea as I do, it will probably be best on my part to wait until she has met your son, so as not to prejudice her against him at the outset. The girl has shown little inclination toward any young man as yet, but I suppose that is not to be wondered at, as she is barely thirteen at this writing."

It appeared obvious from the tone of this last letter that his father had earnestly desired this match. Christian had offered for Miss Beauforth thinking that his father would have wanted him to take up Herschel's betrothal. But it would seem the old Earl had made plans for both his sons.

Earlier, Christian had cursed the very devotion to family honour and his father's memory that had led him to betroth himself to Miss Beauforth. It suddenly struck him now that it would be undutiful, as well as dishonourable, of him to disregard what amounted to his father's dying wish.

So where did that leave him? Honour bound to marry two different women? There could be no question where his inclination lay. Unfortunately, it was equally clear which course was the more honourable. He was already betrothed to Miss Beauforth.

Christian rose. It was high time he returned to London, for it seemed he had quite a lot to sort out.

CHAPTER THIRTEEN

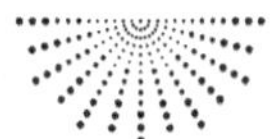

AS IT HAPPENED, SEVERAL DAYS PASSED BEFORE CHRISTIAN WAS able to leave for Town. After directing Lawrence, his valet, to have everything ready for their immediate departure at his word, the Earl went in search of the dowager in order to take his leave of her and to acquaint her with his plans.

He found his grandmother alone in the small parlour she habitually used as her private sitting-room. She had decorated it herself many years before, and it had since become her favourite retreat in the enormous, rambling manor house.

"Ma'am, I am off for London almost at once, but I wished to speak with you first," he said, striding purposefully into the room.

The dowager looked up calmly from her needlework, apparently little perturbed by her grandson's tempestuous entrance. "Certainly, Christian. Pray have a seat." She gestured to the gilt chair opposite her.

Put off his stride by receiving none of the resistance to his abrupt departure that he had expected, Christian dropped into the chair and tugged at his collar, trying to decide how best to begin. Now that it came to the point of actually framing the words, he realized that his dilemma might sound vaguely absurd.

"You wished to tell me something?" Lady Glaedon prompted him.

"Yes. That is... you have expressed certain misgivings about my betrothal to Miss Beauforth, as I recall. I begin to think you may be right."

The dowager waited expectantly.

"In fact, I go to London to discover whether I can honourably extricate myself from it. If I cannot, I suppose I must marry her after all." A sudden depression seized him and he looked pleadingly at his grandmother.

"Not if you do not care for her," the dowager said placidly. "Your happiness has always been my foremost consideration, Chris, and I have been doubtful all along that Miss Beauforth would be likely to secure it. I am relieved you have come to your senses in time." He shook his head disbelievingly, wondering if his grandmother had actually uttered those words or if he were merely hearing what he wished to. "There will be the devil of a scandal if I cry off, you realize," he said cautiously.

"That is neither here nor there," she replied, startling him again. "You had something else to tell me, did you not?" she prompted.

"You know me far too well, I see. Yes, there was something else."

"What is her name?"

Christian passed from surprise to astonishment. "I did not realize that mind-reading was among your many talents, ma'am. Her name is Clayton. Miss Azalea Clayton. She is living in the Beauforth household, which makes the situation doubly awkward."

Now, finally, it was the dowager's turn to look surprised. "Clayton? But that is the Kayce family name, is it not? Lord Kayce has no daughter that I know of. Pray explain everything, Christian, from the beginning. Precisely who is this Miss Clayton, and why is she staying with Lady Beauforth?"

At that, Christian took a deep breath to organize his thoughts and proceeded to relate to his grandmother all that he knew of Azalea: her parents and grandparents, her history, and their few meetings, which had quickly grown into friendship and affection, at least on his part. Finally, he showed her the last letter from Reverend Simpson.

"If possible," he said, "I should like to fulfill my father's final wish."

"Very noble!" said the dowager with barely concealed amusement at the conclusion of his story.

She had watched Christian's face closely during his recital and had a fair suspicion of what he had left unsaid. He was obviously head over ears in love with the girl, but she did not think he had yet admitted this to himself. He had instead convinced himself that it was his "duty" to his late father to offer for her—if he could extricate himself from his current betrothal, also entered into in the name of duty and honour.

Lady Glaedon doubted that such an approach would be likely to recommend his suit to the young lady in question, whatever her feelings towards Christian might be. Not if she had more sensibility than Miss Beauforth, which she must have if Christian had fallen in love with her.

"What do you intend to do, precisely?" she asked. "Hand

her the letter and inform her that she owes it to her grandfather and your father to marry you?"

"Of course not!" exclaimed Christian. "I plan to... well, to continue our friendship and, eventually, explain things to her. She seems a level-headed girl and is sure to realize what a good catch I am." Christian grinned at his grandmother. "Am I not?"

"And what of Miss Beauforth?" she asked quietly, effectively removing all humour from his face.

"That is more difficult," he admitted. "I do not believe her heart is affected, but her pride and ambition assuredly are. Somehow I must convince her that she would not be happy wedded to me. If I could persuade her to cry off, it would be best for all concerned. 'Twill not be easy, however."

From what the dowager recalled of Miss Beauforth, her grandson's words were likely all too true. "My boy, you have a lot of work ahead of you, I can see. However, your 'plan' hardly requires you to rush off on the instant, offending your house guests and placing the burden of entertaining them on me."

This last was a shrewd stroke, for she knew that Christian would never intentionally burden her with responsibilities that should be his. It was rare that Lady Glaedon resorted to guilt to influence her grandson, but she felt that in this instance the stratagem was justified. A few days for thought might significantly enhance his chances for lasting happiness with this girl he had chosen.

Already she was delighted to see a resurgence of his old sense of humour and had no doubt that this Miss Clayton was the cause of it. A delay would also give the dowager a chance to do a little research of her own concerning the young lady involved.

"You are right, of course, Grandmother. I would be the most selfish of beasts to leave you to entertain a houseful of cousins —even if inviting them was your idea."

Christian was well aware that he was being manipulated but he realized, now that the dowager had forced him to look ahead, that he indeed needed some time to think. He knew why the idea of fulfilling his father's wishes appealed so strongly to him— Azalea was all he had ever dreamed of in a woman, and more. But he had to consider how best to go about fulfilling those wishes.

There was also the sticky matter of his betrothal. And his grandmother was perfectly right. He knew very little about how to court a young lady like Azalea. As evidence, he had only to look at the mess he had nearly made of things already with his prejudices. It would not surprise him if she never wanted to see him again.

"Very well," he continued after a brief pause. "I shall put off my departure until Thursday. I believe that between us we can manage to rid ourselves of our guests by then."

With this the dowager had to be content. She knew that young love could not be delayed for long, however good the reasons.

Azalea sat alone in the parlour, trying to keep her mind on the embroidery before her despite her growing fear that Lord Drowling might call at any moment. Lady Beauforth had plainly considered it likely. That was surely why she had gone out by herself, despite the chill drizzle, bidding Azalea to remain at home to receive any callers.

Ever more worrisome, Azalea had overheard her hostess telling Smythe that if her niece should have a gentleman caller while she was out, they were not to be disturbed. Clearly, Cousin Alice expected Lord Drowling not only to call, but to make a declaration in form.

She would refuse him, of course, but how might he react? And if the servants had been warned away, then there might be no one near enough to come to her assistance should he prove obdurate.

Perhaps he would not come at all, she thought, attempting to calm her frayed nerves. Certainly she had given him no encouragement yesterday when he had called. Perhaps he had realized by now that she had no interest in furthering their acquaintance. Somehow, though, she doubted whether that realization would weigh much with Lord Drowling.

A knocking at the front door brought her heart to her throat. *Don't be absurd,* she admonished herself. *He will scarcely ravish you right here in the front parlour!* So saying, she was able to present a calm front when the door opened a moment later so that Smythe could announce her caller.

"Lord Glaedon," he intoned.

Her relief, combined with the intense thrill she experienced at her first sight of him in three weeks, took her completely off guard. She was glad when the Earl spoke first, giving her a chance to collect her suddenly scattered wits.

"Give you good day, Miss Clayton," he said cordially.

"Good-good day, my lord. I fear my cousins are from home just now. We... we were not aware that you were back in Town."

"I returned last night," Lord Glaedon informed her, his smile warm. He seemed not at all put out that Marilyn was absent.

"I trust you enjoyed your stay in the country?" Azalea enquired politely, trying to calm the rapid beating of her heart.

"I found it most— informative," he replied with an enigmatic smile, "but I was unaccountably anxious to get back to London." There was no mistaking the significance of this remark, or the glance that accompanied it. "I missed you."

"And I you, my lord," replied Azalea somewhat breathlessly, scarcely daring to believe the evidence of her ears.

"Please, Miss Clayton, my name is Christian, and I make you free of it. And I've been dying to call you Azalea. May I?"

"Certainly, my... Christian, I mean." Azalea could feel a blush mounting her cheeks, and she hoped Lord Glaedon would not notice it.

" 'My Christian.' I like that," he said teasingly, but with an underlying tenderness that caused her colour to deepen further.

"Oh, you know I did not mean..." she began, then stopped. "You are trying to embarrass me, I think," she finished severely.

"My apologies, Azalea," he replied, obviously savouring her name. "I won't let it happen again."

"I take leave to doubt that, but your apology is accepted." The warmth of her smile now matched his own.

Again Christian felt that strong pull of attraction to her. He had come to Beauforth House in hopes of seeing Miss Clayton again and to discover whether he had imagined her partiality to him. It was an unexpected boon to find her alone. And because of that privacy, he'd said more than he had intended

—more than was probably wise. Sharply, he called himself to task.

Their conversation after that became general, focusing on stories of the Christmas just past, but the physical awareness between them remained. It was several minutes before Christian finally thought to ask about Miss Beauforth and her mother.

"Oh, Marilyn spent the holidays at Alder House with Mary Trentham, and has yet to return, though we expect her daily. Lady Beauforth has gone out to visit Lady Billingsley, but should return within the hour. She will be pleased to see you, I am sure."

"I shall pay my respects as soon as Miss Beauforth returns, of course," he promised.

He knew he should take his leave, but could not quite bring himself to go. Out of the corner of his eye, he saw that the parlour door was closed. Odd that the butler had shut it with only the two of them in here. Slowly, reluctantly, he rose.

Azalea rose with him, standing closer than was strictly necessary. "Will you not stay awhile longer?" she asked softly. "I—I have yet to answer all of your questions about Virginia."

Looking down at her, seeing her so near, Christian struggled to subdue a sudden blaze of desire. He had been trying to place his courtship of her on a more conventional footing —or as conventional as was possible, considering that he was engaged to marry her cousin. But now he wanted to sweep all the niceties aside, to gather her into his arms and kiss her thoroughly, explore her... A shudder ran through him.

"My lord?" asked Azalea softly, noticing it. She had trembled at her own boldness in asking him to stay, but had been unwilling to give up this opportunity of getting to know him better —and of attempting to make him remember.

She had feared that her forwardness might give him a disgust of her, but the look in his eyes was not one of disgust, she was certain. When he remained silent, she reached up tentatively to touch his face, but he caught her hand in his before she could do so.

Her questions abruptly fled. Now she was startled and a little frightened by the naked hunger she saw in his expression.

His eyes locked with hers and she felt a warm stirring deep within her. Was this desire? She wanted it to stop; she wanted it to intensify. Trembling, she licked her lips, needing to say something, anything to break the spell.

Without warning, she was in his arms, his mouth hungrily on hers. After a shocked instant she responded, tasting his lips, his tongue, as he tasted hers. His hands roved greedily over her body, stroking her back, sliding up her stomach, cupping her breasts. Excitement flooded through her at his touch, shocking her in its intensity.

This, *this* was what she had wanted! This would bind her to him, and him to her. Surely it meant that he had finally remembered!

Azalea returned his kisses eagerly. Her own hands began to move, tracing the strength of his jaw, twining through his hair. She felt more than heard a groan coming from deep within him. Suddenly, he swept her up in his arms and carried her to the sofa.

She knew she should stop him. Things were moving more quickly than she had intended. But her will would not respond to her reason. Instead, reason itself was subverted to her surging emotions.

He is my husband, a voice argued within her. *It is perfectly natural that he should love me, and that I should allow it.*

Gently, he laid her on the plush upholstery. Kissing her again, he unfastened the top button of her gown. The second button was nestled between her breasts, and as he worked it loose, he allowed his fingers to wander across her bared flesh. Azalea felt scorched where he touched her. His lips blazed a trail of fire along the side of her throat.

He is my husband.

He had one hand inside her chemise now, stroking her breast, as the other worked on the next button. She leaned her head back, marvelling at the incredible sensations coursing through her.

It is perfectly natural...

He had opened her gown now, and her chemise, and brought his mouth lower, fastening on one breast. Azalea gasped. His tongue teased the nipple and her body responded enthusiastically.

... that he should love me...

Without warning, Marilyn's face forced its way into her consciousness like a splash of cold sea water. Suddenly, she knew why this was wrong.

Christian felt the change in her at once. Her eager, fluid movements, which had been spurring him on beyond rational thought, were suddenly stiff, mechanical. With an effort, he drew back.

"What is it?" His voice was still husky with passion. "Did I hurt you?"

"N-no." Her voice also quivered, but whether with desire

or some other emotion, he couldn't tell. "It is only..." She dropped her eyes.

Sanity returned to him with a crash. What on earth had he done? "Oh, God, I'm sorry," he said. "I never meant..." He stood quickly and turned away, afraid that the mere sight of her, with her gown unbuttoned and her glorious auburn hair in delicious disorder, would tempt him beyond his precarious control. His body throbbed with his need for her.

Azalea thought she understood. He was disgusted with her, now that he was able to reflect on what she had allowed him to do. He was also doubtless frustrated, for she burned with thwarted longing herself, and she had once heard that it was far worse for a man.

"I—I didn't mean—" she began tentatively, but he cut off her words, his back still turned to her.

"No, I know you didn't." His voice was harsh. "I'd better go." Without looking at her again, he strode from the parlour.

Azalea rebuttoned her dress with trembling fingers, tears of shame and frustration burning behind her eyelids. So much for her plan, she thought miserably. Instead of convincing him that she was his lawful wife, she had acted like the veriest strumpet! What must he think of her at this moment?

And how could she ever tell him the truth now? After this, he would no doubt see it as a desperate attempt to manipulate him into marriage. She had spoiled everything!

Smoothing her hair into some semblance of order and blinking back the threatening tears, she picked up her embroidery in trembling fingers, feeling nearly as bereft as she had when she first learned of Christian's supposed death at sea.

∾

The next morning, Azalea prepared for her habitual ride with grim determination. After yesterday she doubted that Lord Glaedon would be in the Park, knowing as he did that she rode there regularly. But if he were, she would somehow have to mend her fences with him. Although any future with him now seemed hopeless, she simply had to try.

Yesterday afternoon, amid the tumult of Marilyn's return from the country and her mother's raptures at having her home, Azalea had sent another query to Mr. Timmons, hoping against hope that the old barrister might be recovered enough by now to see her. The reply, again from his wife, was negative, though she imparted the information that her husband was gradually mending.

Azalea was to have no help from that quarter then, at least at present. No, if Lord Glaedon was to acknowledge her as his wife, it was up to her to achieve it. And achieve it she must.

In contrast to yesterday's drizzle, it was a beautiful, sparkling morning, warm for January, though still crisp enough to be invigorating. In spite of herself, Azalea felt her spirits rise as she and Ginny trotted in the direction of Hyde Park. If nothing else, a ride on such a lovely morning was bound to clear the cobwebs from her brain.

Even as she told herself that it was just as well that Lord Glaedon was unlikely to be there, she glanced ahead and saw him, apparently waiting for her at the Park entrance. Her heart skipped a beat.

"Well met, Miss Clayton!" he called as soon as she was within earshot. "I had hoped that you would not be able to resist riding on such a fine morning."

"I ride nearly every morning, my lord, fine or not," she replied, struggling to match his casual tone. He looked impossibly handsome, his hair gleaming nearly as black as Sultan's coat.

And he was here! Surely that must mean he did not hold her in contempt for what she had done yesterday? "You—you wished to ride with me, my lord?" she managed to say.

"Christian, remember?" he reminded her, making her cheeks grow warm. "Yes, I had to come, of course. I wished to apologize for my reprehensible conduct yesterday. Is it too much to hope that you will forgive me?"

Nervously, she glanced over her shoulder at the groom, who thankfully had dropped back well out of earshot. Further back, she saw a man on foot walking slowly towards them. Even as she watched, however, the man slipped behind a tree as though he did not wish to be seen. Curious, she thought. Was it possible that her uncle was having her followed?

She dismissed it from her mind, however, and turned back to Christian, a tremulous smile playing about her lips.

Though he hid it well, Christian was exerting every ounce of control he possessed to maintain his lighthearted charade. He had come to the Park in hopes of seeing Miss Clayton again, to discover whether she had forgiven him for what he had tried to do.

He had planned this morning's meeting as a sort of test, and not only of his own control in her presence, he now realized. When he had seen her approaching, he'd been gripped by a sudden fear that she would turn and ride away, never wanting to see him again.

Certainly, he deserved it. He had never been in the habit of ruining innocents. But there was something about Miss Clayton that made him forget his rigid control, which he had worked so hard to maintain since resuming his place in Society. With her, he felt far more like the rough, debauched sailor he'd been before his memory had returned. She deserved better than that.

He took her hand and kissed her fingers without a word, but as their glances met, a world of meaning was exchanged. It was as though he asked a question with his eyes and she silently answered. She had forgiven him.

"Shall we ride, then?" he finally asked. In answer, she flicked her reins, sending Ginny into a brisk trot.

As they rode, they fell back into the easy conversation they had enjoyed yesterday, before the madness had taken them both. Slowly, Azalea felt her pulse returning to normal. Still, her troubles were by no means over.

"Marilyn came home last night," she said casually when there was a brief lull in the conversation. To her relief, Christian did not seem unduly affected by the news.

"I trust she had an enjoyable visit in the country," was all he said.

In fact, Marilyn had been in such high spirits upon her return that Azalea had greater hopes than ever that she might be falling in love with Jonathan. She had spoken only vaguely of the other guests at the house party, and Azalea had noticed a certain sparkle in her cousin's eyes whenever Jonathan's name was mentioned.

"Yes, I believe she did," she replied.

She rode in silence for a moment, gathering her courage, then very deliberately said, "Do you know, I was just noticing how very similar your Sultan is to a stallion my grandfather owned back in Virginia."

"Indeed?" He regarded her with interest, though whether

because her words struck some chord of memory or simply because the talk was of horses, she could not be sure.

"Yes. Even their names are similar. Our black stallion was named Spartan."

"You don't say!" Now he appeared almost startled. "Would you believe, that is what I nearly named this fellow when I bought him last year? I finally settled on Sultan because of the Arabian in his lineage."

He went on to describe Sultan's parentage, but Azalea thought that he seemed rather distracted. Clearly he still did not remember everything, but it was a start.

Once or twice during their ride she glanced back to see whether the man she had noticed earlier was still following them, but saw no sign of him. Most likely it had been a stranger simply enjoying a walk in solitude, she thought with relief. But as she left the Park after parting cordially with Christian, a shadow detached itself from the Park gates and ambled off down the street after the Earl.

Back at Beauforth House, Azalea felt more than satisfied with the results of her outing. She knew without a doubt that Christian cared for her, at least a little. And it was clear that she had managed to at least prick his memory. In time it might return in its entirety.

All would soon be straightened out, she was sure of it. Smiling into the mirror as Junie pinned up her hair, she found herself quite impatient to assume her rightful place as his wife, especially now that she'd had a taste of what joys that position might involve.

Azalea hummed softly to herself as she descended to breakfast a few minutes later. "Isn't it a lovely morning?" she asked her cousins brightly as she entered the dining-room.

Walking to the sideboard, she helped herself to a generous portion of kippers and eggs.

"Did you go riding this morning?" asked Marilyn. She obviously considered her American cousin slightly deranged to have formed the habit of being abroad at the uncivilized hour of nine o'clock, or even earlier.

"Yes, I did," answered Azalea, taking her seat and picking up her fork. "And guess who I encountered in the Park?" She had decided that her cousins might need some preparation for what was to occur.

Neither answered, so she continued. "Lord Glaedon! He is returned to Town and promised to call, probably this afternoon." For obvious reasons she had said nothing of his visit yesterday.

Rather to her surprise, Marilyn frowned. "I did not know he was to return so soon. Still, it is flattering, I suppose, that he should wish to see me immediately."

It seemed obvious to Azalea that any pleasure her cousin felt at the news was due to her vanity, and not from any real romantic attachment to Lord Glaedon. Indeed, since her return she had spoken so incessantly of Jonathan Plummer that Azalea doubted there could be much room in her head —or heart —for any other man. Still, if events unfolded as she hoped, it could mean a sore blow to Marilyn's pride.

Lady Beauforth, meanwhile, was agreeing somewhat absently with her daughter's statement, being occupied with the Society news in the *Morning Post*, which she read religiously every day lest she fall behind in the current gossip. Suddenly, she let out a strangled yelp.

"Azalea, you sly creature! Here you are, to be most heartily congratulated, and you never said a word! How wealthy you will be! Wasn't I right when I told you not to discourage him?"

Her expressive face was wreathed in smiles, but Azalea was completely mystified. She chewed quickly and swallowed.

"I am afraid I do not understand you, ma'am," she said when she was able. "Do I collect that my name is mentioned in the paper?"

"Did you not know the announcement was to go in today? Well, then, I suppose I can forgive you for not having spoken. I shall assume you meant to tell us yourself before we saw it in print." Lady Beauforth still looked enormously pleased. "Here. Perhaps you would like to see the wording yourself. He must have called here yesterday after all, though you did not say so." She handed the paper across the table.

It took Azalea a moment to find the item that had caused her cousin such joy. A wild idea struck her as she searched the page, and her heart began to flutter. Surely, Christian wouldn't have... Then, halfway down the sheet, she found it: an announcement of the betrothal of Miss Azalea Clayton to George Bemler, Viscount Drowling.

CHAPTER FOURTEEN

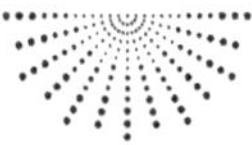

AZALEA STARED AT THE PAPER FOR A FULL MINUTE IN disbelief, trying to understand how that particular combination of letters and words could have come there by accident. For surely this had to be an accident? Who would intentionally play such a cruel joke on her?

The answer, however, came at once and with blinding clarity: Lord Kayce.

Lady Beauforth, meanwhile, was chattering on about the place in Society Azalea would have as Lady Drowling, the balls and routs she could give, and when the wedding would likely take place.

In near panic, Azalea interrupted her in midsentence. "Cousin Alice, you do not understand! There *is* no betrothal. Lord Drowling has not offered for me, and if he had, I most certainly would have refused. I cannot imagine how this announcement comes to be in the paper at all!"

That gave Lady Beauforth pause for a moment. Then she

fastened her attention on what seemed to her the most significant part of Azalea's statement.

"Why ever would you refuse him, child? Drowling is one of the wealthiest men in England. You cannot hope to do better, even as Kayce's ward."

A sudden thought seemed to strike her. "Perhaps that is the answer! Everyone knows that Kayce and Drowling are very close; perhaps he applied for your hand through your uncle — and very properly, too, I may add—and has been accepted. Of course, he should have spoken to you before any announcement was made, but if Kayce approves the match, then no real harm has been done."

"No real harm!" exclaimed Azalea indignantly. "Ma'am, think what you are saying! All of London will believe me betrothed to Lord Drowling now, when I am no such thing!"

And what will Christian think when he sees this outrageous announcement? she wondered frantically.

"Please, Cousin Alice, promise not to discuss this with anyone, unless to deny it, until I have seen my uncle. If, as you say, he and Lord Drowling are responsible for this, then it seems to me it should be up to them to have a retraction printed." And in the afternoon papers, she hoped.

"A *retraction!* Oh, Azalea, my *dear*, how scandalous! Do you wish Society to think you a fickle young lady who accepts a man one day and rejects him the next? 'Twould ruin your reputation, I vow!" Lady Beauforth groped for her smelling salts to underscore how shocking she found such an idea.

"Better my reputation than my life, ma'am," replied Azalea grimly. "And I have accepted no one. Pray have the carriage sent round. I will call on my uncle at once, in hopes of straightening this out. Do cheer up, Cousin Alice! Perhaps it is merely some prank, after all."

Lady Beauforth seemed not at all cheered by this idea, but Azalea had already left the room to fetch her pelisse and reticule.

"Shall I have the carriage sent round, Mama?" asked Marilyn, who had remained uncharacteristically quiet throughout the exchange.

Lady Beauforth nodded gloomily, "We can only hope that Kayce will be able to bring the girl to her senses," she said.

Twenty minutes later, Azalea presented herself at the door of Kayce's mansion to request an interview with her uncle. Her temper had cooled somewhat during the drive, and she now wondered whether the betrothal announcement might truly be a prank, perhaps by Drowling, rather than a plot by Kayce. In any event, she would know soon enough.

After leaving her to wait in the drawing-room some ten minutes, the skeletal butler returned to inform her that her uncle would see her in the back parlour, where he was at breakfast.

Looking about her as she followed the thin, black-clad back, Azalea was relieved to find that the mansion appeared considerably less eerie by daylight. In fact, the parlour she was shown into appeared almost cheerful. A measure of the high spirits she had enjoyed after her ride in the Park returned — until she encountered the cool, appraising expression in her uncle's eyes.

"Good morning, my dear," said Kayce without rising from the small table. His voice seemed pleasant enough.

But as soon as the manservant had bowed himself out of the room, he continued, "I fancy your presence here at such an unseasonable hour means that you have seen a morning paper. I rather expected that you would call."

"You know about it then?" Azalea's eyes narrowed, and anger began to well up in her again, along with a cold touch of fear. "You do not seem particularly surprised or upset that someone would play such a tasteless prank upon us."

"Why should I be surprised or upset at the appearance of an announcement I wrote myself?" returned Kayce with a thin smile. "I regret the shock this may have caused you, but I thought it best not to delay the announcement, when the wedding is to take place so shortly."

His matter-of-fact tone put her off her stride for a moment and she raised her hand to her head, overcome by a sudden feeling of unreality. "Wedding? But there has been no betrothal!"

"Indeed there has, my dear," replied Kayce calmly. "Drowling and I have come to a *most* satisfactory arrangement on the matter."

"Without my consent?" She was aghast. "I refuse to have anything to do with this! I do not even like Lord Drowling, and could not marry him if I did. I intend to send a retraction to the *Post* the moment I return home." Azalea's fear was forgotten in her indignation at this blatant manipulation of her future.

Lord Kayce, however, appeared completely unruffled. "The announcement has appeared in the other papers as well, my dear —did you not see them? In any event, no retraction will be printed. I am your legal guardian, and you will marry whomever I think best suited to the position. The contracts are already drawn up. Pray try to accustom yourself to the idea. Drowling seems to think quite a lot of you, and may even make you happy. He is not unskilled, by all accounts."

Irresistibly, Azalea was reminded of Christian's caresses yesterday, then thought of Drowling in his place. A wave of revulsion swept through her.

"You can hardly force me to take the vows against my will, Uncle," she said in what she hoped was a reasonable tone. "I assure you that I cannot marry Lord Drawling."

"Certainly you can."

The utter confidence in his voice alarmed her. If he *had* been the one behind the attack on Mr. Timmons, he must have obtained the marriage proofs —and had probably already destroyed them. Something of her dismay must have shown in her face, for her uncle again smiled thinly.

"I believe you begin to understand. I wouldn't bother trying to talk Drowling out of it either, if I were you. He stands to gain almost as much as I do from the match. He appears to desire you for other, ah, reasons as well. A most eager bridegroom, in fact. You should be flattered."

Azalea hesitated. It was still just possible that she was wrong. Perhaps Lord Kayce was yet unaware of her existing marriage. If that were the case, then bringing Christian's name into the argument at this point might do more harm than good. She bit her lip, trying to decide her best course.

Kayce's glance became impatient. He disliked having his morning routine disrupted, and though he had known this scene was inevitable, he felt that everything necessary had been said. Besides, there was something in the girl's face that reminded him all too forcibly of his brother, the one person who had exerted a measure of control over him in his youth.

"There is no more to be said," he told her abruptly. "I shall send for you in a few days to discuss the wedding." She was pointedly being dismissed.

"There is quite a lot more to be said, Uncle," replied Azalea determinedly, "but I suppose it can be said later."

Without waiting for the ghoulish butler to show her out, she left the house and re-entered the waiting carriage.

One glance at Azalea's face told Lady Beauforth that Lord Kayce had not been able to change his niece's mind. Looking as grim and determined as she had an hour ago, she proceeded directly to the library upon her return, not even pausing long enough to remove her pelisse.

Although her ladyship knew it would be wiser to say nothing to her young cousin while she was in this mood, her curiosity overcame her good judgement, as it so often did. Following her into the library, Lady Beauforth attempted to find out what had gone on.

"Well, my dear, what did your uncle have to say? Was the announcement a hoax, as you thought?"

"No, Cousin Alice, it was not," Azalea stated flatly. "In fact, this whole thing is entirely my uncle's doing, and he had the effrontery to tell me that I can do nothing about it. I mean to prove him wrong." As she spoke, she was purposefully pulling paper and pen out of the writing desk.

"What— what do you intend to do?" asked Lady Beauforth fearfully.

"I intend to send a retraction to the papers —all of them. If I do so immediately, it might make the afternoon editions."

Lady Beauforth made a last, despairing effort to talk Azalea out of such a disastrous course. "But, my dear, is it not possible that your uncle knows best in this matter? After all, Lord Drowling is a brilliant match, far above what you might have expected as a virtual unknown with only whatever dowry Lord Kayce sees fit to bestow. No doubt he has been very generous on your behalf to bring this about."

Azalea was already writing and made no reply. Encouraged by her silence, Lady Beauforth continued. "Besides, it is not as though Lord Drowling were ugly, or so very old— why, many account him quite handsome, and he is but two or three years older than I. Pray try to accustom yourself to the match, my dear—it will save so much trouble and speculation if you do. And just *think* of the fun we shall have shopping for your trousseau! No doubt Lord Kayce will forward you a substantial sum for that purpose, as he is so set on the match."

At that happy thought, Lady Beauforth looked hopefully at the girl, certain that this last consideration would sway her. She was, after all, female.

Azalea, however, merely folded up the note she had written and addressed it. "Would you mind if I had one of your footmen take this round to the papers, Cousin Alice? I'd like to have it done as soon as possible."

Lady Beauforth's face fell. "Very well," she said heavily, and rang for the footman.

Abruptly contrite, Azalea rose to give her cousin a quick hug. "Please don't worry so. Trust me. This will all turn out for the best."

Lady Beauforth felt somewhat reassured by her young

charge's confident tone. She had always acted intelligently before, after all, and perhaps, just perhaps, she really did know what she was doing.

Azalea, meanwhile, prayed that her words might prove true. In reality, she felt far less confident than she sounded. If Kayce had obtained the marriage documents, she might *not* be able to persuade him to call off this horrible wedding he planned.

As the fashionable hour for afternoon callers drew near, Azalea vacillated between hope and fear that Christian would come as he had promised. Would he have seen the announcement by now? How would he react? Would he be angry? Or, even worse, what if he did not care?

She would have to tell him the truth about their marriage, she had decided, whether she'd prepared the ground well enough or not. With the marriage documents gone, he was her only hope for thwarting Kayce. But when, and where, was she to do so?

She intended to deny her betrothal to anyone who would listen, so there would be no need of privacy for that, at least. Surely Christian would listen to her explanation about the announcement; and, if not, there would be the retraction tomorrow to validate it, she comforted herself. As to the other —she would have to wait until they were alone for *that* explanation.

Did everyone read the Society columns, as Cousin Alice asserted? Surely not. Before today, Azalea herself had scarcely ever glanced at them, though of course she knew that she was not exactly a typical member of the London *haut ton*. At any rate, the majority of the fashionable world would not be in Town until April, and by then all of this would have been long settled. But oh, how she wished that it were settled now!

Christian did *not* come.

While Azalea considered his absence a definite setback to her plans, Marilyn did not appear to notice it at all. This was likely because Jonathan arrived early, then stayed for tea. He was to go to his grandfather's for a few days on the morrow, and clearly wished to spend as much time as possible with Marilyn before leaving.

Lady Dinsmore called as well, fairly bubbling over with congratulations on her friend's betrothal. She, it appeared, did not neglect the social news.

"My dearest Azalea, I had no idea!" she exclaimed upon her arrival. "Did all of this occur while I was gone over Christmas? I would have liked to have been the first to congratulate you, but of that I despair."

"No fear, Barbara," said Azalea wryly. "You are indeed the first, not counting Cousin Alice, but I am afraid congratulations are somewhat out of order. You see, there is no actual betrothal, and I expect a retraction to be printed on the morrow."

Lady Dinsmore looked confused. "Do you mean it was a hoax? You are not betrothed to Lord Drowling after all?"

"Yes, a hoax," answered Azalea, having decided that this would be the easiest explanation. "Lord Drowling has not even offered for me, much less been accepted. So please, if you would be so kind, if you hear anyone else speaking of it, let them know it is all a misunderstanding."

Lady Dinsmore agreed good-naturedly, although she still seemed a little puzzled, and turned the talk to poor Empress Josephine's famed rose gardens at Malmaison.

"I vow, I am dying to see the new tea roses from China, which reportedly bloom nearly all year round —and the centifolias smell like a bit of heaven, I hear." Their conversation revolved about this and other botanical matters until Jonathan managed to break in several minutes later.

"What did I hear you saying about a 'misunderstanding' a few minutes ago, 'Zalea?" he asked with interest. "Did someone actually put a betrothal announcement in the paper as a joke? Pretty poor taste, if you ask me."

She quietly agreed, but tried to convey with her eyes that she wished to speak to him later. Unfortunately, Jonathan had already turned back to Marilyn and missed her unspoken plea.

At least he *is not ready to believe the worst of me*, Azalea thought, vaguely comforted in spite of Christian's absence.

Throughout the afternoon and evening, several notes of congratulation and good wishes were delivered to her, some accompanied by flowers, as well as a syrupy-sweet poem from Lord Chilton, declaring his heart to be broken.

Lady Beauforth had been right, it appeared, and Azalea finally began to realize how awkward her situation was. When the *Gazette* was delivered that evening, she eagerly turned to the Society news. Another announcement of her fictitious betrothal appeared there, but no retraction.

She crushed the pages between her hands in frustration. Now she would no doubt have another round of congratulations to fend off.

Why hadn't Christian come to call?

Though he had already done so once that day, Christian decided to ride again before nuncheon. He had an extraordinary excess of energy, he found, and needed an outlet. As it was well past noon, the Park was more crowded than it was when he took his usual morning ride. He was forced to keep Sultan to a brisk trot, exchanging cheery greetings with acquaintances he encountered.

"Well met, Glaedon!" called Lord Chilton at one point, turning his roan gelding to trot alongside.

"Servant, Chilton," said Christian pleasantly to the older man. He had never particularly cared for the dandified marquess, but he felt in charity with the world today. "Splendid day for a ride."

"Indeed," agreed the other. "It's been an unusually mild winter. Hope the spring shapes up as well. By the way, when do you tie the knot with the lovely Miss Beauforth?"

Christian frowned. He had no intention of allowing the fact that he meant to break off their betrothal to become gossip before he could speak to Miss Beauforth himself. "It's not quite settled yet," he said at last. "The lady is having second thoughts, I fear."

"Oh ho! That dashing American friend of her charming cousin is to blame, I'll warrant. My heartfelt sympathies, Glaedon. Know just how you must feel."

"Do you indeed?" Christian spoke absently, eager to end the conversation so that he could be alone with his reminiscences of the day before.

"I certainly do. I had hopes of Miss Clayton myself, pearl beyond price that she is, but I find she is out of my reach. I am quite desolate, I assure you. Should you need someone with whom to drown your sorrows, I'm your man!" He executed a half bow from the saddle, one hand melodramatically over his heart.

"I'll keep that in mind," replied Chris shortly. "Good day, Chilton." He spurred Sultan down another path and was relieved when the marquess did not follow.

It appeared that Miss Beauforth's growing attachment to Jonathan Plummer was becoming common knowledge, which was all to the good for his purposes, Christian thought. But what had Chilton meant about Azalea? Had he made her an offer and been refused?

He smiled to himself at the thought, for though Chilton's fortune was no greater than his own, his title was. Christian had been right in his estimation that Azalea was no opportunist. The circumstance gave him reason to hope, as well.

A short time later, he returned to his Town house to change before paying his promised call at the Beauforth's.

"Have Cook put a sandwich together for me before I leave, Lawrence," he said to his valet. "I have quite an appetite today, I vow."

Sitting in the library with his feet propped on a stool, a roast-beef sandwich and a mug of ale at his elbow, Christian opened the morning paper, which he hadn't taken the time to read earlier. Munching thoughtfully, he digested the political news and took note of the current prices for sheep. He would have to mention to his steward that it might be a good time to purchase another flock.

Turning the page, he started to skim past the Society news, as he usually did, when a familiar name caught his eye. He went cold inside as he read the announcement of Miss Clayton's betrothal to Lord Drowling.

Suddenly, the roast beef tasted like ashes. He took a long swig of ale to clear his mouth.

Could it possibly be true? She had said nothing of it this morning —nor yesterday, more to the point, when he had nearly ravished her. She had never so much as mentioned being acquainted with Drowling —a thoroughly unsavoury character, in Christian's opinion, despite his wealth and standing in Society. It made no sense.

Lord Chilton's words in the Park came back to him. An avid follower of the current gossip, he must have been referring to this very announcement, Christian realized.

A black rage rose up in his throat, first at Drowling, debauched rake that he was, then at Azalea. No opportunist, he had told himself? Drowling's fortune, he knew, was many times greater than his own.

Unthinkingly, he untied the cravat he had so carefully knotted only a few minutes earlier. Until he'd had a chance to collect himself, he didn't dare go to see her. Rising, he rang for more ale.

The next morning, even before her ride, Azalea opened the *Post* to see if her retraction had been printed. It had not.

Riding did little to lift her spirits. Christian was not in the Park, and the sky was overcast, threatening rain. Though she felt chilled both in body and spirit, she refused to give up. With renewed purpose, she decided to visit the news offices herself.

After forcing herself to eat a quick breakfast, she summoned the coach and departed before her cousins could appear to question her actions. They would not approve, she knew— especially as she also intended to call at Lord Glaedon's Town house before returning.

She went first to the *Morning Post,* since she knew beyond doubt that the announcement had appeared there and the retraction had not. The clerk who greeted her was polite, but very definite in his answers. No, the retraction had not been printed, and would not be unless it came from Lord Kayce himself. Those were his orders, and it was not for him or even his superiors to question a man in Kayce's position.

The clerk managed to imply, without actually saying so, that he considered her a flighty young woman who could not make up her mind and who would do best to let herself be guided by her elders. Furious, Azalea departed.

Her next stop was the office of the *Morning News,* where she met with the same story. Kayce had overlooked nothing, it seemed. She demanded to see someone in charge, and was shown into a smoke-filled office occupied by a very fat man with a thick cigar and a greasy black moustache. He did not bother to rise at her entrance.

"How might I help you, missie?" he enquired insolently.

Fighting down her revulsion and indignation, Azalea explained that her betrothal announcement had been submitted by Lord Kayce without her consent and that she wanted it retracted.

"There will be no marriage," she concluded reasonably, "so it would be wrong to lead your readers to expect one."

The man, who had not given her his name, laughed loudly. "If I only printed what was true, I'd be out of business before you could so much as blink, my girl! Lord Kayce said as how something like this might happen, and paid me well to deal with it his way. There'll be no retraction."

Azalea turned on her heel and stalked out without another word.

There seemed no point in going on to the *Gazette*. Obviously Lord Kayce had these fine businessmen so cowed that they were afraid to do anything that might displease him.

She would have to deal with this problem at its source. She would inform her uncle of her existing marriage and make it plain to him that she would go public with that news if he attempted to push her into this marriage. Once that was settled, she would go to Christian and tell him everything. She would *make* him believe her!

For the second time in two days, Azalea presented herself at Lord Kayce's front door, this time demanding to see her uncle rather than politely enquiring whether he were home.

Almost to her surprise, she was shown into his presence at once, this time in the larger salon where she had greeted his guests at that dreadful dinner party nearly a month before. Kayce rose, smiling broadly.

"My dear Azalea! What an unexpected delight!" he exclaimed in his most affected manner. Oddly, his delight seemed sincere.

"Your coming here like this has saved me more trouble than you can possibly imagine," he continued, with such apparent satisfaction that Azalea began to feel more than a little uneasy. "You see, I had been racking my brains for a pretext to get you here without arousing your suspicions or those of the Beauforths. I very much wanted to avoid a scene, and was not at all sure that you would oblige me in that."

He turned to his butler, who still hovered in the doorway.

"Graves, pray send a footman to Lady Beauforth's to retrieve all of my niece's belongings, and to give her this message, informing her that Miss Clayton will be my... guest until her wedding takes place. He may take Lady Beauforth's carriage, which I imagine is outside."

The butler bowed and departed, and Kayce turned back to Azalea. "I think it best, my dear, considering your recent activities and certain discoveries I have made, to keep you—ah—safe here until Lord Drowling can claim his prize. So much more convenient for all concerned, don't you agree?"

CHAPTER FIFTEEN

CHRISTIAN RAPPED SMARTLY AT THE FRONT DOOR OF Beauforth House, his brisk manner concealing the uneasiness he felt at being there. Last night, and again this morning, he had made a few discreet enquiries about Town, and even at one of the newspaper offices. He had been forced to the conclusion that Azalea's betrothal to Drowling was perfectly genuine, fully sanctioned by her guardian, Lord Kayce. He had come this afternoon only because it would have been cowardly not to.

He would put a good face on it, he was determined. But he also hoped to discover why Azalea, whom he had thought so different from the other young ladies of the ton, had agreed to such a match —and why she had concealed it from him.

"Lord Glaedon!" exclaimed Lady Beauforth in delight when he was announced. "Azalea told us you were returned to Town. We looked to see you before this, in fact. I trust you had a pleasant Christmas and left your grandmother in good health?"

Christian assented, nodding to his fiancée as he noted that Azalea was not present. "And I trust you enjoyed your house party, Miss Beauforth?" he asked pleasantly, though it cost him to maintain his smile.

"Oh! Yes," Marilyn replied, colouring slightly. "I had quite a lively time." She lapsed into silence, but almost before he could notice the change in her manner, her mother launched herself into the breach.

"You will have heard our happy news by now, I presume?" Lady Beauforth twittered. "Our little Azalea, to be a viscountess! And such a wealthy and personable man Lord Drowling is, to be sure!" Gritting his teeth, Christian managed a nod. "Yes, I saw the announcement in the papers. I had hoped to convey my congratulations to her."

"Oh, I fear that will not be possible," replied Lady Beauforth with a nervous laugh. "She is gone to stay with her uncle until the wedding. He, ah, rather *we* thought that more appropriate, as she is to be married from his house."

"The wedding is to be so soon then?" Christian asked, startled. No date had been mentioned in the papers.

"Yes, well, you know how impetuous these young people are," replied Lady Beauforth, fluttering her fan.

Christian raised his brows. Drowling was five and forty if he was a day, he was certain. "Then your cousin is excited about her betrothal?" he could not help but ask.

Marilyn looked up quickly, but before she could say anything, her mother responded, with a brilliant smile, "Why, how can she not be? Lord Drowling is such a wonderful match, and so enamoured of her, too. I wish you could have seen how attentive he was when he called on her just after Christmas."

Christian stayed only the quarter hour that politeness required before rising to take his leave. Closing the door behind him with unnecessary force, he strode quickly away from the house, with no clear destination in mind.

What had he expected? Perhaps he had been hoping that Azalea would be there to throw herself into his arms, denying her betrothal and pledging him her undying love, he thought sarcastically.

For a moment he considered calling on her at Lord Kayce's house but quickly decided against it. It would only be an added torment to him and, perhaps, an embarrassment to her.

He had thought she was different, but it seemed she was no better than any of the other debutantes, out for whatever they could get. Christian had never cared much for the refinements of Society, which too often concealed greed and avarice under a thin veneer of polished manners and polite conversation. Now, that whole artificial world actively disgusted him.

In Azalea, he thought he had finally found someone in tune with his feelings, someone he could trust. But he had been wrong. And that was what hurt the most—he had given his trust, his friendship, and it had been betrayed.

That thought suddenly determined his destination: he would go back to Glaedon Oaks, to the one person he knew he could still trust. His grandmother had always had a remarkable talent for putting things in proper perspective. Right now, he needed her help to do just that.

He turned abruptly, to walk decisively in the direction of his Town house to fetch his horse and a few belongings. As he did so, a ragged little man jumped out of his way with a muttered oath, then turned to follow him.

Lady Glaedon was delighted, though surprised, to see her grandson again so soon. It was perfectly obvious from the constraint in his manner that something was wrong, but she trusted he would confide in her eventually. In fact, as he drifted aimlessly from one piece of estate business to another during his first day at home, she began to suspect that his primary reason for returning was to talk to her.

Several times when they were alone it seemed that Christian was on the verge of saying something to her, before changing his mind and lapsing again into a morose silence.

After a full day of waiting for her grandson to tell her what was troubling him, the dowager decided that some prompting was in order.

"You may as well go ahead and speak to me, Chris," she said bluntly after dinner that evening, when the two of them had retired to her ladyship's sitting-room. "We both know that you will eventually, and the wait is doing neither of us any good. In fact, just being around you in this mood has my nerves nearly as frazzled as yours plainly are."

Christian looked up sharply with a forbidding frown, then nodded ruefully. "I never could keep a secret from you, Grandmother. You are perfectly right. I came here to ask your advice and to seek comfort, but my pride has kept me from doing so. Has it been so obvious?"

"To me, at any rate," replied the dowager. "I take it that your wooing of Miss Clayton has gone less than successfully?" She held her breath, hoping the question would not bring a storm down upon her head.

"Deuce take it, madam, *can* you read my mind?" exclaimed Christian in astonishment.

"When a young man leaves for Town determined to bring back a bride, then returns less than a week later without her, it hardly takes supernatural powers to deduce that his courtship has received a setback. Not a permanent one, I hope? I very much liked what you told me of the girl." And what she had discovered through her own brief research into Miss Clayton's family history, as well.

"Quite permanent, ma'am," replied Christian morosely. "And I fear the girl's character was not nearly so shining as I painted it."

He proceeded to tell the dowager of the announcement in the papers. "I was nearly certain that she cared for me." He decided against mention of the kisses that they had shared just three days ago in Lady Beauforth's parlour. "I was on the point of making her an offer, in fact. I had high hopes of extricating myself from Miss Beauforth, as she has lately shown an interest in someone else. Now I may as well marry her after all, I suppose."

The dowager became thoughtful, choosing her next words carefully. She knew how headstrong her grandson could be if his pride or honour were pricked; and she was aware that much more than honour was at stake here.

"Did she give you no explanation? Why was her association with Drowling not generally known, if he were on the point of offering for her? Did you not press her for the details?"

"I had no chance. When I called, she had already left Lady Beauforth's to reside with her uncle. I saw no particular reason to call upon her there. Besides," he continued angrily, "I understand her motivation well enough. Drowling's fortune is great enough to make me seem a pauper in comparison —it is said that he owns near a tenth of England. Mere affection, even were it genuine, could scarce compete with that." He lapsed back into sullen silence.

"So you never bothered to hear her side of the story," concluded the dowager drily. "Is it not possible that the betrothal was not her idea at all? Perhaps she was sent to stay with her uncle because she was resistant to the idea."

Christian's head came up at that, a glimmer of hope in his eyes. "Do you think it possible, ma'am?" Then the hope faded. "But Lady Beauforth made it quite clear that Azalea was pleased with the match. She told me that she had gone to her uncle because she was to be married from his house. And that is another thing. Azalea never even mentioned to me that she was Kayce's niece. I discovered that from her grandfather's letters."

"I can't say it's a relationship *I* would care to admit to," retorted the dowager tartly. "You say she herself never actually confirmed the betrothal to you?" she prodded then, an ugly suspicion beginning to form in her mind.

He shook his head. "I never spoke to her after learning of it. But Lady Beauforth—"

"A shatter-brained female if ever there was one." The dowager snorted. "She believes whatever Kayce wishes her to, I have no doubt." She leaned forward, putting a hand on her grandson's knee. "Consider this. Suppose there *is* a betrothal, but Miss Clayton had no hand in it."

It was Christian's turn to snort. "Azalea does not strike me as a young lady who would allow such meddling without a fight, Grandmother. She is not a particularly, ah, biddable girl."

"Precisely why her uncle might wish to have her where he can control her," exclaimed his grandmother triumphantly. "Kayce has been a scoundrel since boyhood, and hardly a man I would trust as guardian to an innocent young lady, be she his niece or not."

"Do you think she could actually be in some danger, ma'am?" Christian suddenly sat up straighter, apparently ready now to take up the role of White Knight.

"No *physical* danger, most likely," the dowager replied in a tone that deliberately implied other threats. "Was a wedding date mentioned in the paper?"

"No, but Lady Beauforth implied that it was to be soon."

"Then time may be running out for you to counter Drowling's claim upon her."

"Whatever his claim, I won't allow her to be forced to marry against her will," vowed Christian, in a tone that boded ill for Lord Kayce. The dowager smiled to herself.

"Of course not, my dear," she said soothingly. "Now, if you would be so kind as to set up the table, I could fancy a game of piquet." She realized that her best course now would be to let Christian mull over their conversation. She would be very surprised if he did not find some pressing reason to return to Town on the morrow.

Christian did indeed think over that conversation —many times, in fact— during a long and sleepless night. Could his grandmother's theory be correct? Might Kayce have forced Azalea into a betrothal against her will?

The dowager's carefully chosen words tormented him

until, in the wee hours of the morning, he felt ready to race back to London at that very instant to assure himself of Azalea's safety. He burned to protect her with his name, to comfort her with his words, his body....

The only thing that prevented him from leaving at once was the possibility that the betrothal was genuine. What a fool he would look then! Still, by the time he fell into a dreamless sleep just before dawn, he had resolved to return directly after breakfast. Better to risk looking like a lovesick idiot than to allow Azalea's life —and his own—to be ruined by his own mistaken pride and jealousy.

He acquainted the dowager with his intentions over a late breakfast and was surprised at his grandmother's reaction. She actually seemed to have expected his decision.

"You must do whatever you think best, of course, Christian," was all she said.

They were just rising from the table when an interruption occurred. Semple, the butler, entered with the information that there was a "person" below requesting an interview with Lord Glaedon. Christian felt a sudden certainty that it was Azalea herself, come to explain everything and to beg for his protection against her uncle.

"Is it a young lady, Semple?" he asked eagerly, already starting for the door.

"No, my lord, a man. And not very young," replied that worthy with a lack of expression that somehow conveyed his disapproval. "I would never have admitted him, but he said that you would remember him. He gave his name as Luke Sykes." He spoke the syllables with distaste.

Christian experienced a sharp stab of disappointment. Just for a moment, he had been so sure... The visitor's name meant nothing to him, in spite of his message to the butler. Still, he would have to see him, he supposed.

"If you will excuse me for a moment, ma'am?"

The dowager nodded. "Let me know what it is about, Chris. I could do with some diversion."

When Christian saw the scarecrow figure that awaited him in the front parlour, he understood Semple's reservations. The man was short and wiry, with a shock of brownish hair and several day's growth of stubble on his chin. He was dressed in sailor's garb, little better than rags, and his bleary eyes and red nose proclaimed his fondness for drink. Christian was almost certain he had never seen him before, though there *was* something vaguely familiar about him.

The man rose eagerly at his entrance and stepped forward with a gap-toothed smile. "Thank ye, my lord, I knew ye wouldn't turn me away after all the trouble I had to track ye down," the scruffy little man exclaimed in delight. He seemed to expect Christian to recognize him on sight.

"Mr.—ah—Sykes?" said the Earl uncertainly. "You have some business with me, I collect?" A nasty suspicion began to form. Could this old sailor know him from his days aboard the *Angel* or the *Hyacinth* and have come to blackmail him?

Certainly there were details about that time that he would not care to have come to light. More than anything right now, however, Christian begrudged the time— time he was losing in getting to Azalea. But he would have to hear the sailor out. Perhaps the man was no more than a common beggar, with some cleverly spun tale of woe.

"Ye don't remember me then, me lord?" the man asked, apparently disappointed. "I feared that were the case when ye went past me in Lunnon, day before yesterday. 'Twas the first time I got a good-enough look at ye to be sure of who ye was, and then ye went and left for the country straight off. Devil of a time I had gettin' here, too." He stroked the stubble on his chin. "I guess I *has* changed a bit, and not for the better, since ye see'd me last. But I thought certain ye'd not forget old Luke what saved yer life!"

"My life?" asked Christian skeptically. "And when might this have been?"

"Why, nigh on six years ago, me lord, out o' the wreck of the *Fortitude* afore we was picked up by that filthy slaver, Farris. Course, ye didn't know yer own name then, nor did I. 'Twas just by chance I found out who the lad was that I saved, and that just a couple o' months ago. I been trying to find ye ever since, hoping ye might see fit to reward old Luke for the little favour I done ye."

He had the Earl's full attention now. The man certainly had some of the facts straight —but he could be anyone who had been aboard that slave ship. Christian said as much to the fellow.

"I suppose ye be right, me lord, seein's how ye don't remember me face. I didn't recognize yours right off, neither. I had to follow ye about Lunnon a bit, to be sure. But there must be some way to convince ye. Let's see—do ye remember how Captain Whitten of the *Fortitude* used to yank on his beard when he got riled? Thick red beard he had. No one on *the Angel*— what a name for a slaver, eh?— would know that. The captain was lost afore ever they found us." He watched Lord Glaedon expectantly.

"Whitten... The *Fortitude*... I do remember a red beard. But surely the captain's name was Taylor, and the ship the *Artemis*. I'm certain the captain who told me about the colonies was

Taylor, and dark haired." Christian was becoming more confused instead of less.

"Aye, I remember back then ye kept saying something about a Captain Taylor. There weren't no Taylor, captain or crewman, aboard the *Fortitude,* that's certain. But ye say ye remember the beard. If so, ye must remember the storm, at least!"

At Glaedon's blank look, he continued. "We was two er three weeks out of Virginia, 'most halfway to England, when it broke. It started with that dead calm under a funny-colour sky, then the thunder started rumbling, and almost afore we could batten down the hatches, the wind was on us! The chickens got swept overboard first thing, then we lost two crewmen — one was that tall, skinny fellow with the squeaky voice, do you recollect him?"

Christian nodded vaguely. He was thinking very hard, snippets of old nightmares swimming into focus and then retreating.

"Anyways, we ran afore that wind for two days, losing bits and pieces of the ship as we went. Finally, we was too bad hurt to stay afloat and started to go down. You and me and Jacob got into one of the boats, but Jacob got washed over by a wave, so then it was just you and me. Ye won't remember that part, though, 'cause ye was out cold —a spar knocked ye in the head, I think. Lucky for us, the wind died down a few hours later, but there weren't nothing left of the *Fortitude* that I could see. A couple days later the *Angel* picked us up. Ye was awake, but real dizzy. Neither of us hadn't had no water for prob'ly three days by then."

At this point Christian interrupted his narrative. "Wait, wait! I'm remembering all of this, I think. I certainly remember the chickens going over the side. But you said we were halfway to England? Don't you mean *from* England?"

Sykes looked at him strangely. "Ye never did remember it all, did ye? That must have been a worse knock on the head than I thought. No, we sailed out of port in Hampton, Virginia, in America. Not a real big town, but busy, and with plenty of amusements for sailors with time and a bit o' money on their hands. There was a big church tower in sight of the docks — red brick it was...."

Suddenly, Christian could see that church tower and the buildings surrounding it. He could hear the sound of the bell and... he could see another church, this one of grey stone. The day was bright, but the interior of the church was dim. There were only a few people in it: his father, the rector of the church performing the ceremony and, at his own side, a young girl with bright red curls under a lace veil.

With a suddenness that nearly sent him reeling, full memory returned —the remainder of his westward voyage, his meeting with thirteen-year-old Azalea, their marriage, everything. He sat down abruptly, trying to grasp it all.

Luke Sykes had stopped speaking, and was looking at the young nobleman before him in concern. "Be ye all right, me lord?" he asked tentatively. "Shall I fetch someone to bring ye some water or brandy, like?"

Christian looked at him dazedly. "I am fine, Mr. Sykes. Perhaps for the first time in six years. You shall certainly have that reward —you have earned it twice over now!"

CHAPTER SIXTEEN

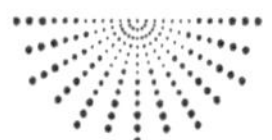

WITHIN THE hour, Christian set off for London at a pace a less skillful driver would never have attempted. He was determined to get to the bottom of the deception Azalea had been practising on him since her arrival in London.

Though *he* might have forgotten that they were married due to the injuries he had sustained in the shipwreck, *she* had no such excuse. Remembering certain looks and words she had sent his way, he knew it must have been on her mind from the first. Why hadn't she told him at once?

He intended to find out.

Before leaving, he had briefly acquainted the dowager with all of the particulars of his suddenly recovered memory. She was at first astonished and then relieved. She informed him that for the past two years she had been aware that something had been haunting Christian, and now she hoped that his ghosts could be laid to rest.

"Of course, you must speak to her at once, Chris," she agreed. "If she is indeed your Countess, you must bring her here as soon as everything is settled. There must be records, if there was truly a wedding, which obviously there was," she continued quickly, encountering Christian's glance. "Those records may well be in America, I suppose." She had chuckled then. "This will be quite a setback for Kayce. I wish I could be there to see his face when you arrive!"

Christian could not help but feel that his grandmother was taking the situation a little too lightly, but he was at least relieved that she appeared more supportive than shocked. Somehow, he thought that she and his bride would deal very well together... if he didn't throttle Azalea first.

Now, he almost laughed at the anguish he had felt at "sullying" the innocent Azalea with his caresses. She was an innocent, there was no doubt of that, but to think that all along she had been his wife —and that she knew it perfectly well. Her lack of resistance was one more thing his full knowledge of the past explained. Already he found himself eager to show her how much more pleasure could be in store for them both.

It was late afternoon when Christian pulled up in front of Beauforth House, where he meant to make enquiries before proceeding to Lord Kayce's. After a great deal of thought during the day's drive, he felt he now partially understood Azalea's reluctance to mention their marriage, when he himself had been so obviously unaware of it.

He had also rehashed each and every detail of their last conversation in the Park, and was now convinced that Azalea had not willingly entered into any betrothal. In only a few moments he would know for certain, he told himself, striding up to the front door.

"Is Miss Clayton in?" he asked the butler the moment the door opened.

"No, my lord," came the expected answer. "Shall I announce you to Lady Beauforth?" At the Earl's curt nod, Smythe showed him into the front parlour with an expression suspiciously like relief on his normally passive face. "Perhaps now something will be done," Christian heard him mutter under his breath as he went to make his lordship's presence known.

"Lord Glaedon!" exclaimed Lady Beauforth eagerly as she came into the parlour a few moments later, her hands fluttering nervously. "One of the very people I was hoping to see! Perhaps you can offer me advice, for I am very nearly certain that something is not quite right. But I was unsure what I could do about it even if that were the case, for Kayce is her guardian, after all. But maybe nothing is truly wrong, in which case I would feel terribly foolish for interfering! I would have asked Mr. Plummer, except he is out of Town. But, of course, you understand." She dropped into the chair closest to him and fanned herself vigorously.

"No, ma'am, I am afraid I do not understand at all," said Christian more severely than he had intended. Lady Beauforth's disjointed manner had never been more irritating. "When I was here last, if you recall, you told me that Miss Clayton was excited about her upcoming nuptials. Are you now saying that she is in some sort of trouble? What has Kayce done to her?"

"Well... nothing, so far as I *know*," said Lady Beauforth, twisting her fan in her hands. "She is staying with him until the wedding, as I told you before, but I fear that I did deceive you a bit on one point. She was not at all pleased with the betrothal, I confess. At the time I thought I was acting for the best, but now..."

"I think you had better tell me the whole, madam," said Christian, striving for patience he did not feel. "Start with the betrothal announcement. You say that it was not Azalea's idea?"

"No, she was quite surprised, even angry, I fear, that it had gone in. Apparently it was all her uncle's doing, and I must admit it seemed odd at the time that he would not consult her first, even though Lord Drowling *is* such a good match. I do know that she sent retractions to all of the papers, but they never appeared in print. At least not in the *Post*, which is the only one I seem to find time to read."

Distractedly, she moved from the chair she'd been sitting in to the sofa, and motioned him to sit opposite.

"And?" he prompted, seating himself on the edge of the chair indicated.

"Yes, I suppose that is neither here nor there. At any rate, on the morning of the day you last called, Azalea went out without telling anyone where she was going, and the next thing I knew I had received a message from Lord Kayce saying that in the interests of convenience, she would be staying with him until the wedding, which is apparently to take place much, sooner than anyone told me about." Lady Beauforth paused to catch her breath.

"When?" snapped the Earl. "When is the wedding taking place?"

"Why, as I just said, no one has told me anything. And I've practically acted as a mother to the girl these two months past! I have sent a note round twice asking Azalea for particulars, and whether she wants my help in selecting her trousseau — her uncle is hardly the one she would prefer for that sort of help, I am certain —and all I have received in reply is a formal note from Kayce saying that poor Azalea is too busy at present to answer her correspondence. So, as I said at the first, I am beginning to worry, for it is not at all like her to ignore me. She has always been most considerate and sweet-tempered with me."

"Could Kayce be keeping her prisoner, do you think?" asked Christian sharply. Why had this shatter-brained female not done something the day Azalea disappeared?

"That is precisely what I am beginning to fear," answered Lady Beauforth worriedly. "At first I thought that perhaps it was for her own good, as she kept declaring that she would never marry Drowling no matter what arrangements had been made. I thought she was merely being headstrong, as young people can be, and that her uncle likely knew best. Such a good match, you understand, my lord! *Much* better than she could have hoped for in the ordinary way."

At Lord Glaedon's scowl, Lady Beauforth broke off uncertainly, before continuing in a slightly different vein.

"Anyway, the more I thought about it, the more wrong it seemed. Azalea really has become almost a daughter to me, and not for the world would I wish to see her truly unhappy in marriage. I fear her temperament is such that even great wealth may not compensate for her dislike of Lord Drowling. And so I would like your advice. Do you see any way that I might help poor Azalea? Without creating any sort of scandal, of course," she added hastily.

"Lady Beauforth, I believe you can leave this entirely to me. Was there any man of business —a solicitor, perhaps —with whom Azalea has consulted since her arrival in London?"

"Why, yes, a Mr. Timmons," replied Lady Beauforth in surprise. "Why?"

"Do you have his direction, by chance?" Lord Glaedon was becoming more impatient by the moment to be gone. He must not arrive too late!

"Well, I did at one time... Ah! The coachman will know," said her ladyship, increasingly bewildered. "He drove her there more than once."

"Thank you, I'll speak to him on my way out. I shall be in touch with you on the matter shortly." Christian rose to depart.

At that moment, Marilyn hurried into the room. She was stunningly dressed in a powder blue gown that matched her eyes to perfection, but Christian scarcely noticed.

"Mother, Smythe told me... Oh! You are still here! Good afternoon, my lord."

Christian nodded curtly, impatient to be gone. "Your servant, Miss Beauforth." He took a step towards the door, but Marilyn stopped him.

"Might— might I have a word with you, Lord Glaedon — in private?"

"Marilyn, Lord Glaedon is in something of a hurry just now, I'm afraid," put in Lady Beauforth, to Christian's relief. "Perhaps later—"

"But Jonathan will be back tomorrow, and I promised to speak to Lord Glaedon before then," protested Marilyn, earning a startled look from her mother and a frown from the Earl. "And you have been from Town as well, my lord." She turned back to Christian accusingly.

He sighed and sat back down, realizing that he might as well get his unpleasant business with Miss Beauforth out of the way, as well.

Before he could speak, however, she hurried on, with a distracted glance at her mother. "It—it is about our betrothal, my lord. You see, I have thought much about it and I fear that — that we should not suit."

"Marilyn, my angel, have a care!" interjected Lady Beauforth, but her daughter shook her head.

"No, Mother, I am persuaded that I will not be happy as Lady Glaedon. You see, it is Jonathan that I love!" She turned apologetically to Christian, who was striving to conceal a smile. "I am so sorry to break your heart in this way, my lord, but I pray you can become reconciled to losing me. You would not wish me to marry you when I love another, would you?" Manfully, Christian kept his expression serious. The fishlike opening and closing of Lady Beauforth's mouth did not make it any easier.

"Certainly I cannot hold you to our betrothal under the circumstances, Miss Beauforth. You may consider it at an end. And now, I really must be going." He nodded to both ladies and strode quickly from the room.

"He took it remarkably well," Marilyn commented after he had gone. "Doubtless he wished to leave before he could betray what he truly felt. Men do not care to express their sorrow publicly, I have noted."

Lady Beauforth finally found her voice. "My love, do you realize what you have just done?" she wailed. "You would have been a countess!"

"I have discovered that there is more to life than being a countess, Mother," replied Marilyn loftily. "I do feel badly for poor Glaedon, though. And after he came directly to see me first thing on returning to Town."

"Actually, my dear, I believe he came to speak to Azalea," returned Lady Beauforth somewhat distractedly, trying to sort out everything that had just occurred.

"Indeed?" asked Marilyn in surprise. "I thought... Oh, well, no matter. What do you think of this dress, Mother? Jonathan —er, Mr. Plummer —is due back from his grandfather's estates tomorrow, and I thought I would wear this when he comes to call." She pirouetted for her mother's evaluation.

"What? Oh, very nice, my love," said Lady Beauforth, scarcely looking at her. Oddly, she discovered that Marilyn's broken betrothal did not upset her as much as the thought of Azalea's possible danger. What could Lord Glaedon possibly do for her? And would he be in time?

Azalea raised herself on one elbow and shook her head, trying to clear the fog from her brain. How much time had passed since her uncle had imprisoned her in this sumptuous bedroom?

She clearly remembered arriving at Kayce's Town house, and that she had tried to leave after he informed her that she was to be his "guest" until the wedding. Two footmen —a fancy name, she thought, for hired thugs —had blocked the front door, while Kayce told her she had a choice between being carried to her chamber and being escorted to it. She had chosen the latter only because open resistance would obviously do her no good, whereas a show of submission might.

Bit by bit, she pieced together what had occurred afterward. First, there had been hours of solitude, broken only by the delivery of a meal tray at noon, and another shortly after dark. That had given her ample time for thought, and for regret.

She had believed that the surest way to avert her uncle's

plan was to inform him of her marriage to the Earl of Glaedon, much as she would have preferred to tell Christian first. But the very fact that he had imprisoned her implied that Kayce must already know of it, and must know also that she no longer possessed any proofs. By coming here instead of going to Christian, she had unwittingly played right into her uncle's hands.

As long as he held her prisoner, she could have no opportunity to convince Christian or anyone else of the truth, so that they might come to her aid in preventing a lawless union with Drowling. Which meant her only recourse was escape.

Accordingly, that night, after all was quiet in the house, she had climbed down the tree outside her second-storey window. She remembered bolstering her courage by thinking how she would love to see her uncle's face when he received her note from Lady Beauforth's in the morning.

But alas, her ambitious scheme had come to naught. Kayce had evidently been suspicious of his niece's uncharacteristic compliance and had posted a guard in the garden below her window. The man had seized her before her feet touched the ground and dragged her ignominiously back into the house through a rear entrance.

When called to the scene, Kayce had chuckled at her obvious chagrin and had ordered her taken back to her chamber and the window to be locked, in addition to posting an additional guard outside her door.

The next morning he had allowed her to descend and join him at breakfast. He had conversed on general topics as though absolutely nothing were amiss, while Azalea remained stubbornly silent, refusing to play along with his dreadful charade. Her uncle had completely ignored the glares she sent his way, and she had finally decided to devote herself to the excellent breakfast set before her with the rationale that if she were ever to make good her escape from this monster, she would need her strength.

That, apparently, had been a mistake.

She realized now that something in glass or plate must have contained a drug, for it was at that point that her memory failed. All she could recall after that were hazy images of being carried back to her bed, of being fed and ministered to at intervals by a large, grey-haired woman with a deep voice, and of disjointed sentences being spoken over her by Kayce and this woman, who was presumably some sort of nurse. Now she tried to organize her confused thoughts, to remember anything that they had said, feeling vaguely that it might be important —but she could not.

At that moment, Azalea heard voices outside her chamber door and the rattle of a key in the lock. Hoping to discover something of use, she closed her eyes to feign sleep. She heard two sets of footsteps enter the room, one heavier than the other, and then detected a glow against her closed eyelids. Presumably, the bedside lamp had been lit.

"Still sleeping, my lord," said the deep female voice she remembered. "Shall I give her another dose to be safe?" Before Azalea could begin to plan some way to avoid swallowing the drug, Kayce's voice responded.

"No, I think not. We can hardly have an unconscious bride, after all. Check in on her periodically, and when she begins to stir, give her just enough to keep her quiet without putting her back to sleep. I have paid the clergyman well, but he still might balk if she were to protest too violently during the ceremony. We certainly don't want any repetitions of those claims to a previous marriage she was ranting about earlier, even if they were mere fancies brought on by the drug. Report to me when she wakes."

"Yes, my lord," replied the woman, and Kayce's footfalls receded.

Azalea forced herself to remain limp as the big woman turned her body from side to side, washing her and changing the cotton shift she wore.

She had told her uncle of her marriage? She had no recollection of it. Had she mentioned Lord Glaedon by name? Had her uncle perhaps *not* obtained the marriage proofs, as she had feared? Or was he merely hiding that fact from this servant? She had no way of knowing.

The woman completed her ministrations and left, and Azalea cautiously opened her eyes again. The door and window were no doubt still locked, nor was she at all certain that she could walk yet, in any event. Experimentally, she tried to sit up in bed, and the room rocked crazily about her. No, even standing would be impossible for the present. She would try again later. In the meantime, she could at least think through her situation.

Why had Lady Beauforth not come to enquire about her? Of course, she very well might have, Azalea realized, and been fobbed off by some story of Kayce's. She would have to assume that there would be no help from that quarter. Lady Beauforth had always been strongly in favour of a match with Drowling anyway, and would hardly work to prevent it.

What about Marilyn then, or, better yet, Jonathan? She was positive that he would help her if she could somehow get word to him. But he would know no more of her situation than the Beauforths did—he might not even be in Town.

Hadn't he been about to leave for his grandfather's estates the last time he called? Who else might possibly help her?

Involuntarily, her thoughts turned to Christian. If only she had gone to him and explained everything before coming here! He had called himself her friend, and had implied much, much more. And somehow Azalea knew that he would have no trouble dealing with Kayce and Drowling if he chose to do so.

But such fantasies were pointless. By now he would think that she had entered into a betrothal with Drowling willingly, since that was doubtless what Lady Beauforth would tell people. Even if she were somehow to escape, could she really bring herself to go to him and tell him that she was his wife, as she had once thought to do? Undoubtedly he would laugh and shut the door in her face.

No, she would return to America, she decided. Even if her uncle somehow forced her to go through with this wedding — which would not be a true one, she consoled herself —they could hardly keep her under guard for the rest of her life. Somehow, someday —very soon —she would escape and make her way back, if not to Williamsburg, then at least to the New World, where no one would know of her humiliation here in England. If she could not have Christian's love, then she would take the secret of their marriage with her to the grave.

And that was another option, she suddenly realized. While her conscience recoiled at the sinful idea of suicide, a practical voice somewhere in her still-fuzzy mind told her that it would be infinitely preferable to a marriage with Drowling.

Thrusting that thought hastily aside, to be considered again only if no other solution presented itself, Azalea forced herself to prepare arguments that would convince any clergyman —even a well-paid clergyman —that this wedding ceremony could not possibly take place.

By the time she again heard footsteps, she had composed a speech, to be delivered at the altar, if necessary, that she was nearly certain would free her, at least temporarily. She again pretended sleep, hoping to avoid another dose of whatever she had been given. Only if she were fully in control of her faculties would she be able to convince the clergyman not to perform the ceremony.

So far, her ruse appeared successful. The woman merely looked closely at Azalea and shook her gently by the shoulder before leaving the room.

It might have been two hours later when the door reopened. By now, Azalea had managed a brief walk about the room and was fairly certain that she had shaken off most of the effects of the drug. As before, she appeared to be sound asleep when her uncle and his henchwoman entered.

"Time grows short," said Kayce impatiently. "Surely she should be awake by now?"

"Aye, she should, my lord," replied the woman. "Mayhap we gave her a bit too much last time. She's smaller than anyone I've dosed before."

"Well, let's sit her up and see if we can bring her to. If possible, I'd like to have some conversation with her before the wedding."

Curiosity almost caused Azalea to open her eyes. What could Kayce wish to speak to her about? Should she try to convince him one last time, or would it be safer to pretend to be drugged until she could talk to the clergyman?

The beefy arm of her erstwhile nurse raised her into a

sitting position while Kayce's footsteps receded across the room, then returned. Before Azalea could decide how to react, the decision was made for her— cold water was unexpectedly flung in her face.

She gasped and sputtered from the shock of it, her eyes flying open in astonishment.

"There!" said Kayce in evident satisfaction. "That was easy enough. Now, my dear, as soon as you have your wits about you, we must have a talk."

Azalea glared at him, forgetting in her anger that she should pretend to be still under the influence of the drug. "May I have a robe first?" she asked icily, glancing down at her wet cotton shift, which clung to her body in a most immodest manner.

Kayce nodded to the nurse, who brought Azalea's own velvet wrapper, apparently transported from Lady Beauforth's during her long sleep. Pulling it closely about her, she looked defiantly at her uncle.

"Well?" She knew she should try to placate Kayce somewhat if she were to talk him out of his plans, but she was simply too angry at the moment to care. "What do you need to say that necessitated waking me in such a manner?"

"You seem to be in complete possession of your senses," said Kayce, with a significant glance at the nurse. "Perhaps now you will tell me what your ravings about a previous marriage signified."

So he did not have the marriage papers! Azalea felt a surge of relief and triumph, suddenly seeing an easy way out of her predicament.

"I had intended to inform you of it, dear Uncle, had you but given me a chance," she said with false sweetness. "I did, if you recall, tell you that a marriage with Lord Drowling was impossible, but you did not believe me."

Kayce's eyes narrowed. "And who is this alleged husband? Some American commoner whom you abandoned to seek your fortune —or rather, my fortune —in England? Is he here to step forward and claim you?" Disbelief showed openly in his face.

"Hardly that, Uncle," retorted Azalea, stung. "Lord Glaedon is no commoner, nor is he in America. And he *will* be here to claim me—in time to stop this ridiculous marriage you want so badly." She knew this last was a lie, but prayed that Kayce would believe it.

He did not.

"Yes, I knew about your partiality for Glaedon —your meetings in the Park have been reported to me. But my sources also tell me that he is presently in the country with his dear grandmama." Kayce's features twisted with dislike as he mentioned the dowager Countess.

"A pretty story, my dear, but most improbable. I fail to see why either of you should have desired a secret wedding. Where are the marriage papers? Why was there no announcement? And what of the small matter of his betrothal to your cousin, Miss Beauforth?"

Azalea's sudden confidence began to crumble. Without any proof, her story of a wedding in Williamsburg when she was but thirteen sounded absurd even to herself. The only person in England who could corroborate her tale was Mr. Timmons, and as far as she knew he was still bedridden.

At her silence, Kayce smiled unpleasantly. "I thought as much. No, my dear, it will take more than such a fable to change my plans. And I warn you— one word of this during the ceremony and I might have to arrange an unpleasant, ah, accident for young Glaedon."

He smiled as Azalea's eyes widened in horror. "I shall return for you shortly. Mrs. Melkin," he said, turning toward the nurse, "help her to dress."

The wedding gown Mrs. Melkin held up was beautiful, but did not serve to distract her a whit. Somehow, she must get out of this!

Since there was obviously no chance of overpowering the massive nurse, Azalea allowed herself to be fastened into the exquisite dress without a word, hoping that some opportunity for escape would present itself after she left the bedchamber.

True to his word, Kayce returned in less than an hour to escort her downstairs to a large room at the rear of the house —the dining-room, she realized, with the table removed and the chairs placed along one wall. Drowling was there, along with the skinny butler and a man she assumed was the clergyman. If anything, he appeared even less sympathetic than the others, she thought despairingly.

Drowling turned to smile at her, but there was more lust than affection in his glance. His look made her skin crawl, and Azalea suppressed a shudder, knowing that he would show no more pity than her uncle.

As if in a nightmare, she allowed Kayce to guide her to her place at Drowling's side.

Now? Should she deliver that carefully prepared speech? But what of Kayce's threat? Azalea had no doubt whatsoever that he was capable of carrying it out. She could not risk Christian's safety, or possibly his life, even to stop this travesty of a wedding.

Oh, Chris, where are you now? she moaned silently to herself.

After driving at a reckless pace through the dark London streets, Christian finally drew to a halt a few doors from Lord Kayce's Town house. He did not wish to call attention to his presence just yet. For the sake of Azalea's safety, he thought it might be wiser to discover all that he could before pounding down Kayce's front door.

Proceeding on foot, he went around to the rear of the house to check the stables, hoping to gain some useful information there. Sure enough, drawn up outside them was a handsome travelling carriage with a crest on the side that he recognized as Lord Drowling's. Here to visit his reluctant bride, was he?

Though not well-acquainted with the man, Christian had developed a dislike for Drowling after an occasion several months before when he had found him in a tavern forcing his attentions on a terrified young serving wench. The idea of that bully laying so much as a finger on Azalea made his blood boil.

Just then, a stable-lad came out of one of the stalls and stopped short when he saw a stranger, obviously one of the nobility, standing there. Plainly unsure of his responsibilities in this circumstance, he came forward hesitantly.

"How can I help you, guv'nor?" the boy asked in as deep a voice as he could muster.

"With information, my good man," answered Christian with a wink.

When the boy hesitated, he reached into his pocket and brought out a gold guinea. "This is yours, if you can help me," he said, flipping it expertly into the air and catching it again.

The lad's eyes gleamed as he watched the glinting coin. He

was only an under stable-boy, and had never possessed so much money in his life as this liberal stranger was offering. Lord Kayce was not so generous that he commanded unswerving loyalty from his lower servants.

"What might you be wanting to know, milord?" asked the boy, suddenly respectful.

"Who is within with Lord Kayce right now?"

"Just the swell what owns this coach, and the parson, milord," answered the boy eagerly, his eyes never leaving the guinea.

"No one else?" asked Christian sharply.

"Oh, there's the young lady, the master's cousin or niece or some such," replied the lad, "but she's been here since day before yesterday. I thought you just meant whose horses was here."

"Thank you. A parson, you said?" The boy nodded. "Does he come here often?"

The lad had to stifle a laugh. "Never before that I've see'd, milord. Lord Kayce ain't exactly the church-goin' type, if you take my meaning."

"I understand," said Glaedon. "Then what might he be doing here now?"

"Oh, I reckon he's to do the wedding, milord. The young lady be going to marry that swell as I mentioned. Harry, the groom, told me so."

Christian was already striding toward the house. "Thank you, my lad, you have earned this." He tossed the guinea over his shoulder and the boy caught it with a grin and stowed it in his pocket. It was by far the easiest money he had ever earned.

Walking softly now, Christian approached the kitchen entrance. No one seemed to be around, but he had no desire to raise the alarm prematurely. He peered into the scullery: empty. Closing the door silently behind him, he passed swiftly through the kitchens and into the passageway beyond, then stopped. He could hear voices behind the door on his left and pressed his ear to it, trying to make out the words.

CHAPTER SEVENTEEN

"MISS CLAYTON?" ASKED THE ACERBIC CLERGYMAN WITH increasing annoyance.

Azalea knew she was supposed to be repeating his words at this point in the ceremony, but could not bring herself to speak, regardless of the threat Kayce held over Christian. Instead, she looked first pleadingly, then defiantly at her uncle. He could force her to stand here, but not to repeat wedding vows!

Kayce returned her look with a frown. "She does," he said firmly.

The harassed cleric looked from the defiant girl before him to the man who had paid him so well to perform this wedding. Really, this was most irregular! Still, for fifty pounds... "Very well," he said. "And do you, Lord Drowling—"

"I do not!" broke in Azalea, speaking just as firmly as her uncle had.

"A moment, please," said Kayce with deceptive pleasantness. He pulled his niece aside and beckoned to Mrs. Melkin, who had been standing unobtrusively in the background. "Must we drug you again, my dear? I had thought concern for young Glaedon would ensure your cooperation, but I am prepared to take other measures."

"What I told you is true, Uncle," said Azalea grimly. "Even if I say the vows, this marriage will not be legal. I swear it upon my life."

Kayce glanced over at Drowling, who was watching them with a mixture of curiosity and amusement. "If Glaedon were to die, then the point would be academic, would it not?" he asked in low tones.

Azalea gasped at this bald threat. "You would not!"

"My dear, you have no idea what is at stake here. There is very little I would not do to achieve my ends." Kayce watched her face shrewdly and nodded in satisfaction when he saw that she was finally defeated.

While Azalea was convinced that Christian would have no trouble besting Kayce, Drowling, or even both of them together in a fair fight, she knew that her uncle would never engage in one. What chance could even the bravest, most skilled man have against a paid assassin striking unexpectedly from behind?

Slowly, she resumed her place and the ceremony continued. As the clergyman droned on and on, she closed her eyes, praying for the miracle she knew was not to be. The service was nearly over.

"By the power vested in me—" the pastor was saying, when he was interrupted by a resounding crash from the other end of the room as the door to the kitchen slammed open.

"There will be no marriage!" proclaimed Lord Glaedon

loudly, striding into the room and effectively halting the proceedings.

The clergyman's mouth dropped open. Even fifty pounds was surely not worth this kind of agitation to his nerves!

"Christian!" gasped Azalea, starting toward him. Then, at a sudden, violent movement on the part of Lord Kayce, she cried, "Watch out!"

Glaedon turned to face the older man, his anger at what he had tried to do to Azalea matching Kayce's obvious fury at being thwarted. Almost without thinking, Christian felled Lord Kayce with a single blow from his fist before turning to face Drowling, who was now also advancing menacingly, having recovered from his surprise at the intrusion.

"By what right do you come bursting in here, Glaedon?" he demanded. "This is my wedding! "

"I think not, Drowling." Glaedon's voice was as cold and sharp as steel. "I am here by right of being the lawful husband of this lady. Do you care to name your seconds?"

Drowling's face became a study in astonishment. "Husband? Are you serious? Why was nothing said about this?" He looked accusingly at Kayce, who was struggling to rise, holding a handkerchief to his bleeding mouth.

"There is no proof!" shouted Kayce hoarsely. "The girl all but admitted it!"

"You are mistaken, Kayce," said Christian calmly. "I have the proof in my pocket. Your thugs did not do a thorough enough job on Mr. Timmons, I regret to tell you, and he is very much on the mend. He told me where the papers were hidden." At his words, Kayce paled visibly.

"By the way," Christian continued, "you may be interested to know that one of his assailants has been apprehended and has named you as his employer on this and one or two other occasions. I believe a magistrate is likely on his way here at this moment."

With a wild look, Kayce darted from the room.

Christian turned to Lord Drowling.

"'Twas all Kayce's idea, Glaedon," the Viscount said, shrinking back from what he saw in the other man's eyes. "He thought that if I married into the family, I would remain silent about the trick he played on his brother Walter, back in '91."

"And what trick was that?"

"The duel he was goaded into fighting. He thought he'd killed his man, but it was all a sham. The pistols had been tampered with and the surgeon paid off. Walter fled the country, which was what Kayce wanted." He glanced at Azalea, who was regarding him incredulously, then back at Christian. "I never knew a thing about a previous marriage, though, I swear it!"

Christian regarded him coldly. "That may well be, but I cannot think you believed Miss Clayton amenable to the match. Get out of my sight, you piece of filth."

Drowling's life was infinitely dearer to him than his honour. He left nearly as quickly as Kayce had done.

"Just as well," said Christian, turning at last to Azalea. "I had no desire to flee the country myself just at present."

He opened his arms and she ran to him without a word.

During the short walk to Christian's waiting carriage, Azalea managed to find her voice. She was still shaking from the ordeal she had been through, as well as from the after-effects of the drug, but she felt it was imperative that she speak.

"I was never so happy to see anyone in my life, Christian," she began in a trembling voice, "but I don't understand—"

"Shh!" He laid a finger on her lips. "There will be time enough later for explanations. Right now, I intend to restore you to Lady Beauforth so that you can recover from this very disagreeable experience."

In fact, Azalea did feel unequal to any lengthy conversation, and it was obvious that a short one would never do. Since she had not yet had time to organize the chaos of her thoughts and emotions, she lapsed gratefully into silence.

Christian helped her into the carriage, where she nestled comfortably against him, to his complete satisfaction. By the time they reached the Beauforth mansion, she was sound asleep.

Azalea awoke to find herself back in her own cozy green-and-gold chamber, the sunlight of early afternoon streaming through the half-open curtains. She smiled and stretched lazily, enveloped in a glorious sense of well-being. What a dream she'd had!

The door opened as she sat up to admit the ever-vigilant Junie, breakfast tray in hand.

"Good morning, miss—or, should I say, good afternoon. It's a treat to have you back with us, I must say! I trust you slept well?"

Full recollection flooded back, and Azalea's smile broadened. So it hadn't been a dream! "Marvellously, Junie, thank you," she said. "That breakfast smells delicious. I declare I am ravenous!"

"Cook thought you might be, so he fixed you up something special," said Junie, placing a tray bearing hot chocolate, creamed sole, ham and popovers for her mistress. "Ring when you want me, and I'll help you to dress."

A short while later, Azalea descended to the front parlour to find Lord Glaedon and Lady Beauforth deep in animated conversation. Seeing her in the doorway, Christian rose. She came forward hesitantly, looking from one to the other questioningly. Lady Beauforth spoke first.

"Oh, my dear, dear Azalea, it is wonderful to see you looking so refreshed! Christian has just been telling me the most extraordinary tale… I vow, I don't know what to think! Are my wits addled, or is it true?"

Azalea glanced shyly at Christian, who smiled down at her in a way that made her heart skip a beat. "Yes, Cousin Alice, it is all true," she admitted. "I am sorry that you had to learn of it in this way. Pray believe I never meant to hurt you—or Marilyn. Especially when you have both been so good to me."

But Lady Beauforth was smiling, though she still looked thoroughly bemused. "Well, you *have* been the sly one! But there, I mustn't scold, for Christian here has been telling me why you never dropped a word about it before. And to think that I was in alt over the idea of a match with Lord Drowling!" Her ladyship dismissed that previous favourite with a flick of her fingers.

"But we have many, many plans to make if this information is to be made public without a scandal! However, we can discuss that later. Christian tells me you were too tired last night for any talk, and, indeed, I believe him, for you could scarcely stand when he brought you home. So I'll leave you two alone for a few moments —not that it will be improper, I suppose, under the circumstances." She shook her head again. "But you must have quite a lot to say to each other. My, my, what an amazing turn of events... "Her voice trailing behind her, she bustled out of the room.

Christian led Azalea to the white-velvet sofa and seated himself next to her. She thought he had never looked so handsome, with his dark hair curling around his ears— curls she longed to touch. With him beside her, as she had feared he never would be again, a storm of emotion swept over her. But first, the explanations.

She met his eyes then, to discover that he had been regarding her intently.

"Can you ever forgive me?" they both asked abruptly, then laughed uncertainly.

"Christian, can you possibly understand why I said nothing to you at the start?" asked Azalea after a moment. His very nearness seemed to be affecting her ability to speak, or even to think.

"I think so," he answered with a gentle smile. "Are you certain you still wish to acknowledge me after the way I treated you?"

Azalea nodded silently, her confused spirits rising. "How did you find out? I know you honestly did not remember anything of your visit to Virginia. Do you now?"

"I remember everything." Christian told her about the old sailor who had visited him at the Oaks and how his memory had suddenly returned as a result.

"No wonder you seemed familiar to me from the first," he concluded, winding one of her auburn curls around his finger. "And to think that that familiarity was a part of what fascinated me about you when we first met— here in England."

He was openly laughing at himself now, and Azalea's last fear evaporated. Miraculously, Christian seemed to be again the carefree young man she remembered from Williamsburg rather than the moody stranger he had been in England.

Impishly, she reached up to touch the dark curl that had been intriguing her, and their eyes met again. Her breathing quickened as he bent his head towards hers.

His kiss, deep and passionate, brought back vivid memories of earlier caresses here in this very same room. She felt that she was being transported on a golden cloud to heavenly regions undreamed of.

She responded eagerly, wanting Christian to have no doubt of the true state of her feelings —or desires.

"So where do we go from here?" he asked huskily at length. Before Azalea could answer, Lady Beauforth bustled back into the room.

"I have been thinking, my dears, and I have a plan to put before you. What would you say to another wedding ceremony, this time in St. George's, Hanover Square? That way we need say nothing about your having been married all this time, for you must realize that it will look excessively odd to everyone."

She gazed pleadingly at them. Azalea knew that her cousin really did want them happy and was delighted that they had reached an understanding, but that her horror of scandal could not be overcome.

"Dear Cousin Alice, what a lovely idea," said Azalea, rising to embrace her. "If Christian agrees, that is."

"On two conditions." Both ladies turned to look at him questioningly. "That it can be arranged within the month, and that we spend the intervening period at Glaedon Oaks. My grandmother has expressed a strong desire to meet my Countess."

Azalea agreed readily and they all fell to discussing wedding plans. In the midst of arguing the merits of lilies over white roses, a topic Christian could not find as interesting as his bride apparently did, Marilyn and Jonathan walked in, flushed from a walk in the Park. Both looked extremely pleased with themselves.

"Might we make it a double ceremony?" asked Jonathan when all had been explained to them. Lady Beauforth, open-mouthed, looked at Marilyn, who nodded happily. "If you approve, that is, my lady," he concluded more formally.

"Approve?" exclaimed Lady Beauforth. "My dear boy, you are already like one of the family. I am only surprised that you waited this long."

"There was the small matter of her previous commitment, if you recall," he reminded her. "In addition, I wanted to be sure of my prospects first. Lord Holte has made me his legal heir, as of yesterday, so I am now a man of substance both in England and America." He smiled fondly down at Marilyn.

"But we are to honeymoon in Virginia, as you promised," she reminded him.

"That I did," he returned. "Did you by chance plan on a wedding trip there as well?" he asked, turning to Azalea and Christian.

"No, I had something else in mind," replied Christian, grinning with delight at their news, "but I have yet to discuss it with my bride." He turned to Azalea. "Would you care to take a drive? My carriage is at the door."

She nodded, too happy to speak.

He took her firmly by the hand and led her outside to his

waiting carriage. "Care to take a guess where we're going?" he asked. The intensity of the gaze he turned on her made her heart flip over.

"To the Park?" she asked shyly.

"No, to my Town house. It occurs to me that my Countess might care to see the place, as she will have the managing of it shortly."

Azalea felt as if she were melting in the warmth of his regard. "Yes. Yes I would," she agreed.

On the way there, Christian told her about his arrival at Beauforth House the afternoon before and Marilyn's timely request. They chuckled together as they climbed down from the carriage, but when they stepped into the house, their laughter stilled. No servants were in evidence, by prior arrangement. Silently, hand in hand, they mounted the stairs.

Once in his own bedchamber, Christian closed the door softly and held out his arms. She came to him willingly, with no reservations. This was Christian, the man she had loved for so very long —and her husband.

"To think I was consumed by guilt for kissing my own wife," he said, echoing her thoughts. "Were you very angry?"

"Only that you stopped. I shall remember that time always, Christian." She smiled up at him, her heart in her eyes.

"I won't hold back this time," he warned her. "Prepare yourself for something even more memorable."

Azalea doubted that could be possible, but she soon found that she was wrong. Thoroughly, without any indication of haste, he kissed her, running his hands over her body. She returned his kiss passionately, the fire that he kindled within her suddenly bursting into roaring flame.

He chuckled deep in his throat as he sensed her response.

She fumbled at his clothes, eager to have his skin against hers. What she had felt before was as nothing compared to the rage of desire that now had her in its grip.

Christian fastened his mouth on hers again and with eager hands began to strip away her gown. Azalea unhesitatingly responded to his ardour, opening to his kiss. She continued to fumble with his cravat, and in a moment had it undone. Her nimble fingers went on to the studs of his shirt, finally baring his chest even as he released her from the bodice of her gown. He ran his hands down her back, the sensation of her nipples against his bare chest nearly driving him mad.

Softly, wonderingly, Azalea's hands explored the contours of his torso, her fingers combing through the hair on his chest, sliding down the plane of his hard stomach. Christian untied the sash of her gown and slid the garment down past her hips until it lay in a shimmering heap at her feet. For a moment, he pulled back to feast his eyes upon her lush curves.

She did not cease her explorations, but slid one finger beneath the waistband of his breeches, which were now stretched tight over his straining arousal. Quickly, he helped her to unfasten them and a moment later stood as free of encumbrance as she.

Kissing her deeply again, he lowered himself onto the bed, drawing her with him, his whole length pressed against hers. This time there was no stiffening in her, no hesitancy, as he traced the curves and hollows of her body with his hands and then his mouth.

Azalea had never dreamed such sensations could exist. As his hands stroked and caressed, lower and lower, she arched her back to greet them. Heat pulsed between her thighs, spreading, licking over her until her whole body was aflame.

Slowly, maddeningly, his fingers approached the source of the inferno.

She gasped as he fastened his mouth over one of her breasts, teasing and tantalizing the nipple with his tongue. At the same time, he inched his hand lower, into the curly tangle between her legs. One finger stroked the spot that had become the very centre of her being and waves of pleasure and insatiable need washed over her. Without fully understanding why, she slid her hands around to his back to pull his lower body to hers.

Releasing her breast with a final, lingering kiss, he obliged her, allowing his hardness to slide up her thigh until it just rested against the fiery spot his finger had been massaging. Arching again, she pressed herself against him.

He moved from beside her to above, supporting himself on his arms, and slowly, gently rocked back and forth, barely grazing the place where her sensations were focused. Arching higher, she felt him slide inside her, into the void that cried out to be filled.

"Oh, Chris, yes!" she breathed.

He rocked faster, each movement now thrusting him deeper. Suddenly, she felt a sharp pain, a stretching, tearing sensation inside her, and then it was gone.

He had slowed for a moment, but now thrust with renewed vigour. Azalea wrapped her legs around his to pull him in further. Her ability to think was gone—her whole world was a kaleidoscope of emotions and senses. She rocked with his rhythm, her passions rising to a dizzying crescendo until they exploded in a rush of pleasure so intense that she cried out in ecstasy.

Christian thrust twice, thrice more, then arched his own

back, shuddering, as he spent his own passion. Carefully, he lowered himself next to her, kissing her gently on the lips. She had been all that he had known he would be, and more —far more. Still deep inside her, cradling her to him, he felt that he could happily remain here with her for the rest of his life. He had never felt so complete.

But slowly, reality intruded. Loath as he was to move, he knew that he had to get Azalea back to Beauforth House if her reputation was not to be sunk beyond repair —at least, if they were to go along with Lady Beauforth's scheme.

"You realize that you will have to marry me now," he said softly, kissing a curl at her temple.

She looked up at him with those glorious green eyes and smiled. "If I had known what being your wife entailed, I would have told you my first day in England," she breathed.

"Let that be your punishment," he said with a tender grin. "You missed two months of pleasure for your silence."

After another quiet moment of contentment, Azalea asked him, "Didn't we come here to discuss our wedding trip?"

"Insatiable minx! That's not why I brought you here at all."

"Cousin Alice will wonder at our being gone so long," she prompted gently, though she had no desire to leave.

"As you say. I had another setting in mind for my surprise, anyway."

He would not answer her excited enquiries, but helped her to dress, then held the door for her to precede him out of the suite and down to the waiting carriage.

"Chris, you are driving me to distraction," she declared as they pulled up before the Beauforth house.

"Only fair," he replied. "You have been doing that to me since the moment I met you— again."

Once inside, he did not take her back to the parlour as she had expected, but led her through the house and out into the deserted gardens behind. The sunlight made it cheerful despite the fact that only the conifers were green. They stopped under the rose bower, covered now with gnarled grey canes awaiting the warmth of spring to bring them back to life.

"Happy as I am for your cousin and Mr. Plummer, I have no intention of sharing my wedding trip with them. It strikes me that we have a lot of catching up to do, old married couple that we are." His smile made her want to leap into his arms again. "But not necessarily in America."

She looked up at him questioningly.

"I thought we might tour the Continent," he said at last. "I hear the roses at Malmaison in June are well worth seeing."

Azalea gasped with delight at the prospect of having that botanist's dream fulfilled. How could he have known?

When she would have asked, he stopped her with a kiss at first gentle, then demanding.

"I made a promise nigh on seven years ago to make you happy," he murmured at length. "It is time I began to fulfill it, don't you think?"

Keep reading for a sneak peek at *Ship of Dreams*, book 2 of the Americana Dreaming series, a richly detailed historical romance that will sweep you into the world of the California Gold Rush and the SS Central America. Half a century before the Titanic, there was another…

SHIP OF DREAMS (PREVIEW)

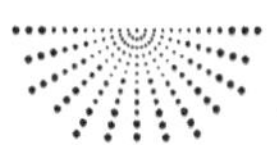

The bride hath paced into the hall,
Red as a rose is she;
Nodding their heads before her goes
The merry minstrelsy.

—Samuel Taylor Coleridge
The Rime of the Ancient Mariner

SAN FRANCISCO — AUGUST, 1857

"MURDER? IMPOSSIBLE!" DELLA STARED AT HER LANDLADY in disbelief, but the woman only nodded her neat gray head.

"Murder," she repeated. "That's what they're saying in the streets. Mr. Potts claims it was the Doctor Mirabula's Sovereign

Remedy for Ague you sold him that carried off his wife last night. And that apothecary, Mr. Willis, is telling everyone who will listen that it must be true."

The bristle brush she'd been pulling through her thick, carroty curls hung suspended as Della absorbed the words. "That's preposterous! I mixed that remedy myself. It contains nothing but vanilla, quinine, and a jigger of brandy. It may not cure the ague, but it's perfectly harmless. More likely it was one of Mr. Willis' own brews at fault."

Mrs. Lewis shrugged. "I wouldn't be surprised. But be that as it may, I've turned away four people already this morning wanting their money back on your remedies, and I fear there'll be more. This could take an ugly turn, dearie."

"Yes. Yes, I suppose it could." Remembering the vigilante sweeps of the previous year, Della shuddered. More than a few accused 'criminals' had been hanged without benefit of trial, based on sketchy evidence, at best. Standing up from the dressing table, she crossed the tiny room in three steps and cautiously parted the yellow chintz curtains to peer out at the street below.

A crowd had gathered two blocks away, in front of the *Euphemia*, once a landlocked ship and now converted to a hotel. Even from this distance she could hear the high, nasal voice of Mr. Willis as he shouted and gestured toward Mrs. Lewis' boarding house. The apothecary had been trying to put her out of business for months, seeing her as his greatest competitor. Now it looked as though he might succeed.

Selling patent medicines had been Della's most successful enterprise yet, first in the outlying mining towns, then in Sacramento, and now in San Francisco. A dash of this and a dash of that, and she could command far higher prices than her sewing or produce had ever brought in. Of course, most of her remedies were useless, which caused her the occasional twinge of conscience. Still, she'd always made certain they would cause no harm, in accordance with Hippocrates—and in contrast to others peddling medicines, to include Mr. Willis.

"They're getting louder. What will you do?" The landlady wrung her hands vigorously, as though to compensate for Della's immobility.

"Do?" She turned from the window and shrugged. "Why, leave, I suppose."

Mrs. Lewis stared. "Leave? Leave San Francisco, you mean? But if you're sure your tonic did no harm—"

At that moment, Della felt far older than her twenty years—older even than Mrs. Lewis. "Of course I'm sure. But that may not matter." Quickly, she weighed her options.

She could face her accusers, attempt to prove her innocence and clear her name. But the Coroner was a friend of Mr. Willis, as was the Chief of Police. And even if she prevailed against all odds, most of her customers would desert her.

Two weeks ago she'd squandered most of her money on a new dress, in hopes it might elevate her social standing—a business investment of sorts—and she had yet to be paid for most of the past two weeks' sales. Now she likely wouldn't be, which meant she'd have nothing to pay *her* creditors when they came knocking. Which they would do any moment, as today happened to be Steamer Day, the twice monthly date when all San Francisco businesses—and individuals—settled up accounts.

"At best, my business is ruined," she said to Mrs. Lewis, at the end of her ruminations. "At worst, I'll be charged with murder. Leaving is the sensible thing to do."

She left unsaid what they both knew: once a charge was brought, the verdict would depend as much on public sentiment as on the truth of the matter. Justice was too often swift and careless in this sometimes overly exuberant young city— especially when a prominent man like Mr. Willis had incentive to affect the outcome.

"You're paid through the end of the month," Mrs. Lewis reminded her, pale blue eyes crinkled with worry.

Della smiled at the woman's kindness. "Consider next week's rent my gratitude for your help in this matter." She glanced out the window again, at the milling crowd. "They'll be heading over here at any moment. Hold them off as long as you can, while I slip out through the kitchen. You've always been kind to me, Mrs. Lewis, and I thank you." She absently kissed the landlady on the cheek, already planning her escape.

As the woman bustled out of the room clucking to herself, Della's mind worked rapidly. With a decisive nod, she pulled out her largest valise—the trunk would be too heavy—and began throwing necessities and her most valuable possessions into it. The brooch and rings that had been her mother's, her real silk scarf, her silver handled hairbrush. No room for her bottles of Carter's Consumption Cure or Doctor Brown's Brain Tonic. Nor for her new hooped dress, the beautiful but expensive green dimity with the seed pearls that had taken her savings.

She'd wear that, she decided. Being dressed like the cream of society might give

her more choices. Besides, she couldn't bear to leave it behind. She could pack the old lilac one she had on. Her mother's wedding ring she slipped onto her left hand. She could pose as a married woman—a widow, perhaps. That would give her more freedom.

Unable to afford a maid, Della only owned dresses with front closures, so she was able to change quickly and unaided. Throwing an ivory shawl over her tell-tale red hair, she tucked her few remaining twenty dollar gold pieces into her bodice and headed down the back stairs, suitcase in hand.

"She's not here, I tell you!" came Mrs. Lewis' shrill voice from the front of the house. "She went out just after breakfast to make some deliveries."

Dear Mrs. Lewis. Della would miss her—the nearest thing to a mother she'd had in years. Just now she had no time for sentiment, however. At any moment, someone might think to check the back of the house.

Lifting her skirts out of the dirt with one hand, her valise clutched tightly in the other, she set out at a brisk pace up Front Street toward the wharves, grateful that at least there was no mud just now. And what another stroke of luck that this had happened on Thursday, the day the steamer sailed!

Lady Luck had always been Della's good friend, getting her out of more than one tight place in recent years. She trusted the good dame would come through for her again today. With a glance at her pocket watch, she quickened her pace. This was going to be close.

When she neared the crowded docks a few minutes later, passengers had already begun boarding the elegant Pacific Mail side-wheel steamship, *Sonora*. Steerage passengers, from ragged to respectable, stood in lines to have their tickets and papers checked, while those sailing second and first class proceeded with more decorum. Della focused on the latter, thinking hard.

She'd be safest in first class, and she could just about afford a ticket, assuming any were still available, but it would take every bit of her money. Many of those aboard did not plan to sail, she knew, but were merely seeing friends off, and would debark at the final boarding call. Perhaps she could pretend to be acquainted with a first-class passenger, then buy a steerage ticket once aboard? It would be risky ...

"Hoy, there!" came a shout from behind her. "Has a Miss Gilliland boarded this ship?"

Her heart in her throat, she forced herself to keep walking along the wood-planked street, which at this point became a wharf, extending out into the bay. Out of the corner of her eye, she saw a uniformed policeman hurrying to question the crewman taking the steerage tickets. What a mercy she hadn't joined that line! Without slowing her stride, she veered toward the first class section, keeping as many people as possible between herself and the police officer. Dressed in her finest, she easily blended in.

A loud cheer from behind her made Della glance back. A luxurious, decorated carriage had stopped, and as she watched, a couple, obviously just married, stepped out. Their wedding party and other well-wishers cheered again. Then they were being swept toward the steamer—toward Della.

Seizing her chance, she donned a bright smile and joined the throng. Carried along by the crowd, she hurried up the gangway and onto the promenade deck—and away from the police search, which had now progressed to the second class passengers.

Hordes of wealthy people jostled each other politely as they made way for the large wedding party. Even in her tight situation, Della couldn't help analyzing the faces and voices, trying to guess which ones had made a killing in the gold fields, which had made fortunes in business, and which had been born into money. Experience had made her an excellent judge of character.

Moving a little bit away from the wedding party before someone realized she didn't belong, she scanned those on deck for a likely face—someone who might be persuaded to help her. The nouveau riche tended to be less generous than those who'd had their wealth longer, she'd discovered ...

Ah! That tall, dark-haired man. He had the aristocratic bearing of one who'd grown up with a sense of his own importance. At the same time, something in his handsome, patrician features told her he just might listen to a hard-luck case. He appeared to be alone at the moment, too, which would make this easier.

A glance back at the dock showed that two other police officers had joined the first, one of them now questioning an important-looking man with a top hat and walking stick, clearly a first class passenger. She had no time to lose.

Pasting a winning smile onto her lips, she moved toward the man she hoped would save her.

Kenton Bradford, of the New York Bradfords, stood near the top of the gangway, irritation warring with impatience. Where the devil was Sharpe? They were supposed to have met an hour ago, before he boarded the *Sonora*. He had important business to discuss with the man, but now it looked as though they might miss each other altogether.

The riverboat bringing Bradford south from Sacramento

yesterday had hit a snag in the river, necessitating repairs and delaying him by several hours. When he'd finally reached San Francisco late last night, he'd immediately sent a message to Mr. Sharpe explaining, and suggesting they meet at the *Sonora* before he sailed. But Sharpe had not yet appeared, and the ship was due to depart in a quarter of an hour.

Though he had done so only a minute or two earlier, Bradford pulled out his finely-chased gold watch and consulted it yet again before thrusting it back into his pocket. Sharpe had been the one to convince him to attempt establishment of a California branch of Bradford Shipping & Mercantile, and had promised to become an important investor. Without his support and influence, its success would be far from assured.

He had run across more than a few slick talking shysters since reaching California six months ago, men adept at parting the foolish from their money. Was Sharpe another such a one? He'd had nothing beyond a few letters from the man since meeting him in New York last year, when he'd so enthusiastically expounded upon the opportunities for established businesses expanding to California. Those opportunities still abounded, no doubt about that. But to convince local businesses to patronize his company over others would take some doing. Competition was fierce.

Already, Bradford Shipping had received pledges—and gold—from numerous merchants eager to take advantage of the lower shipping rates he offered. Not enough, however. If only Sharpe—Ah! Was that him? Tilting back his silk top hat, Kenton scanned the shifting, richly dressed throng on the promenade deck and caught another glimpse of the man. Yes, it was definitely Sharpe. He'd seen Bradford now, and angled toward him, laboriously making his way through the press of bodies.

Kenton stepped forward, raising a hand in greeting. "Sharpe! I was afraid you wouldn't make it."

"Bradford! Kenton Bradford. It's good to see you again. I only received your note this morning, about having been delayed on the way from Sacramento," explained the shrewd-eyed, sandy-haired young man, raising his voice to be heard above the general clamor. "It's been all of a year, hasn't it? How have you been?"

"Fine, fine," Kenton said quickly, impatient with this small talk. "We have only a few minutes, I fear, and I have a lot to tell you."

"A lot to tell, indeed," came a feminine voice from behind him. A slender hand took his arm, and he turned in surprise to see a flame-haired vision—a striking young woman he had never seen before in his life—extending her other hand to Mr. Sharpe.

"I'm so pleased to meet you at last, Mr. Sharpe," said the young lady. "I'm Della—Della Bradford. Kent's wife."

~

Order ***Ship of Dreams*** now to keep reading!

AUTHOR'S NOTE

Azalea was actually the very first book I ever wrote, though it was my seventh published (after some much-needed revision). It is set in the same "world" as all of my Regency-set books, both my traditional Regencies and my single title Regency historicals, with a few of the same (fictional) peripheral characters. As you may have noticed, with *Azalea*, I expanded a bit beyond the strict confines of traditional Regency—perhaps one reason it did not immediately sell. It also serves as a transition from the world of my traditional Regencies to my <u>Americana Dreaming Series</u>, opening up a gateway to two more stories that heavily feature the adventure and romance of colonial America: *Ship of Dreams* and *Bridge Over Time*. Though each of my books stands alone, complete in itself, some readers prefer to read them in order. For all of these reissues, I have taken the opportunity to clean up a few small errors of fact and proofing, and am delighted to again share my stories with you in this new format.

Thank you so much for purchasing and reading *Azalea!* If you enjoyed it, please consider leaving a review wherever you buy or talk about books to let other like-minded readers know they might enjoy it, too.

ABOUT THE AUTHOR

Brenda writes novels of sparkling romantic adventure spanning Regency England, Americana, contemporary teen science fiction and more. Which ever you pick up, you'll find excitement, romance and, always, an uplifting happy ending. In addition to writing, Brenda is passionate about embracing life to the fullest, to include scuba diving (she has over 60 dives to her credit), Taekwondo (where she's currently working toward her 4th degree black belt), hiking, traveling…and reading, of course!

Connect with Brenda at:
brendahiatt.com